HELLO,
GOODBYE

HELLO, GOODBYE

a Novel

KATE STOLLENWERCK

spark press

Published by SparkPress, a BookSparks imprint,
A division of SparkPoint Studio, LLC
Phoenix, Arizona, USA, 85007
www.gosparkpress.com

Published 2022
Printed in the United States of America
Print ISBN: 978-1-68463-145-2
E-ISBN: 978-1-68463-146-9 (e-bk)

Library of Congress Control Number: 2022902193

Interior design by Tabitha Lahr

For my Gigis: Philo Mae,
Jaxie Ruth, and Jimmie Frances,
with love and gratitude,

and to my parents,
for everything.

CHAPTER ONE

My summer plans went up in flames exactly six days ago. My best friend, Livi, imploded, and she took my summer down with her. I told her not to send those pics to Caleb, but she did it anyway. He betrayed her, the pictures went viral, and her mom lost it. It didn't help that Livi had a long-standing lack of interest in achievement unless you considered multiple TikToks a day a healthy benchmark. Her mom confiscated her phone and shipped her off to wilderness camp for the entire summer.

Wilderness camp? For Livi Ramos? Livi's idea of roughing it is a day without a Starbucks run. I feel terrible for Livi. I really do. But I'm being punished as well, and I didn't do anything! Her banishment means I've not only lost my best friend, but I've also lost my ride. I don't turn sixteen until the end of summer.

It couldn't get much worse.

My bedroom door pushes open and Dad walks in. He's still wearing his business suit. "Hi, Peanut."

"The name is Hailey."

He sits down on the bed where I'm spread out. "Ah, yes, Hailey. I forgot. My apologies. How was your day?"

Dad doesn't look good. Bits of gray pepper his black hair and stubble covers his chin. His blue eyes are bloodshot, red lines fanning out in squiggles from the pupil to the corner of each eye. The skin over his nose is dry and flaky, and his lips are slightly chapped. He appears to have some sort of condiment stain on his tie. "The better question is, how was your day? You look like hell. I mean it."

He pats my leg and sighs. "Just another long day at the office."

"Sucks for you," I say, with a lopsided grin. "Was it an *Office Space* kind of day? Like, you stared at the clock and pushed paper around as you plotted the demise of your boss?"

Dad lets out a laugh, his eyes coming to life. Dad is one of the funniest people I know and making him laugh always fills me with pride. I'm pretty sure his sense of humor is how he landed my beautiful mother.

"More or less. You know that movie's in my top five."

"It's not that I'm lazy. It's that I just don't care," I reply, and we both break into smiles. It makes Mom crazy when Dad and I start the movie-quote banter. I pull out that *Office Space* gem whenever Mom grills me about my subpar performance, usually related to school. Of course, this never ends well for me. She rages while Dad gives me an approving wink. But only behind her back. He's as scared of her as I am.

"What did you do today?" he asks.

I stick my hands out, dangling my fingers in front of him. "I painted my nails."

But I don't tell him how depressing it was to paint my nails alone. Livi and I love to paint our nails. It's kind of our thing. We keep a box of our collective colors under my bed and between us have close to a hundred bottles.

During the school year, she would come over after dance team practice, and we'd pull out the box, painting our nails while catching up on the day's tea.

"Nice job. Fuchsia works for you. But anything else? I can see cleaning your room didn't make the cut."

Clothes, hangers, and dirty towels litter the floor, and old school papers sit in disorganized piles on my desk. I ignore his last comment. "No other excitement today besides the polish change. I'm starting to think summer vacation is a little overrated."

Dad shakes his head like he gets it. "So, you don't have any definite plans for the summer?"

What kind of question is that? I should have guessed something was up. When does Dad ever just show up to my room to talk before first changing out of his suit? His normal evening routine is a quick wardrobe change before he's out the door for a run. "You know I don't," I say. "Spill it. What's this about?"

"Okay, here's the deal. Gigi needs some help, and I think you're the perfect candidate."

My body freezes. Did he just ask me to spend the summer helping my grandmother? He can't be serious. I like Gigi fine, but I hardly know her. We see her on holidays, but not much in between. I stare at Dad for a long time before replying.

I finally open my mouth. "What sort of help are we talking about? And why is Mom sending you to do her dirty work? Gigi's not your mother."

Dad takes his suit coat off and places it neatly beside him before jerking his necktie loose. "I think Mom was scared that if the request came from her, you'd shoot it down because, you know, it's Mom asking. Gigi is having a harder time getting around, and she needs someone to help her out."

I'm still not buying it. "Dad, come on, is she sick? What's going on? Can't she hire someone to help her? I admit, yeah, my summer has been pretty boring so far, but this is a big ask."

The skin on his forehead bunches together and his eyes turn to slits. "Wait. Don't give me that look," I say, backpedaling fast. "Gigi's nice, but we never see her, so it will be awkward. And what would I do all day? Does she even have Wi-Fi?"

Dad lets out a laugh. "Peanut, you're acting like it's a death sentence. Plus, you'll have your phone, and that's where your face is pointed ninety-nine percent of the time anyway."

"That's not true. I do other things besides look at my phone."

He gives a closed-mouth smile, but I know that smirk lingering around his eyes. He's locked and loaded, ready to spray fire at me. "Only because you're kicked out by our parental time limits."

I get two hours a day, *even in summer*. My parents won't budge on this rule. "Do you honestly expect me to spend my entire summer break with Gigi? What am I going to do, move in with her? Hello, I don't have my driver's license yet."

"Yes, yes, I know. Of course, you wouldn't move in with her. Mom or I could drop you off in the mornings, or you could ride your bike to her house."

Dad has gone off the deep end. I must shut this down now. "Excuse me? Ride my bike? It's June in Texas! I would show up sweaty and dehydrated and might pass out from heat exhaustion. Or I might even get myself killed! What if a car doesn't see me because of the sun's glare? I'm sorry, it's too dangerous."

Dad gives a half-grin. "Well, it's good to know your mother's melodrama has passed to the next generation."

"Dad!"

"Okay, okay. No biking to Gigi's house. Mom or I will drive you."

My shoulders relax, and relief washes over me, but this isn't over yet. "Well, I can't do it every day. That part has to be negotiable. You can't take my whole summer."

Dad gives me his "I feel you" look where his eyes turn

up at the corners. He bites his lower lip, nodding slowly. Dad just has this way about him. Even in dire circumstances, I always feel safe with him.

He gazes at me with the same blue eyes I have. "Okay, let's make a deal," he says. "How about you spend two days a week with Gigi? Does that sound fair? And by the way, Gigi's pretty rad for someone her age."

Did he just say rad? I let it go. Now isn't the time to make fun of him. He might retaliate with a longer jail sentence, and two days is okay. I can handle two days. "Dad, fine, I'll try. But, no offense, I think we have completely different ideas of cool."

"Oh, really. Well, you might be surprised. Gigi has lived quite a life. You could learn a thing or two from her."

I'm having a hard time believing that one. "One last question. Are you going to pay me?"

Dad arches his eyebrows. "Pay you money?"

"Well, I mean, it sounds like a job."

"Spending time with your Gigi *is a job*?"

"Dad, come on. Throw me a bone here."

"Okay, five dollars an hour."

"Um, *hello*? That's not even minimum wage. I could work at Dairy Queen and make more money."

"Um, hello, I don't see you working at Dairy Queen, so be grateful to be offered any money," he fires back.

"Fine."

He stands, his jacket slung over his forearm. "One more thing. Don't tell Mom that I'm paying you. It will upset her."

I wave my hand at him. "My lips are sealed."

As he pulls the door closed behind him, he stops and turns his head over his shoulder. "Thanks for being a team player. Gigi needs us now. I think this actually might make your summer better than you can imagine."

Yeah, whatever. This year will officially enter the history books as the worst summer of my life.

CHAPTER TWO

The alarm buzzes in my ears, but I bury my head under the covers. I should *not* be up this early in the summer. Lifting the pillow off my face, I shout, "Alexa, off!" and my room returns to a state of quiet bliss. I roll slowly out of bed, a yawn falling out. After giving my long brown curls a firm shake, I stumble over to my closet and throw on my jean cut-offs and a white tee.

I head for the refrigerator downstairs and grab my much-needed caffeine. I pop open a Dr Pepper can, and my foul mood lightens at the sound of the familiar fizz of my favorite drink. Mom's not going to like me drinking soda in the morning, but I need it to deal with this day.

I drop a waffle in the toaster as Mom breezes into the kitchen, her high heels clacking on the wood floor. She wears a white sheath dress, and gold necklaces of various lengths dangle from her neck. Her silky blond hair is styled with beachy waves; her lips glimmer with gloss. She pours her coffee and looks me up and down. "You're wearing *that* to Gigi's?"

I lower my eyes, examining my outfit. "It's summer. I look fine."

"Could you have at least ironed your shirt?" she asks.

I may look slightly disheveled with bedhead, puffy eyes, and wrinkled clothes. Whatever.

My little brother, Kyle, sits at the kitchen table and giggles with a mouth full of cereal. I walk over and smack the back of his head before returning to stand guard over my waffle. Kyle's been known to pull off a sneak attack and snatch my Eggos while I'm not looking.

"Hey, that hurt," he whines.

"Stay out of my business, and I'll leave you alone."

Mom frowns at me. "Hailey, it's too early for the fighting. Enough." She walks to him and rubs his back while talking to him sweetly. Will she ever stop babying him? He's eleven, not five.

She turns toward me and raises a finger in the air. She's about to lecture me. "A few reminders about Gigi. Please use proper English and don't say, 'yeah.' Remember your manners and be respectful. Oh, and she's having problems with her hearing, so be sensitive if she asks you to repeat something."

"Got it," I reply flatly.

She sips her coffee, studying me. "Have you started the ACT prep class I registered you for? Any progress on my suggestion you find a volunteer job on the days you aren't at Gigi's?"

I know she means well, but a little breathing room would be appreciated. "Mom, it's summer. Can you give me a few weeks to relax? I work hard during the school year with cross country and my course load. I think a mental break is deserved."

"Well, colleges today expect you to do something during summer break. You need a story to tell, a summer narrative that weaves into the rest of your high school experience and defines who you are."

That's gonna be a tall order considering how my summer is unfolding so far. "I'll think about it."

Dad strolls in, his suit jacket on and a tie knotted around his neck. "Peanut, we need to leave. I have an eight-thirty call I can't miss."

He does a roundup up motion with his hand like this is some freaking cattle call. "We gotta go!"

Dad, unlike me, is a morning person, which is super annoying. I don't budge from my position in front of the toaster. "But I haven't had breakfast."

He scrolls through messages. "Well, as they say, the early bird catches the worm. Sorry, Hales. We need to bounce."

I grimace. "I have to eat something first. It's rude for me to show up to Gigi's hungry and that reflects poorly on the two of you," I say, wagging my finger at them both.

His eyes raise from his phone, and a smile spills from his lips. "You know I appreciate a clever comeback. Two minutes on that waffle, and you're taking it in the car with us."

Dad stops at the coffeemaker, filling a giant Yeti. He's not messing around. That thing holds a full three cups. With mug in hand, he plants a kiss on Mom's cheek. "Good luck with the new client," he says.

He then gives Kyle's hair a tousle on his way to the garage. "Hales, I'll be waiting in the car."

My waffle pops. I grab my bag and head out the door.

We slide into the Volvo. Dad's coffee is in one cup holder, my Dr Pepper in the other. As I reach for the radio, he blocks my hand. "Sorry, but I've got a call with my partner to prep for our meeting."

"Fine," I garble out, my mouth stuffed with waffle. I pop my AirPods in and put on my favorite playlist.

The commute to Gigi's house isn't bad, about a fifteen-minute drive. Gigi lives in an older part of town. Our community is newer, and the homes have better upgrades—things like walk-in closets and open-floor plans, but her neighborhood has prestige. Her house was built in the 1950s, and she's lived in it forever. Mom, on the other hand, is always itching for a new address.

We currently reside in our fifth house of my short life, and I've recently surmised the root of the problem: Mom's addiction to HGTV. She binges shows like *Fixer Upper*, *Love It or List It*, and the one with the twins, and then she gets all these wild ideas about what's wrong with our perfectly acceptable home. She'll adore the house we live in, and then after a couple of HGTV weekend benders, she's nothing but complaints. She'll get the bug to move and will nag Dad until he can't take it anymore. Then sure enough, our house will be on the block.

I peek in my bag to make sure I didn't forget any essentials. Last night, I had the foresight to pack an emergency kit with supplies to save me from boredom. I don't know what to expect at Gigi's. What if she takes a two-hour nap after lunch? I have my AirPods, my cell phone, my copy of *Twilight*, and of course, my nail polish.

I'm only on my third song when Dad taps me on the shoulder. "We're here. I need you to hop out. I'm cutting it close on time."

I remove my earbuds and stare at him, slightly bewildered. "You're not going in with me? Not even for a few minutes?"

He points at the clock on the car's dashboard. "Sorry, but I've got fifteen minutes until my call. But you don't need me to go in. It's Gigi. I'm sure you'll have a great day."

I consider making a desperate plea, but I can tell he's in work mode. I climb out of the car but flip back before closing the door. "Thanks for the ride. I'll make sure to turn in my timesheet this evening. I assume I'm getting paid after each day worked, right?"

He waves his hand at me, like he's shooing a fly away. "Fine, fine. Gotta run."

I shut the door, and the Volvo zooms down the street.

I stand on the sidewalk and take a moment to admire Gigi's house. Gigi lives on Oxford Street, a block that bustles with kids on bikes, adults out for runs, and a constant stream of yard crews and pool guys. Her home is a traditional brick bungalow, painted pearl white, the shutters sky blue, and her wooden door stained a butternut brown. She lives in one of the few remaining original cottages; most of her neighbors tore down and built mega mansions, every square inch of the lot filled with house.

I head up the walkway, which splits the yard into two equal parts. A short porch juts off to the right of the door where Gigi has placed a wicker rocking chair with a needle-point lumbar pillow that says, "Home Sweet Home." I walk a few steps down the porch and peek in the window. Gigi sits in her living room chair, engrossed in her newspaper. I return to the door and tap the bronze knocker three times.

At least a minute passes but still no answer. Then I remember what Mom said about her bad hearing. I give several loud knocks and press the buzzer. After a few moments, the door swings open, and Gigi greets me with an ear-to-ear grin.

"Hailey! Don't you look lovely this morning," she says in her soft twang, pulling me into a hug.

I'm taller than Gigi; she's barely up to my chin. I awkwardly squeeze her back. The role reversal of me enveloping her in my arms throws me, but she's still soft and squishy like always, even though I no longer burrow into her bosom. As she holds me longer than is customary, I get a whiff of her perfume. She smells sweet, like fresh soap, with a hint of jasmine and vanilla.

I break away and fidget with my backpack's straps slung down around my knees.

Gigi looks healthy this morning, her cheeks full and rosy. Her frosted blond hair falls delicately at her shoulders, and she's done her makeup, her lips a bright shade of red. She wears a cream silk blouse paired with beige linen pants and flower-embroidered espadrilles. I am doubting this whole "Gigi needs your help" story.

She motions me inside, and I step into the entryway. Gigi babbles at me. "I was so thrilled to hear you would be able to help me this summer. I'm so looking forward to our time together. It's been ages since we've spent quality time, just the two of us."

"Yeah, Gigi, me, too," I say, and give a half-hearted smile.

I draw in a breath at my mistake. I just broke rule number one from Mom. I said, "yeah" instead of "yes." This is gonna be one long summer.

"Well, come in, come in. Let's head to the kitchen and sit down and have a chat. I brewed us a kettle of Earl Grey tea, and I baked banana-nut muffins last night. Come, come!" Gigi says. She waves her wrinkled hands, and her gold bangles clatter loudly on each wrist.

I follow Gigi's lead as we cut through the living room en route to the kitchen. I catch quick glimpses of the Persian rugs, the antique end tables, the porcelain vases, and all the blown glass. Rich and heavy fabrics upholster the sofas and chairs, and paintings line the walls.

Her collection is a mixture of impressionist street scenes, portraitures from other centuries, and rolling landscapes. The people in the portraits are so unattractive, and the old landscapes make me thankful for modern living. Why does she have these hanging on her wall? "I forgot how beautiful your home is."

Gigi smiles at me. "Thank you, dear."

She must think our house is awful. Mom, with her modern and monochromatic taste, favors clean lines, furniture in crisp white, and little clutter. Gigi's house is a cornucopia of color and texture, pattern layered upon pattern, every inch filled with a knickknack, book, or antique. It's a little bit of a wonderland, something catching my eye in every corner of each room.

I stop as my attention settles on the Steinway piano that anchors the living room. Gigi's piano is massive. Covered in an ebony black casing, the piano sits with the lid propped open, the dampers, strings, and hammers on display. One of my favorite memories of Gigi is me perched on her lap in front of the piano with her arms stretched around me. Her fingers danced on the keys as she sang nursery rhymes and silly songs with her beautiful voice.

I point at the piano. "Do you still play?"

"All the time."

We sit down at the oval kitchen table, and she places her finest china in front of me. Mom only busts out the china at holidays and then complains the entire time about how taxing it is to handwash it, yelling at Kyle and me to make sure our utensils don't scrape the plates. But Gigi acts like her china is everyday wear.

She pushes a plate of muffins in front of me. "Hailey, please eat. Have you had breakfast?"

As she drops a banana-nut muffin on my plate, I smile. Bananas send my gag reflexes into overdrive; I can't even stomach banana-flavored bubble gum. But now doesn't seem like a good time to bring it up. "I actually had a waffle and don't usually eat much in the mornings, but thanks."

I sit upright, my shoulders slack against the chair and my ankles crossed, trying my hardest to have proper etiquette. I move my hands from the table to my lap and then back to the table. Where do they go? I've blocked out the awful memories from my sixth-grade cotillion classes, but I'm pretty sure where to put your hands at all times was covered.

She pours the tea, and once again I give my obligatory smile. I detest tea as well, especially Earl Grey, but I'd better fake this one or she might catch on that all her attempts to welcome me have failed. She passes over the milk and sugar, and I dump both in my cup, altering the color to a whitish hue. I stir my spoon for a solid minute before taking a swallow. My throat constricts as it rushes down, warm and nasty. There's still not enough milk to make the taste tolerable. God, tea is awful. I'm going to have to make up a story for the future about how I'm tea-intolerant or have some moral dilemma with the consumption of tea to get out of this torture.

Gigi is happily drinking, the cup slightly shaking as she brings it to her lips. A sadness builds in my chest. Maybe Dad was serious. Maybe she's not doing so great. "How are you feeling?" I ask in a soft voice.

She gently places her cup down, and then rubs her thumb over the red stain on the rim of her mug. Cocking her head, she blinks her long eyelashes repeatedly. "Oh, some days are better than others, but what do you expect at seventy-four years?"

I nod. I know she's getting up there . . . I mean, she is my grandmother . . . but I didn't realize she's that old. "Well, you look good," I say. "Any big plans for your seventy-fifth?"

She lets out a girlish giggle and waves her hand at me, light pink nails catching my eye. I'm guessing she's wearing Essie's Mademoiselle shade. Maybe Gigi has a secret stash of nail polish I can pilfer through for me and Livi?

"Lord, I haven't given it a thought. It's still a few months away. But being a Capricorn, we're known for enjoying birthdays," she says, giving me a wink.

I slurp down another shot of tea, but the bitter taste makes me wince. "Cool. I don't know a lot about astrology, but I'll take your word for it."

She tilts her head to the right, her eyes twinkling. Gigi has beautiful green eyes, round like a full moon, and in a certain light, bright and shiny like emeralds. Mom and Kyle have the same eyes.

Why couldn't I have inherited anything from Mom's side?

"Well, there is a lot of truth in the stars. I'm quite well-versed in it, so if you ever need any celestial guidance, you let me know."

A laugh escapes the corners of my mouth. She's a little out there. "Will do."

We sit in silence, and I wonder how the heck we're going to pass the next eight hours. I assume Gigi has a master plan, so I figure I might as well find out what's in store for me. "So . . . what are we doing today?"

Gigi glances up at the ceiling, then lowers her eyes back to mine. "I was going to do a little reading, work on the cross-word, and I hope you and I could go to the grocery store."

Why am I here if she's just going to read all afternoon? Shifting in my chair, I try to keep my composure, but I've never been good at hiding my emotions. Dad always says I'd make the worst poker player.

Gigi taps her fingers on the table. She's on to me. "Well, there are some other chores, but I don't want to burden you on your first day here. I thought you might want to relax before I ask you for help with a few things."

I should have guessed Gigi is looking out for me. But what's in my best interest is getting things wrapped up so this gig can end early. "Oh, Gigi, really, I'm here to help, so let me know what you need me to do."

Her wrinkles pop out as she gives me a broad grin and claps her hands together. "Marvelous. That's a great attitude you have. Let me grab my reading glasses and list."

Oh, man. She's made a list. Gigi glides into the office off the kitchen, so I dash over to the sink and dump out two-thirds of my tea and pitch half the muffin into the garbage can. I race back to my seat and listen to Gigi talking to herself. "Now, where did I put my glasses?"

"Hailey, do you see my glasses out there?" she shouts.

"No, they aren't on the table or the counters!" I yell back.

She returns to the kitchen. "Could you be a dear and check my bedroom?"

"Yeah, sure."

I walk through the living room and down the long hallway, passing two guest rooms before arriving at Gigi's bedroom. Searching for her glasses, I gaze toward the bathroom. Holy jackpot! Stacks of lipsticks overflow from acrylic trays piled four high. There must be at least thirty tubes. I'm no Sherlock Holmes, but I think this discovery all but guarantees she has a decent haul of nail polish to go along with this mother lode.

As I continue my search, I move toward her vanity. The antique piece is a mahogany color, with brass handles on the drawers, curved legs, and a trifold mirror. A bottle of Chanel No. 5 and a silver hand mirror and hairbrush sit on display. I pick up the perfume bottle and raise it to my nose. With touches of rose, oak, and vanilla, it's definitely the sweet and fresh scent Gigi wears. I then lift the mirror, studying the ornate pattern of flowers, swirling garland and ferns, noticing "Tiffany and Co. Sterling" stamped on the edge.

I run my fingers over the soft white bristles of the oval hairbrush. I wonder if it's made of horsehair or some other exotic animal. Even though I should ask permission first, I brush through my curls, the bristles snagging my thick brown locks.

"Did you find my glasses?"

The hairbrush slips from my fingers.

Gigi stands in the doorway and smiles at me. Turning my back to her, I bend down and yank out several dark strands to remove the evidence of my crime. I flip around and wave the brush in front of me. "I got distracted by this hairbrush. It's so beautiful."

She leans on the doorframe. "I bought it years ago at an estate sale. It's quite old. I love things that carry someone's story in them. Most everything in this house has history, including me," she says, her smile extra bright. She then adds, "You're welcome to use any of my things. Ask away. *Mi casa es su casa.*"

Heat rises to my cheeks. She totally knows I was snooping. I dart my gaze around the room to avoid eye contact. I spot the glasses on the bedside table and scoop them up. "Got 'em."

We return to the kitchen and sit down at the table. Gigi rests her hands on the pad of paper. I slide the reading glasses over to her, and she smiles at me, wrinkles exploding around her mouth. Gigi is old, but she's still attractive. Her strong features—a straight-edged nose, bow-shaped lips, and large eyes—are strikingly in balance. I bet she was gorgeous back in the day.

She reviews her list. "Ahh, yes. I was hoping we could go to the grocery store, the pharmacy, and stop by Home Depot. I also have several projects around the house I could use your help with."

"We really are diving all in," I say in a chipper tone.

She removes her glasses and folds them up. As she gazes over at me, her lips turn down. "Your mom said you have your learner's permit, so I was hoping you could handle the driving today. My eyes aren't what they used to be and although I'm generally fine, I do get anxious with crowded parking lots."

I get her apprehension. Crowded parking lots are the most nerve-racking part of driver's ed. Well, that is, after merging on the highway and parallel parking. "My parents didn't tell me I would drive you. I forgot my permit. How about the next visit?"

Gigi smiles from ear to ear, her eyes crinkling at the ends. "The next visit is fine. Let me see what else is on my list."

I peer over at the piece of paper, and I'm transfixed by her exquisite handwriting. Her upper- and lowercase letters perfectly loop together, and her spacing is impeccable, even on a silly to-do list. Dad's penmanship is trash, and Mom's a weird combo of cursive and block.

"You have the most beautiful handwriting," I say. "Where did you learn to write like that?"

"School, of course."

"They don't teach us anymore."

She raises her hands to her chest and crosses them over her heart, shaking her head. "I will never understand the decision to abandon cursive in school."

"I guess with computers, it isn't necessary."

More wrinkles appear as she snaps her brows together. "Handwriting is quickly becoming a lost art form. Your great-nana was such a stickler about things like penmanship. She is rolling over in her grave on this one."

She touches the end of her pen to her lips. "We would spend hours working on our cursive. Letter-writing was our means of communication with the world. For my entire life, putting pen to paper has been a daily ritual." She shrugs and sighs deeply. "And now no one writes letters anymore. I feel sad that your generation won't experience the thrill of receiving a love letter."

Gigi writing love letters is hard to imagine, but she's piqued my curiosity. I'm a sucker for a love story. "Yeah, a text message of incomplete sentences and emojis is probably the closest I'll ever get to receiving a love letter."

She crinkles her nose, her mouth dropping into a frown. "Abandoning handwritten letters is one of the modern world's great tragedies. Computers and phones are useful and efficient, but there isn't any magic in digital font. Humanity has communicated by the handwritten word for hundreds of years and now, within the span of a generation, it has almost completely vanished."

Her hands swirl in the air. "With a handwritten note, you can feel the passion of the writer in the slant and size of the letters, whether the writing appears frantic or thoughtful. The writer conveys emotion by underlining, writing in all caps, doodling around words, or filling an entire page with a drawing or picture. The beauty of someone pouring out their soul comes through in the writer's handwriting. You *feel* their heart on the page. Did you know that every single person's handwriting on this planet is unique? Just like our DNA."

A giggle falls from her lips. "When I was young, we would lace our letters with a lipstick kiss or perfume."

I'm intrigued by this side of Gigi, but it's difficult to imagine her at my age. "You wrote a lot of love letters when you were young?"

"I did. We all did back then." She taps her fingers on the table. "Do you have a boyfriend?"

Is Gigi seriously asking me about boys? Mom knows not to go there with me. "No."

A smile circles her lips in a way that makes her seem more like a co-conspirator than an authoritative figure. I find myself admitting one of my secrets that I haven't even shared with Livi. "I do want a boyfriend. Well, I don't know if a boyfriend is what I want or just some excitement or adventure in my life, someone that finds me interesting."

Gigi's expression shifts and her eyes cast to the side, like she's been transported somewhere else. A few seconds pass before she returns her attention to me. "In time, Hailey. One thing I have learned on my journey is that life can unfold in unexpected ways. But if you want something to happen, be brave and step off the ledge. Whether you fall or fly is up to you."

I give a nod, but I'm always perplexed when adults speak in cryptic language. What does that even mean? Nothing unexpected is going to happen to me this summer, especially if I spend most of my time at Gigi's house.

Gigi's morning task list isn't so bad. I take down some clothes from the top of her closet, and we sort things into piles: keepers, trashers, and Goodwillers. Gigi owns a lot of clothes, and we have fun cracking up at some of her zany outfits: jumpsuits with shoulder pads, dresses in wild animal prints, and sparkly tops and skirts, mostly by some designer named Joan Rivers. Gigi says she was super-famous and hilarious, but I've never heard of her. I make a mental note to check her out on YouTube.

We take a break for lunch. Gigi makes us turkey sandwiches, and we eat together at her table. "I like to spend the afternoon reading. Would you like to join me?"

Man, things move slow around here. I guess it's not so bad. I do enjoy reading, which I always assumed I got from Dad since Mom never reads. Maybe it skipped over her, and my love of books is from Gigi?

We retreat to the living room, and I grab my copy of *Twilight* out of my bag. Gigi sits in a club chair, and I slump into the wingback chair across from her. "What is *Twilight* about?" she asks.

I pass it over, allowing her to take a closer look. "It's the first book of a series about an ordinary high school girl who falls in love with a gorgeous and mysterious guy who turns out to be a vampire. But the novel isn't about blood-sucking vampires. I mean, there are gory parts and fight scenes, but it's really about the love story between Bella and Edward."

Gigi lifts an eyebrow. "Are you a romantic?"

Who asks that? "I enjoy a good love story."

She returns *Twilight* to me, and then pushes herself off the chair. She walks over to the bookshelf behind the piano and runs her finger over a row of leather-bound books. She stops, pulls one from the shelf, and wipes off the front cover. Returning to her chair, she then lowers herself gently into the seat, and places the book in her lap.

"Well, you come from a long line of romantics, and I would like to make an exchange. You give me that copy of *Twilight* to read, and, in return, I give you my copy of what I consider one of the great American tales about love."

She's flamed my curiosity again. Gigi is building quite the cliffhanger, and I'm taking the bait. "I'm up for it. But I'm not sure we have the same taste in novels."

She crosses her ankles, that dang twinkle in her eye drawing me in. "Well, let's both take a read and then compare notes. I am going to hand you a first edition of *The Great Gatsby*."

I've heard of this book but don't know anything about it. She passes it to me, but it's in a navy box. The novel's title and the author's name are etched on the box's spine in gold lettering.

"Go on," she assures me. "You can open it. I had that box made to protect the book. It's quite old and valuable. This novel is one of my most prized possessions."

I've never held a first edition book, and my stomach twists as my fingers tap the box. "I can't possibly take something this valuable out of your home. What if I lost it or damaged it? Mom would kill me."

"One thing growing old has taught me: What's the point of having things if you don't enjoy them?" says Gigi. "I want you to experience the beauty of this novel, and I'm not taking the book with me to my next destination, now, am I?" She lifts her chin, prodding me along.

I remove the novel from the box and rest it in my lap. The book is light. How can an amazing story unfold so quickly? I study the tattered dust jacket, a beautiful set of sad eyes staring at me from a sea of blue. "This picture is hypnotizing."

"This dust jacket is one of the most famous in modern literature," replies Gigi. "It's supposed to represent the excess of the Roaring Twenties. Do you mind placing it in the box? It's easier to read without the jacket."

I carefully remove the dust jacket. The book's cover has faded to an army green, like it molded from age like stale bread. The binding is wilted and stained with a few dark spots. I delicately open the front cover. The inscription on the inside page reads:

Ilse,
To my sweet, embraceable you.

Always and forever,
Jack

My heart thuds. I raise my eyes to Gigi. "Who are Jack and Ilse?"

Gigi grows quiet. "Ilse and Jack were my parents, and this novel was a big part of their love story."

Jack and Ilse. Why have I never heard these names? I thought Mom always said Nana's name was June. But I might have it all wrong. With Nana having passed years before I was born and Dad's mom as well, the names jumble together. I need to pay better attention.

"Life is a long and winding road, my angel. Read the book, and once you understand this story, I'll fill you in on Jack and Ilse," says Gigi.

I slowly turn the page. My brows arch at the publication date of this book—1925—close to a hundred years ago! I flip the pages with cautious dexterity; each page is thin and fragile, like it might tear with a light touch.

I skip forward to the last page. "There are only two hundred and eighteen pages in this book. That's short for a novel. *Twilight* is close to five hundred pages."

Her eyes flash at me. "Yes, but don't be fooled. Short doesn't mean any less engaging. Fitzgerald is a master with words, and every sentence serves a purpose. He easily accomplishes in two hundred pages what most authors barely scratch the surface with in twice that amount."

"Are you up for the challenge?" she asks. "Should we make a wager on which novel tells a better tale?"

I cackle, but it sounds like more of a throat clearing. It shouldn't surprise me that Gigi's a gambler. "I'll take that bet. But I'm warning you, Edward is easy to fall for."

"You haven't met Jay Gatsby yet," she says.

"Touché. What's the wager?"

Twinkle, twinkle go her eyes. "Perhaps I get a third day with you each week for the summer?"

I nod, like I'm contemplating her proposal, but Gigi wanting to spend more time with me makes my insides shine. "That's fair. But what if I win?"

"You could drop down to one day a week."

I think that would hurt her feelings, and she's turned out to be way more interesting than I would have guessed. "Oh, no. I want to spend two days with you."

A ginormous smile lights her up like a Christmas tree.

"I think I know what the perfect wager would be."

"Yes?" Gigi asks.

"To rummage through your lipstick and nail polish collections." Before she can reply, I add, "When I went to your bedroom, I stumbled upon your lipsticks stacked on the counter. I'm impressed."

Gigi throws her head back and howls with laughter. Her

giggles are high-pitched bursts of joy, falling out of her in a stuttering pattern, and I can't help but laugh alongside her. "Deal. Let's shake on it. We each have three weeks to finish the books, and then we can have a lengthy discussion. In fact, let's have a party to celebrate our favorite novels."

When I extend my hand, she leans forward and clasps it with both of hers before squeezing tightly. "Three weeks? Gigi, I can knock this out in a few days!"

She reclines into her chair, falling into laughter. "You've always had a wonderful spirit to you. You remind me of my younger self."

I beam at her.

Mom picks me up promptly at four. I hop in her car and take out my AirPods.

"Not so fast. I'd like a report first."

I bite my tongue, but she was rude to Gigi. Rather than coming to the door and saying hello, she texted me to come outside. I haven't paid much attention before now, but she's prickly toward Gigi. I find this strange since Mom's the one behind my summer stint.

"It was good. What do you want, like a play-by-play of our day?"

Mom grips the steering wheel with both hands, her lips pressed together. "I was concerned since I know you weren't exactly enthusiastic when asked to help Gigi out."

I'm not about to let her know I enjoyed the day. I might need to milk Gigi duty to get my way on a few things on the home front. "I helped her with chores around the house. We cleaned out her closet, and I loaded and unloaded the dishwasher. She had me take the trash out. That's about it. She likes to read, so we spent an hour with our noses in books."

Mom bobs her chin up and down. "Well, I'm glad to hear it. I appreciate you pitching in since work is so busy."

I don't point out the obvious: Mom could stop by on the weekends or after work if she wanted to help. "You're welcome. Oh, and she wants me to drive her around, so don't let me forget my permit next visit."

"What did you and Gigi talk about?" she asks.

Why does Mom always want to know every single detail of my day? "She asked about high school—things like my running and what subjects I like. And then we talked about her home. I had forgotten how beautiful Gigi's house is, with all the antiques, colorful rugs, and old books. She owns a lot of fancy stuff like china, and she was teaching me about Herend, which are these little porcelain animal figurines, and I love all her blue pottery."

Mom is eerily silent, not even a "yep" response. "Why are you so quiet? What, you don't like Gigi's taste? Her style is super traditional, but it's still nice."

Mom takes in a deep breath and releases a long sigh. "Her home is lovely."

I turn my head and gaze out the window, popping in my AirPods.

CHAPTER THREE

It's my second day with Gigi. I hop out of Dad's car and don't bother to look back. I hope the time flies by like last time. Gigi had shown me where she keeps her spare key, so I can let myself in if she doesn't answer on the first knock. She's discreetly hidden it in her yard under a decorative rock, which is way better than Mom and Dad's hiding choice under the planter next to the front door. I'm like, "Why don't we just leave the house unlocked and post a 'Burglars Welcome' sign?"

Using the key, I let myself in. "Hello! Gigi, it's Hailey! I'm here!" I shout.

Gigi calls out that she's in her office. I drop my bag on the living room sofa and march toward her voice.

She is sitting in front of her computer, hunched over the screen, reading glasses perched on the tip of her nose. "Good morning," I say cheerily.

She swivels her office chair toward me, greeting me with a warm smile. "Good morning. I was just getting caught up on my email."

I didn't expect Gigi to be computer literate. "You know how to use a computer?"

Her head pops back. She crinkles her nose and squares her jaw. "I'm not *that* old. We've had home computers since the '90s, dear. I just have a difficult time seeing the print on this screen."

I bend over her shoulder to view the monitor. "I can help with that. Let me adjust the font size and the background color of the screen."

I quickly make the changes, and her eyes widen. "Thank you," she says. "That would have taken a five-hour call to tech support to accomplish on my own."

My brain suddenly registers that if she is sending an email, she must have Wi-Fi. I'm way too slow in the mornings. "You have Wi-Fi?"

"Yes, I have Wi-Fi. Not that I know how to work any of it. One of the neighborhood kids helps me when issues arise."

Her hands are perched perfectly over the keyboard and her fingers move at a dazzling pace. "Where'd you learn to type so fast?" I ask.

She stops, and her hands hang in the air above the keys. "All girls were required to take typing when I was in school. We didn't have the career opportunities young women have today," she says.

She turns her head over her shoulder. "You don't take typing? Your mother took typing."

"Nope. We take computer classes, but they teach us programming."

Her fingers fly again. "That's called progress. It's good to know all that bra-burning wasn't for naught."

I think she's making a joke, but I don't get it.

She pauses to review her message, and then hits the send button with a dramatic press of her forefinger. "You ready to run some errands?" she asks.

I stick both thumbs up. "I brought my permit. We have a busy schedule today, huh?"

"Yes, and I hope you can keep up."

I let out a laugh. She sure is spunky for an old lady.

She pushes herself out of the chair. She's wearing navy capri pants, a hot pink gingham button-down, and thick, white running shoes—not a brand I recognize. We might need to add "buy a new pair of kicks" to her to-do list. Bangle bracelets line her arm, jangling as she walks toward the door. "Come on, let's grab my list and head out."

We enter the garage, and my eyes lock on the monster car she drives. It's a four-door Lincoln town car and at least ten years old. The car is big, boxy, and brown. Is there a car with less personality than a four-door sedan in a shade of brown? I'm gonna look ridiculous driving this tank. Please, Lord, don't let me run into anyone from school today.

Gigi opens the garage door and sunlight pours in, but she doesn't move toward the Lincoln. "Not that car. Today, we're going to drive Betty," she says.

I scrunch up my face. "You have another car? And you named it Betty?"

She waves at me to follow.

We walk outside. Adjacent to her back fence stands a separate one-car garage. She pulls out a clicker, and a loud clanging follows as a mechanical chain slowly lifts the door to the smaller garage.

Gigi sure is full of surprises. A car covered with a tarp fills the entire space.

"Could you give me a hand?" she asks.

We each take an end of the cover, pull it over the top of the car, and dump it in a pile beneath the bumper. My eyes about pop out of their sockets, and my mouth falls open. I'm staring at a gorgeous, powder-blue convertible with shiny chrome wheels. "This car is insane! This is yours?"

Gigi gives a triumphant grin. She opens the door and reaches in, releasing the levers, cranking the top down. "I had a feeling you would love it."

She steps back to admire the car with me. "This beauty—also known as *Blue Betty*—is a Cadillac Eldorado. Convertible, of course. Your grandfather bought this car for me as a wedding gift. It's the only decent thing that man ever did for me."

I stand there dumbfounded at this car and its connection to my grandfather. I've never heard a word about him from Mom. I just know he walked out when she was little. "What year did you get this car?"

"1970."

My mind races. "You've had this car for fifty freaking years? Oops. Sorry for the bad language."

She raises her eyes to the sky, tapping her index finger on her chin. "I hadn't done the math but yes, about that long."

We approach the car, and she pats the side door, running her fingers back and forth, like she's stroking a favorite pet. "I could never part with Betty. She and I shared a lot of good times through the years. I haven't driven her in ages, so she may need some encouragement from us."

I walk around the car, gawking at her beauty but also completely intimidated by her size. This car is a boat, easily measuring double the length of the Volvo I've learned to drive on. But man, she's lit, like *on fire*.

"This is amazing, but I don't think I can drive a car this long and wide."

Gigi steps toward me and wraps her arm around my shoulders. "I believe you were looking for a little adventure this summer. I suggest you grab the bull by the horns and go for it!"

Gigi disarms me with her confidence. It's like she's trying to help me when she's the one needing assistance. "Are you sure? What if I get into an accident or bang her up?"

She moves to the passenger side of the car and slips into the front seat. "Utter nonsense. You take after me, which means you'll master her quickly. Now, let's get going because it's going to be incredibly hot in a few hours, and then we'll have to put the top up. What fun is a convertible if your hair can't blow in the wind?"

I slide into the driver's side and reach for the seat belt, but the material is flimsy and stretched out. Pulling it over my shoulder, I struggle to clip it into the rusty silver buckle. The belt droops, loosely falling around my waist. "Is there a way to tighten this?" I ask.

"The car has some wear and tear, but honestly, we didn't use seat belts back then."

"No seat belts? I don't think I've ever not worn one."

She smacks her lips loudly. "No seat belts, no car seats for children. In fact, most babies rode on a parent's lap in the front seat! I brought your mother home from the hospital in this car. I drove, and your grandfather held her in his arms. I never trusted that man to drive Betty."

Another grandfather reference! He's definitely sounding like bad news.

I scan Betty's interior. Plush, white leather seats perfectly complement the baby-blue exterior. Only an arm rest separates me from Gigi, and the front seat could easily fit three people.

I'm mesmerized by all the old buttons and gadgets. The radio and air conditioning controls are on the driver's side dashboard; nothing is digital, from the speedometer to the gas gauge. I notice another radio under the passenger-side dashboard, but it looks so strange. I point to it. "What exactly is this, and does it work?"

Gigi licks her thumb before wiping the dust from the dials. "It's called an eight-track stereo. And it most definitely works. Have you ever heard one play?"

"Never."

"The eight-track tape was a precursor to the cassette and CD."

She opens the glove compartment and pulls out a cartridge, popping it in. I read the name: *Abbey Road*.

"Nothing brings me joy like driving around in Betty and listening to The Beatles," she says.

She hands me the key, and I place it in the ignition. Betty roars to life with a loud boom. I let out a light squeal and Gigi laughs.

I face her. "What happens now?"

She taps her finger on the gearshift. "Put her in reverse and slowly back out. It will be a tight turnaround, but we've got plenty of time."

It takes me about twenty half-turn rotations of the steering wheel to get her ready to exit the driveway. I turn to Gigi, my hands squeezing the wheel tightly. "The alley is so narrow. I'm scared I'll scratch her on a fence or ram into a row of garbage cans."

She pats my leg. "Take it easy and you'll be fine."

She sweetly sings the song from the eight-track. I vaguely recognize the music. As I lurch the car out into the alley, I push on the brake to recheck both ways. "What's this song called?"

"Don't pull out. Put the car in park," she says tersely.

My stomach tightens. What just happened? "Did I do something wrong?"

She purses her lips and glowers at me. "No, but I'm deeply troubled that you don't know the name of 'Come Together' by The Beatles. Hailey, if there is one gift I'm going to leave you with before I die, it is a love and appreciation for the greatest band of all time."

I'm starting to think Gigi is a little crazy. "You're upset because I didn't know the name of this song?"

Gigi's eyes pinch together as she adjusts the bracelets on her wrist, untangling them from each other. "Yes."

She continues, "The Beatles have been the soundtrack to my life. I own all their albums on eight-track, so we're going to have to spend a lot of time driving around in Betty so you can learn their music."

I wait for her to tell me to keep driving, but she's not finished lecturing me. "Now *Abbey Road* is their last studio album, which came out in 1970, the year I got Blue Betty. You can bet your boots I burned a hole in this eight-track that year."

She rummages through the glove box and selects a different cartridge. She removes *Abbey Road* and pops the new one in. "You do like music?" she asks.

"Of course. I'm a teenager!" I smirk. "But no one I know listens to The Beatles."

She's the one smirking now. "Well, that's a shame. You should start a new trend."

Yeah, I'm gonna take a hard pass on that one. I'm not the type of girl that gets things trending. I don't have followers or a following. I'm not weird, but I don't run with the popular crowd.

She claps her hands together. "Let's start at the beginning. I first heard The Beatles in 1963, when I was about your age. After that my life was never the same. They were the first boy band in the world, captivating young girls' hearts, minds, and *sex drives* with their melodies, good looks, and charm." She winks. "George was always my favorite."

I bust into giggles. She is reminding me of Livi with Shawn Mendes. When we we're thirteen, she became totally obsessed with him but thankfully outgrew it last year. If I don't hear "Stiches" ever again, it will be too soon.

"This album is called *Please, Please Me* and is filled with Lennon–McCartney-written songs, including two of my favorites, 'I Saw Her Standing There' and 'Love Me Do.'"

The music plays, and Gigi loudly sings along. Thank goodness she has such a beautiful voice, or this drive would be excruciating. She stops singing and says to me, "You may pull out into the alley now."

We return to Gigi's in time for lunch. I'm relieved to be finished driving Betty. Although it was a thrill to be in such a cool car, I was anxious the entire time. She's so long and feels so heavy, and the steering wheel is a beast to turn. But, man, a convertible is fun!

I carry in the groceries, place them on the kitchen counter, and ask for instructions on where to put things away.

"Oh, anywhere in the fridge works."

I begin unloading, and unconsciously slip into Mom's strict rules about refrigerator organization: top shelf for dairy products and other ready-to-eat foods, raw meats on the middle shelf, and fruit, vegetables, and salad in the bottom drawer.

We eat turkey sandwiches and Sun Chips (Gigi's favorite), followed by a few Oreos. Gigi likes to dip them in milk like I do. After a big dunk, I say, "Betty is a rock star. I think five people stopped us to ask questions about her. Does that always happen?"

She holds up a finger, taking a moment to chew her cookie. She dabs the corners of her mouth with a napkin before returning the linen cloth to her lap. "Yes, she always collects a crowd of admirers. I just haven't taken her out in so long that I had forgotten her magnetism. It felt so good to have the top down, listening to my favorite band, with my best granddaughter." She touches my hand, wrapping her fingers around mine, rubbing her thumb over my palm.

"That was fun. I loved driving her." I add, "Just so you know, I'm aware of a few Beatles songs, like 'Yesterday,' 'Twist & Shout,' and 'Yellow Submarine'." I'm drawing a blank on other Beatles hits. "What's your favorite song?"

"That's like asking who's your favorite child," she says.

Huh? Doesn't everyone have a favorite child? Because Dad favors me, and Mom is all over Kyle.

"Tell you what," she says, "I'll make you a couple of lists of Beatles songs to take home with you. I'll share a few of my favorites, and then you can take a listen and tell me what you think."

I can't imagine that I'm going to like her musical suggestions, but she's an entertaining old lady, so I'll indulge her. "Sounds like a plan."

Gigi rises, pulls open a kitchen drawer, and returns to the table with a pen and paper. While Gigi works on her lists, I load our plates in the dishwasher. I sit back down at the table, and she pushes the sheets of paper over to me. "I made you a few compilations because The Beatles have so many wonderful love songs, and then a list of my other favorites."

Perusing the song titles, I recognize a few, but don't know most of them. "Gigi, there's almost forty songs here. All these songs jumped off the top of your head in, like, thirty seconds?"

"Well, I've had fifty years to think about it. Now I have the albums in my living room and the cartridges in Betty, so no excuses to not take a listen."

I gently fold the piece of paper in half and lift my body up. "Don't worry, I plan to listen to them all. We can have a music hour to go along with our reading hour."

A buzzing alarm blares from another room of the house. She jumps up, her face as frantic as her body. "Shoot, I need to take my medication. If I didn't set that alarm, I would never remember."

I wasn't aware Gigi took medication, but from the commercials always running on TV, it seems like most old people take something. "What do you take medication for?"

"I have high blood pressure. It's a common ailment of old age."

She exits the kitchen, disappearing down the long hallway toward her bedroom. I retreat to the living room and grab *The Great Gatsby* from my bag. I sit in my regular spot— the wingback chair across from Gigi's club chair. With the book in my lap, I lean my head back and close my eyes.

I stayed up way too late last night watching a marathon of *Criminal Minds*, and then I couldn't fall asleep. All the bad guys kept running through my thoughts.

I'm not sure how much time has passed when I hear Gigi call my name. I snap my head forward, catching a little drool with my tongue as I close my mouth. Gigi stands over me, her brows furrowed together, her lips pushed to one side. "Do you need a nap? You're welcome to go rest in the guest bedroom."

Mom would kill me, but a bed sounds like heaven. "Thank you. Are you sure you don't mind?"

Gigi places her arm around my shoulder and lifts me from the chair. She guides me to the first guest bedroom. While I take my shoes off, she pulls down the bedcovers. I shouldn't take advantage of Gigi when I'm the one supposed to be helping her, but I'm so tired. I lie down, and she raises the comforter up to my chin. She sits beside me, tucking a few curls behind my ear.

My eyes flutter open and shut under the haze of impending sleep. She rubs the tip of her thumb over my cheek, moving her hand to stroke my hair. "You are such a beautiful girl. You're what I always imagined she looked like, with your dark curls and fair skin."

Gigi's not making much sense, but I'm so tired I might not have heard her correctly. I utter a few *ums*, and my eyes close. A faint voice talks to me, but everything quickly fades to black.

My eyes pop open, and I glance at my watch. I slept for two hours! Throwing back the covers, I swing my legs out of bed. After taking a moment to tidy the room, I pick up my shoes and tiptoe down the hallway. Gigi is asleep in her chair.

My book still rests where I left it, so I quietly sit down and start reading.

My phone rings. I scramble to grab it from the bottom of my bag and press decline to silence it, even though it's Mom. Gigi jerks awake. "I'm sorry if my phone woke you," I say softly.

She straightens her shoulders in the chair. "I wasn't asleep. I was just resting my eyes."

I check my messages and see the following string:

Here.
I'm waiting.
Hello??
I'M ON A CALL AND CAN'T COME GET YOU.
COME OUT NOW!

Mom reverts to all caps in text messages when she's annoyed, and she enters DEFCON 1 when we get off schedule. I check the clock on my phone and realize she's been waiting ten minutes. This is not going to be good. I stand and jam *The Great Gatsby* into my bag. "Mom's here to get me so I gotta run. Thanks for letting me drive Betty."

I take a few steps toward the front door before flipping around. "Oh! And thank you for The Beatles recommendations."

Her posture remains upright. She isn't frazzled like I am about Mom. "We had fun together. We completed the trinity of a perfect day: we read a good book, we listened to a great song, and we drove around in a cool car."

I break into a smile. "I like that."

"You'll be back next week?"

"Yep." I catch my mistake. "I mean, yes, ma'am."

I blow her a kiss, and she gives me a twinkling wink.

CHAPTER FOUR

It's been four days since I've seen Gigi, and I must admit I miss the old bird. I have a little pep in my step this morning, unsure of what surprises might unfold over on Oxford Street.

I spent the weekend listening to The Beatles and reading *The Great Gatsby*. I've read the first three chapters and just met Gatsby. He's super rich and throws elaborate and glitzy parties, but no one seems to actually know him.

I made better headway with The Beatles, moving through most of the songs on the first list. I won't tip my hand right away, but, man, those guys know how to write a love song! I'll have to show Gigi my Beatles playlist on Spotify. But considering she doesn't own a smartphone, it's highly unlikely she knows how to stream music. She whipped out one of those funny flip phones last time I was at her house, and I about fell over.

I have a genius idea. My family should surprise Gigi with a smartphone for her seventy-fifth birthday! I'm not sure Mom will go for spending hundreds of dollars on Gigi, considering she hasn't even stopped in to say hello, but I'll work on Dad.

Gigi's out in front of her house inspecting her lawn when Dad and I roll up. "Good morning, Celeste," Dad says through my open door.

Gigi approaches the car, holding her hand up to shield her eyes from the bright sun. "Hello, Dashing Dave," she replies with a toothy grin.

She's always called Dad "Dashing Dave," which I don't get because he's not dashing. A line drive pummeled his nose in high school, leaving a crooked and bumpy snout. His almond-shaped eyes and warm smile help offset the nose, but dashing? Not a chance.

He laughs, and they chitchat for a minute about the weather before he takes off.

She outstretches the shears she holds in her garden gloves. "Could you be a dear and help me pull a few weeds? The heat will soon make it intolerable outside."

We walk the perimeter and peek our heads in bushes and flower beds, digging out persistent pests that attack her yard. The main culprit is called nutsedge. It's a weed that requires the actual nut buried down deep in the dirt to be dug out, or the weed will keep coming back to life, wrecking her lawn.

I had snapped the first few from the top of the root without procuring the nut before Gigi caught my mistake and steered me in the right direction.

As we work on the weeds, I ask her about the different flowers scattered around her yard. She answers like a walking encyclopedia. She throws names at me in quick succession as I try to match the name to the flower she points to in each pot and bed. "Those beautiful pink flowers are penta, and they come in white, red, or deep pink."

Gigi continues the botany lesson. "I have impatiens in those beds under the magnolia. They are fabulous flowers but require shade."

She wags her finger toward the beautiful magnolia tree. The tree is the focal point of her front yard, with tall limbs that majestically barrel toward the sky. It's a tree that calls to be climbed, but I was always too little to jump up to the first branch.

"I bought this house because of that tree," says Gigi. "The homes were all similar on this street, but that tree spoke to me." She shuffles toward the side. "I love the deep purple of these Angelonias, and they do well in the sun and heat. Oh, and those yellow flowers are lantana and are another wonderful hot weather plant."

Gigi continues the rapid-fire education as she stops in front of her navy planters by the door. "I adore these petunias, and they are so stunning in the spring. Unfortunately, with this heat picking up, they are about to be done. What if you and I go by the nursery and find flowers we both like that will survive July and August's onslaught?"

"Yes, let's add that to the to-do list. I've never been to a nursery."

She stares at me, her lips parting slightly. I expect her to lay on some criticism of Mom and Dad for my lack of education, but then her face brightens. "Prepare to be awed by the endless flowers. I can spend hours roaming the aisles of the nursery, mesmerized by the colors and aromas."

We then loop around to the backyard to her prized possession: her beloved rosebushes. I remember the pricklers from when I was little because I had kicked a ball in the bushes, and it was the only time Gigi ever raised her voice at me. I think her flare-up was a combination of her fear I might damage her roses and concern the bushes might bang me up. The roses won that battle, a few thorns nicking me bad enough to draw blood. I'm pretty sure I can remember every incident from childhood that resulted in pain—bee stings, rose pricks, and rollerblade wipeouts are a few that come to mind.

She rattles off names again as she approaches the bushes and gently inspects them. "Please hand me those shears."

She clips a few blooming roses at the stem and carries them inside with us. She places the flowers down on the kitchen counter. "Could you please fetch the vase from the top of the pantry?" she asks.

Dragging a chair over, I then step up to reach the top shelf. I jump down and hand the vase to her. She gently removes the leaves from the roses, plucking them off one by one. She then cuts the stems at an angle and pours a little sugar into the vase. "Flowers have always made me so happy. It's important to find simple things in life that bring you joy." She lets out a chuckle. "It's a cliché but rings true: Always remember to stop and smell the roses."

Gigi is a trip with her mantras and advice.

"Where did you learn about flowers?" I ask. "Mom doesn't exactly have a green thumb." Mom outsources all aspects of the yard.

Dad used to mow our grass, but she would get frustrated when jobs weren't completed with military precision. For the sake of Dad's sanity, they hired a lawn crew.

Our yard is sparse when it comes to flowers. Mom prefers the low-maintenance bushes that bloom in spring and magically come back every year.

Gigi arranges the flowers, crafting a perfect centerpiece. "Nana loved flowers. She would spend hours in the beds in the backyard in Waco. When she and Papa moved here to live with me and your mom, she planted those rosebushes."

"Those were Nana's?"

She nods slowly. "Yes."

I lean against the kitchen counter. "And her name was Ilse?"

Gigi glances down at the flowers. "No, Nana's name was June."

I was right! What does it all mean? "So, Nana, your mother, is named June. But you said the names in the book—Ilse and Jack—were your parents."

She raises her eyes. We face each other in the small kitchen nook, only a few feet separate us. "Have you finished *The Great Gatsby*? That was our deal. Read the book and then I will tell you about Jack and Ilse."

I squint. "I'm working on it. These people aren't very likeable. I like Gatsby and Nick, but I'm not sure about the rest of the characters."

Her mouth twitches. "Well, you're perceptive."

"Have you read much of *Twilight* yet? What do you think of Bella and Edward?"

She walks to the sink and turns on the faucet to rinse her hands. She shifts her head toward me as she rubs her palms together under the running water. "I understand your attraction to Edward. He's handsome and thoughtful, but I find Bella boring."

"But she's sweet and good where Daisy is shallow."

Gigi dries her hands with a paper towel and then pitches the crinkled paper in the trash beneath the sink. She stops to look at me and totally disarms me with her stare. It's like she's examining every angle of my face. Heat creeps up my neck and I look away.

I step toward her. "Could you give me a few teasers on Jack and Ilse to help motivate me to finish *The Great Gatsby*?"

She moves her gaze around the kitchen before returning to meet mine. "Did you ask your mom about Ilse?"

I stop myself from telling her the truth. Mom never mentions Gigi. But I wouldn't tell Mom anything Gigi confides in me. "No, I sensed that Jack and Ilse's story was something private, so I wouldn't share it with anyone else."

She raises her hands to my cheeks, cupping them under my chin. "I knew you were going to be the one."

What is she talking about now? "The one for what?"

"To hear my story and keep my secrets."

Goosebumps spike up my arms and down my legs.

She motions with her head toward the living room. "Come on, let's get to reading."

We sit and read in silence. I try to focus on Gatsby, but my mind is on what Gigi said about keeping her secrets. Raising my eyes from my book, I watch her read *Twilight*. She only has a few pages left. A grin spreads across her face. "You look engaged over there. So what's the verdict?"

She fights an unwilling smile, then closes the book and drops it to her lap. "I've been mildly entertained. I'm almost finished with the epilogue. Are we honestly to believe she didn't know they were going to prom? But I'm quite confident that *The Great Gatsby* is going to stay with you in a more profound and meaningful way. It's hard not to fall in love with Jay Gatsby and his optimism."

We sit quietly for a few moments. My mind drifts to Jack and Ilse. "So, a few hints about your parents to keep me motivated to finish?"

Removing her reading glasses from the end of her nose, she places the specs and book on the table beside her. "I have never shared their story. It's a long and complicated tale. I almost don't know where to begin."

She draws in a long breath. "My parents, Jack and Ilse, met in Germany after World War II. Jack was a soldier in the US Army who had fought in many battles, including the Battle of the Bulge. The war ended, and they met and fell in love. They moved to Paris to start a life together, but Ilse had lingering health issues from the war. She passed away shortly after I was born. Jack brought me to America, to Waco, Texas, to live with his sister, June. Nana is really my Aunt June."

My head spins, and a stabbing pain settles in my chest, my heart breaking for people I don't even know. This might be one of the saddest stories I've ever heard. I have so many questions, but two that burn brightest inside me. "Why is this a secret? Why doesn't Mom know this story?" I ask.

Gigi's face contorts in a strange way. Her eyebrows push together and wrinkles huddle around her cheeks. "Life is complicated. Decisions were made to protect the both of us."

What does that mean? What could they need protecting from? "I don't understand."

She releases a deep sigh. "I've shared enough for today. Hurry up and finish the book so you can fully understand Ilse and Jack's story."

I wrap my arms around Gigi, and she hugs me tightly. I fumble in my mind, trying to figure out what to say. I'm only fifteen, but I'm starting to realize sometimes words are useless.

I step away and she rises. Her face is no longer wearing a frown; her wrinkles settle back to a resting state. How does she flip the switch so fast? "All right. Enough sadness today. Let's go have some fun. I think we should take Betty out for ice cream."

"I'll never say no to ice cream, but I'm not sure about driving Betty. Turning her is super scary and parking near impossible in crowded places."

She walks toward the kitchen, and I trail after her. "There is an easy solution for that problem. Let's head over to the high school parking lot and give you some practice. Your school will be empty during summer, correct?"

She packs her handbag and ties her straw hat on, looping the fabric straps under her chin, a decision apparently made. "Yes, it should be a ghost town up there. I'm game for that."

As expected, it takes me a solid ten minutes to back Betty out and turn her around to exit the alley, but Gigi doesn't seem to notice as she rifles through her Beatles tapes. "Let's skip ahead to *Sgt. Pepper's Lonely Hearts Club Band*. This album has so many great songs."

We cruise over to school, singing, "With a Little Help from My Friends." Gigi claps her hands to the song. "John and Paul wrote this song for Ringo. He sings only a few songs, and this is his best. Ringo ends every concert with it, which is my absolute favorite part of his show."

Gigi keeps surprising me. "You've seen The Beatles in concert?"

"Is the Pope Polish?"

Now I'm confused because I'm pretty sure the Pope is from Argentina.

She continues, "I saw The Beatles play in Dallas on September 18, 1964. That concert was one of the greatest nights of my life. The boys stood on stage in their suits, their floppy hair bouncing to the beat, their faces full of joyous smiles. I screamed the entire time, losing my voice completely. I was thrown into such a tizzy that it took me weeks to recover. I've seen Ringo and Paul numerous times through the years, but nothing on this earth matches seeing John, Paul, George, and Ringo together."

Livi must meet Gigi. Our moms took us to see Taylor Swift last year, and I thought Livi might spontaneously combust from all the screaming and freaking out that night. I love Taylor, but Livi falls into that slightly concerning fangirl crowd. Gigi is giving off the same vibes.

As we sit at a red light, I peer over at Gigi. She shakes her head to the beat, her face joyful as she sings along to the song. I'm totally convinced she does get by with help from her friends.

She points her finger at me. "The Beatles have provided me with the three guiding tenets of my life: I get by with a little help from my friends, all you need is love, and let it be."

I think she's being serious, so I hold in my laughter.

"Ahh, and now we segue into 'Lucy in the Sky with Diamonds.'" She sings along to the music, doing this weird car dance. I mean, the song is pretty eclectic with that organ at the beginning, but she's moved into the trippy mood fast. I throw my head back in laughter. Livi's going to die when I tell her my best summer memory is spending the afternoon in a convertible watching my grandmother's psychedelic dance moves as we sing Beatles songs.

I join in for the chorus and belt out, "Lucy in the Sky with Diamonds," as we arrive at the high school parking lot. I maneuver Betty over to the large empty area by the football stadium and throw her into park.

Gigi grabs the dial and turns the volume down. "Time to practice."

"Can you first give me some advice on turning this bad boy?"

She opens the car door and steps out. "Yes, but first let me drive her to remember the feel. It's been a few years."

I scooch over to the passenger side, and she takes the wheel. Next thing I know, Gigi guns her, looping us around fast. I squeal in delight.

She slams on the brakes, and my wild eyes lock on her. She delicately adjusts her hat in the rearview mirror as if she just finished a lovely stroll in the park, rather than driving like a homicidal maniac. "It's all coming back to me. You must turn the steering wheel before you want the car to turn. She's got a little delay. Then just lean into it."

Did she honestly just advise me to lean into a car? This isn't like a bike where my body weight will have an impact, but I'm not going to debate physics with her. "Any other tips?"

She pushes open the driver side door, springing from the car to return to the passenger side. "No. You just have to get used to her, so let's get practicing."

Moving myself over to the driver's side, I take the wheel and try to follow her instructions. I practice backing her out of a parking spot and pulling her in as well. I'm starting to get the hang of turning this beautiful boat.

We're parked having a laugh as she sings, "When I'm Sixty-Four," which she modifies to "When I'm Seventy-Four," when we're interrupted by approaching voices. I gaze in their direction, and my stomach drops. A crowd of football players are exiting the stadium; the shiny, perfect boys with muscles and good hair and straight teeth. I slump down in Betty, hoping my head is no longer visible and that they'll just casually walk by the old lady in the classic car.

But I hear male voices shouting near me.

"Yo, check out that car."

"Man, that is so dope."

"Bruh, look at those chrome wheels."

Please don't let them see me. *Please don't let them see me!*

"Who's in the car with the old lady?"

It's official. I've entered the gates of hell. I try to disappear within my mind, but they quickly approach the car, like a stampede of wild mustangs.

All I can think is please don't let this be happening. Please let this be a joke. Sweat drips down my spine and the hairs on the back of my neck spike up. And then it happens. My absolute worst freaking nightmare.

Gigi is waving her hand. "Hello there, boys!" she says.

She is speaking to the football team! Does she not understand the precarious nature of the high school social strata? For the love of God, please make this stop!

I inch myself up to brace for impact. My first one-on-one with the football team, and I'm with my grandmother. This is not the impression I want to make! I finally lift my eyes and settle on the gang's leaders standing closest to the car—our star quarterback, Cody Myers, his number one receiver, Blake Alexander, and the national blue chip running back, DeMarcus Thomas. These three guys are the trifecta of high school status, power, and popularity. They don't know me, or at least I don't think they do. DeMarcus and Cody are rising seniors, and Blake is a rising junior, like me.

Blake gives a half-smile. "Hey, Hailey. Sweet car. Hi, Mrs. Turner."

I have officially entered the Twilight Zone. Did Blake Alexander just call me by name? More importantly, how does he know that Gigi's name is Mrs. Turner?

My cheeks are aflame; I'm sure my face has turned bright crimson. With my pale skin, blushing is never subtle. "Hey," I reply.

DeMarcus slaps Blake in the chest. "You know this girl?"

Blake's eyes catch mine, and I'm momentarily lost in their amber glow. "Yeah. We've had a few classes together. English and chemistry last year, right?"

Blake Alexander knows we had classes together? *Blake Alexander knows we had classes together!* We've never exchanged a word, even though he sat in front of me for part of the year. Adrenaline courses through my veins. My head swirls. "Yeah, that's right."

Gigi takes her sunglasses off, twirling them in her hand. Her eyes twinkle.

Crap.

"Would y'all like to hop in and go for a spin with us?"

I must have misheard her. I look over again at Gigi, and her eyes are still twinkling.

Double crap.

Absolutely not. I cannot drive these boys. I'm on the verge of a nervous breakdown. I grab my thigh, trying to stop the shaking.

"Yeah, that would be awesome," replies DeMarcus, and he does an incredible athletic jump, pitching his body into the backseat. Blake and Cody fall in beside him.

Somebody save me!

My entire high school reputation hinges on my ability to

drive Betty and impress these guys. What was Gigi thinking? I exhale the breath I've been holding in. "You need to drive. I can't—"

She holds up a hand and cuts me off. "Let her rip, and I'll make sure the music matches. I have the perfect song!"

Gigi and the freaking Beatles! Can't she see I'm having an existential crisis? She clicks in a new cartridge. "You boys ever listen to The Beatles?"

The guys snicker. The first few guitar riffs of "Revolution" play, and the music is a jolt of energy, lifting my courage, and propelling me forward. "Can one of y'all tell your friends to back up?" I ask.

DeMarcus barks at the lingering others who do as commanded, but they remain a captive audience. I back Betty out and turn her around. Gigi gives me a thumbs up, and I haul ass, throwing Betty into a series of donuts. The boys in back hoot and holler as we whip around again and again. I slam the brakes, and then watch them in the rearview mirror as their heads jerk forward and their forearms jut out to catch the back of the front seat, deflecting the impact of the sudden stop. At that exact moment, the song ends, and they nod and smile. One by one they hop out of the car.

"Impressive driving," Blake says, his face wrapped in a grin as he pushes his thick brown hair from his eyes.

Electricity rockets through my body with such force that I press my fingers to my wrist to check that I have a pulse. Okay, still alive.

Clearing my throat, I squeak out, "Thanks," but my voice pitches to such a high note I'm not sure the sound is audible to the human ear. I'm speaking dolphin.

DeMarcus taps the side of the car, before raising his arm up, and we share a high-five. Cody lifts his chin at me and gives a half-smile.

A compliment, a high-five, and a smile from those three? I'm dead.

Gigi directs her megawatt grin at the boys. "Nice meeting you," she says. "Blake, tell your mother hello for me."

He waves and walks away, jabbing his friends on the shoulders as they share a laugh.

As exciting as that was, I need to flee this scene. I peel out, black marks covering the parking lot.

"Watch out, Mario Andretti!" Gigi says in delight.

Who the heck is Mario Andretti? More importantly, how does Gigi know Blake Alexander?

As Gigi and I sit inside the ice cream shop licking our cones, I marvel at what just happened. Unlike me, Gigi is totally unphased by speaking to three of the best-looking and most famous faces at my high school. Those three are supposed to guide our team to a state championship this year, which is the pinnacle of Texas high school sports. Heck, our entire community's dreams hang in the balance with these guys. They already have ardent and loyal fans, including every kid I know. It's like being sprinkled with stardust to have DeMarcus, Blake, and Cody acknowledge you.

I take a bite of chocolate chip. "How do you know Blake Alexander?" I ask in a gargled voice.

Gigi stuffs the last bite of her cone in her mouth, chewing completely before answering. "Oh, he lives down the street from me. He's the young man who helps me when I have technology issues."

"He's been in *your house*?"

She pitches her napkin in the garbage can behind her. "Yes. His mom is so lovely, always checking in on me when there's a bad storm or any neighborhood alert about robberies and the like. A wonderful family and such a well-mannered, polite young man."

I nod and fiddle with the napkin on my cone.

"He's a little dreamy, huh?"

Gigi gets it. She gets me. I lift my eyes and confess my sins. "You have no idea. I've had a crush on him since we were, like, ten. But so do most girls I know. Everyone at our school likes Blake—nerds, athletes, teachers, coaches. And what's not to like? He's super smart, a star football player, friendly to all, and so easy on the eyes. I mean, have you seen his eyes?"

Gigi laughs, and I laugh with her. I release a big sigh, about to reveal what I'm sure she already knows. "But I'm not pretty enough to get a guy like Blake. I'm not like Mom."

Gigi reaches over and squeezes my hand. "You are quite mistaken on that front," she replies. "You may need to get a different mirror because I'm staring at a young woman with a timeless beauty and soul. I guarantee you I'm not the only one who sees it."

I know parents are required to give kids encouragement—it's like part of their job—but Mom and Dad do it so frequently that they've lost all credibility with me. But something about Gigi makes me believe she's sincere.

She bobs her head from side to side. "I'm glad to know you have good taste in men. I don't have the best track record in that department."

She's talking about my grandfather, the scoundrel, right?

CHAPTER FIVE

It's Saturday morning, and I'm in bed reading *The Great Gatsby*. I haven't bothered to dress yet because I have no plans for the day. As I work my way through the novel, I try to process the enigma that is my grandmother. It's like she's launched a grenade in my life, blowing up every preconceived notion I had of who she is, who I am, and what my summer might be.

I've made it through the first hundred pages. This novel is filled with a sorry bunch of unlikable characters. Tom is horrible. Myrtle is gross. I'm not sure about Daisy, but I'm enchanted by Jay Gatsby. He's charming and mysterious, and obsessed with Daisy; he would do anything for her love. The previous chapter just ended with their kiss. Totally swoon worthy.

My phone buzzes, and I look down to see Dad has messaged me.

Want to go for a run?

Dad and I have been running buddies since elementary school. He's a dedicated runner and competes in 5Ks, 10Ks, and the occasional marathon. Mom hates running, so he roped me into the sport. I'm a talented runner, but I wouldn't say I enjoy it.

I text back,

Sure. Give me five minutes.

Our Saturday morning runs have been a ritual this past year, except in the last few weeks I've balked, claiming excessive heat when the real reason is extreme laziness. I should be gearing up for the fall race season, but it feels so far away. The truth is I've been running for so long, I just don't have to work as hard as my teammates. Running has always come naturally to me.

I rummage through my dresser drawer for my Dri-FIT tank and shorts. Standing in front of my mirror, I weave my hair into a braid and grab my running shades. Mom's insistent that I protect my blue eyes from the sun, claiming I could cause myself to go blind. Of course, I don't believe her. It sounds like one of those made-up parent urban legends, like it takes seven years to digest gum, swimming after eating can cause drowning, or drinking coffee stunts your growth. But I figure this isn't the one to chance it on.

I take the stairs two at a time and grab a mini bottled water out of the drink fridge as I pass through the garage. I gulp it down before pitching the bottle into the recycling bin on my walk to the street.

Dad is waiting for me, flexing a leg on the curb, his hands resting on his hips. "How far do you want to go?"

Dad loves to have a set course before we head out. I tend to wander when I run, letting my mood dictate the distance. "I don't care about the route, but can we keep it under six?"

"Sure. You ready?"

We start jogging an easy eight-minute pace. Dad usually kicks it up with each mile, so we'll end close to seven. His pace is a little slow for me, but I don't let on. We both know I'm faster than him now, so I try not to rub it in.

Dad likes to chat when we run. We generally have light-hearted conversations, discussing things like Bart Simpson's best pranks or funniest guest characters on *Friends* or the terrible music of his youth. I love to tease him about '90s grunge, eviscerating the "Seattle Sound," and sending him into a tailspin because the dude thinks Eddie Vedder is the Second Coming.

Occasionally we'll talk about something serious. Sometimes he's a little sneaky and casually tries to pry info out of me, but I'm usually onto his game. I've already surmised this morning's conversation is a recon mission from Mom to find out about my week with Gigi. Mom has been strangely quiet, so I bet Dad's been sent to get the dirt.

As we pass neighbors' houses, air conditioners hum, clicking on and off as they run on full blast, ready for a day of sweltering heat. We hit our stride and our breathing settles.

"How was the week with Gigi?" Dad asks.

Bingo.

Where do I even begin? I trust Dad not to tell Mom every-thing I say, but he's required to pass along some information. Do I give him bad intel? I decide to test the waters out to see what he'll share.

"It was better than expected. I hate to admit it, but you were right. She's interesting," and I say with a laugh, "and a little unusual."

He nods, like he already knows this. "How so?"

"Did you know she's obsessed with The Beatles? She's instructed me to listen to every album and even made me specific lists of songs."

Dad lets out a chuckle. "She did the same thing to me

when I first started dating your mother. But she's right to educate you on The Beatles. They're widely considered the greatest band of all time."

I look over at him. "I'm quickly learning."

Should I share with him about Jack and Ilse? The problem is I do think he'll tell Mom. I trust Dad, but Gigi is Mom's family, which puts him in a dicey situation. I don't even know the story yet, and I can't break Gigi's confidence in me.

Instead, I focus on the fun side of Gigi, sharing stories with him that I won't care if he retells. "Have you seen Betty?"

He gives me side-eye as we run. "Her convertible?"

He knows about the car as well! I don't understand how Gigi could have such an amazing car, and Dad hasn't talked about it before. "Dad, that car is so cool, and it's so fun to drive."

"She let you drive it?" he asks.

"Yeah. Is that a problem? I told Mom she asked me to drive her around."

He nods but doesn't say anything else.

Gigi and Betty. They really are a wild combination. I fall into fits of giggles thinking about them and halt in place. Dad has this rule we never stop running. Even if I'm about to hurl, we drop to the slowest jog possible, walking not allowed.

"What is it?" he asks, bouncing on his toes.

I look at him, unsure of whether to share my big news. "You promise you won't tell Mom this story?"

He crisscrosses his fingers over his heart. I hope he means it. As we return to our pace, I tell him about taking Betty to the high school parking lot and the madness that followed with Cody, Blake, and DeMarcus going for a ride. I've been dying to share with someone the biggest story of my life. With Livi away, he's the closest thing to a confidant I have.

Dad laughs when I tell him about my donuts, Gigi playing "Revolution," and the boys cheering me on. "I told you Gigi was cool," he says, with genuine affection in his voice.

We start our cool down walk, and he raises his hands over his head. "How much do I owe you for this week?"

I don't admit that was a jerk move but simply play it off. "I was just giving you a hard time. I would never make you pay me for spending time with Gigi."

His face breaks into a wide grin. I think I just earned a little redemption.

It's Monday morning, and I'm back at Gigi's. She's obsessed with having her lawn pristine and weed-free, which requires a lot of work, and it now falls on my shoulders. Just like last week, I arrive at her house, and she has the gardening gloves and shears ready for me.

The sun shines brightly over a cloudless sky. We're thirty minutes into de-weeding her yard, and the heat is unyielding. Sweat drips down my back and legs, and I can even feel it between my toes. The thick humidity hangs in the air, my arms and legs heavy like limbs made of cement. I'm bent over a flower bed, digging out another annoying nutsedge when I hear Gigi's voice.

"Good morning to you as well! Hailey, come say hello."

I pop up and notice my shirt is damp with sweat, clinging to my arms and stomach. A loose curl tickles my face and I tuck it away. Yanking on my sticky top, I look over at Gigi.

Blake Alexander stands beside her.

I. Am. Dying.

He's also a sweaty mess, his Dri-FIT tank glued to his torso. His hair is wet, and droplets run down the side of his cheeks, which he flicks off with his finger. "Hi, Hailey."

I wave but remain tongue-tied. What does one even say in reply?

"We were just finishing up some yard work and about

to have a refreshing glass of iced tea," says Gigi. "Would you like to join us?"

He shifts back and forth, not nervously, but in a confident, cool-guy way that tells me he's completely comfortable standing in the heat with my grandmother and me. His gaze seems to be stuck on me. He smiles, and his left cheek dimple appears. The ground tremors beneath my feet. How can one guy be so gorgeous? I, of course, have noticed his dimple before. I've watched it since second grade, but it's never been directed at me.

I will be gracious and provide the guy an easy out. "Gigi, that's so polite of you, but I'm sure he's got a busy day." I lift my chin at him, telepathing the message, *Thanks for being nice to the old lady, but you're off the hook.*

He raises his arm up to his forehead and brushes off sweat with the back of his hand. "It's so hot today. I'd love a glass of iced tea."

Gigi snaps her fingers. "Let's head inside then," she says, a giddiness to her voice that makes her sound more like a teenager than an almost-octogenarian. I cringe, hoping she regains her composure soon.

Gigi heads toward the kitchen, leaving me to make small talk with Blake. As I close the front door behind us, I struggle to find the right words.

"This house is so cool," he says, breaking the silence sitting between us.

I stop beside him, and he towers over me. He's close to Dad's height, about six feet. Both of us survey the room of books, art, and antiques. "Yeah, she owns a lot of unique stuff. Gigi loves to tell stories, so feel free to ask away."

We arrive at the kitchen and take a seat at the round table. Gigi walks over with the pitcher of iced tea and glasses, and I discreetly sniff my pits. I scoot my chair a few feet away from Blake just to be safe.

Gigi pours the tea and hands us each a glass. "Blake, what are your plans for the rest of the day?"

He takes a sip. "I'm not sure. We don't have practice, so it's one of my few days off this summer. I was out for a run when I bumped into y'all."

"Hailey's a runner as well. She made varsity as a freshman," Gigi says, a smile in her voice.

"Impressive," he says. "You run track?"

Ugh. Why couldn't I run track? Everyone knows track is the cooler, sexier running sport. "Cross country."

"She had the fastest time in the fall meet last year, beating all the other girls in the city," Gigi says.

Oh, man, please make it stop. I know Gigi means well, but running cross country is not something to brag about to one of the stars of the football team. "In our conference, not the city. And it was a tight race. I just got lucky and was able to hold on to my kick at the end."

"You can't beat luck," says Gigi, "but I think your hard work and natural talent pushed you to victory."

This lady needs to take it down a notch!

"What's your pace?" Blake asks.

I pretend to sip my tea, but the truth is I detest iced tea as much as the kettle version. I've got to remember to bring some Dr Pepper over to Gigi's house. Gazing over at Blake, I contemplate whether to make myself sound amazing or tell the truth. Would he even know the difference? I stick with the facts on this one since they're impressive on their own. "My race pace is around six-fifteen, but I train closer to seven."

"For what distance?"

"Most of my races are just over three miles, but I train for five or six miles usually."

He takes his lower lip between his teeth like he's reevaluating my stock. "We should go for a run some time. I could use the help of someone fast."

I'm pretty sure all the color and heat just drained from my face. Did Blake Alexander just ask to spend time with me? I realize it's to improve his own running . . . but still. If he thought I was a super nerd, he wouldn't ask me. "I'm betting the star wide receiver is a good runner," I say, trying to play it cool.

"I'm fast, but I need to work on my endurance. Coach is on me to pick up distance running to build my stamina. So, honestly, you'd be helping me."

Am I about to be running buddies with Blake Alexander? Hell yes, I am!

"Okay, cool. I train most mornings," I lie, "so let me know what days of the week work for you, and I'll link it up to my visits here."

I'm glad I didn't fib about my speed earlier because now I just launched a big one, and I don't need to be piling lies on top of more lies. Saturday was my first run in two weeks, and with the heavy summer air, I struggled. I'm gonna have to start two-a-days to get ready for Blake.

"Cool. Let's exchange numbers, and I'll text you."

My heart stops beating.

"Pass your phone over," I say flatly, as the butterflies have a dance party in my stomach.

He slides it to me, and I'm hit over the head by his screen saver. It's a picture of Blake and Bree. Bree Billings. The two Bs are boos. She and Blake are the beautiful, power couple of our high school. Bree's a stereotypical ditzy Texas blonde with bleached hair and big boobs. Guys apparently don't mind the emptiness between the ears in high school.

Seeing her face is a good gut-check that this running arrangement is to improve his game and nothing more.

My fingers type quickly, and I push his cell back over to him. "I'm in your phone now."

He tips back his tea, drinking the last sip. "Mrs. Turner, may I load my glass in the dishwasher or help you with anything before I leave?"

Gigi picks up his glass and places it next to hers. "You are such a dear. No, we are all set."

She raises a finger, and I worry about what might come out of her mouth next. "But Hailey is spending time over here this summer helping me with various projects around the house. If we run into any trouble, and need an extra pair of hands, can we ring you?"

"It's text, Gigi," I say. "No one rings anyone in the twenty-first century."

Blake laughs. "Yes, ma'am. Happy to help."

"Hailey, walk our guest out, please."

I do as Gigi orders and escort Blake to the door. We stand there, a few awkward seconds pass.

"I'll text you," he says.

"Cool."

He jogs away, and I shake my head in complete wonder.

CHAPTER SIX

I did it. I finished the novel, and I'm exhausted. What a tragic and awful ending to all their lives. I felt sucker-punched at the end, and so sad for Jay Gatsby. I want to ring the neck of that dang Daisy Buchanan! But now I get to learn our family history and the truth about Ilse and Jack and discover more about Gigi.

I've been trying to imagine what Jack and Ilse's story will be and how it relates to *The Great Gatsby*. I hope their ending isn't as sad and terrible as this book. It's strange but I'm feeling connected to these mysterious people from the past in a way that's hard to explain. It's like my DNA carries their story, and I need to know what happened to them.

I arrive at Gigi's and can't hide my excitement. She opens the door and I hug her, holding her tight, and she embraces me with equal force. She knows I've finished it. She knows I've been wrecked by this novel. It's heartbreaking and horrible, and just like Gigi told me, it stays with you. The story's themes and characters fester, percolating in the back of your brain and deep in your soul. It's crazy how a novel from a hundred years ago is still relevant to today's world. It makes me think about these "influencers," who all day long push material objects, pursuing money and fame as the gold standard of a successful life. Daisy and Gatsby chased the wrong thing and ended up empty and hallowed, and poor Nick had to flee it all.

Gigi and I discuss the book at length, and I wave my white flag, accepting defeat. But Gatsby and Daisy don't make my heart happy; they make my heart ache. They make life's cruelties painfully real, and their story makes clear how love's obsession can destroy everyone and everything around you.

We are in our regular spots—I'm in the wingback chair and Gigi's across from me. I can't take it any longer. "I've finished my end of the deal. Please, please tell me about Ilse and Jack."

She rises from her chair without a word. Crossing the room to the piano, she sits down, moving her fingers through a series of warm-up exercises. "Come join me," she calls to me.

I sit down next to her on the tuffet bench beneath the grand piano. "Let's start with their song."

Her fingers dance over the keys, a haunting melody filling the air. The words tumble out of her mouth and my heart thuds.

"Embrace me, my sweet embraceable you . . ."

The words falling from her lips are so romantic, an enduring and deep love coming through the song's lyrics. The music is slow and soothing; I've never heard anything like it. I feel the emotion of the song with each repeat of the chorus. Closing my eyes, I imagine Jack and Ilse holding each other as they slowly sway to this song.

She plays the last few notes, and we sit in silence. I lean my head on her shoulder, and she gently touches my cheek. "I could always play the piano. For as long as I can remember, the piano has been in my life. It was a gift from God to me. I remember being four years old and sitting down in front of the keys. My mind saw the notes, and my fingers followed along. Uncle Jack would always ask me to play this song when he visited us. I never knew why until Nana gave me the book many years later."

I keep my head on her shoulder, her heart telling me her truth.

"Uncle Jack was in and out of our lives for years. We never knew when he would turn up, always unannounced, and usually intoxicated. He would drop off lavish gifts, staring at me with curious eyes. His intense focus unnerved me. I didn't know what I did wrong to elicit such looks. Then when I was twelve, he sat with me on the back porch one evening when Nana and Papa were at a church meeting and told me his story, *their story*, my story."

She continues, "It wrecked me, which I don't think was his intention. For years, I thought he had made it up, that I must have misheard him, or that he was just telling tales, even though his words were crystal clear in my memory. But as I got older, there were too many things I couldn't explain away.

"Everyone is dead, so there is no one to ask about the past. I pushed it out of my mind for so long. As I sit here an old lady, I find myself longing for the truth about who I am and where I come from."

She stands and walks to the bookshelves behind her, picking up a framed photo. She runs the tips of her fingers over the picture, and then hands it to me. It's a black-and-white photo of a man in a military uniform with a buzzed haircut. A cigarette dangles from his mouth as he smirks at the camera.

"Jack," I whisper.

She nods and retreats to her chair. I follow, bringing the picture with me. I sit and study the image. A date is written in ink at the bottom of the photo: "1944."

"Jack served in the army in World War II and fought in many battles." Her eyes mist. "But nothing could prepare him for April 29, 1945."

I don't know much about World War II. I have no idea what this date signifies.

"His regiment ended up at the Dachau concentration camp the day it was liberated."

She lets out a deep sigh, like a weight on her shoulders, a burden that has held her down. "Certain moments in your life burn into your soul and that conversation with Jack is one I can remember as if it occurred yesterday."

She draws in a deep breath, squinting her eyes as water builds on the edges. "He walked into Dachau, his senses overwhelmed by the ghastly sights and smells, death all around him. He was surrounded by emaciated, sickly bodies," she says, her voice trembling. "People barely still alive, holding on out of sheer will, the wounds and illnesses too many to name. He and the other soldiers gently lifted up bodies that weighed nothing, wisps of life, bones so brittle, faces so fragile, tears of joy dripping down their faces as tears of horror ran down those of Jack and the other soldiers."

A faint smile forms at the corners of her mouth. "And then he saw her. A young woman who looked more alien than human, her head bald and nail beds nothing but skin, her cheeks sunken into her face, her body like a small child. But her eyes, these amazing, green eyes that sparkled, *twinkled*, amid all this death."

Gigi's eyes.

Mom's eyes.

"He was drawn to her, gently scooping her up, carrying her to safety. He vowed to never let her go."

She wrings her hands and raises a pinky to her eye. I swipe my cheek.

"He stayed by her side, nursing her back to health over the next several months. During this time, they got to know each other, and he tried to help her find her family. Three sisters and a brother, parents and grandparents, cousins, and neighbors. But there was no one to find. All were gone."

Gone. Everyone gone. This is Gigi's family. My family. I can't catch my breath; it's like an elephant has sat on my chest, crushing my lungs. Gone. Gone. Everyone, everything gone.

"Jack finagled jobs to keep him in Germany, even when he was ordered to go back home. He spoke of kind officers that knew he was trying to save this girl."

She slowly presses her lips together. "After a year, he took his discharge from the military. She had gained weight, rehabbed well, and was ready to flee Germany, swearing she would never set foot on its soil again. Ilse planned to come to America with Jack, but she wasn't yet strong enough for the weeks-long boat journey, so they moved to Paris. They married in 1946, and I arrived shortly thereafter."

My mind floods with questions, so many things I want to ask Gigi, but I start with the most pressing ones. "What happened to Ilse? And what happened to Jack?"

Her voice croaks, and she lifts the glass from the end table, drinking a long sip of water. "She wasn't supposed to get pregnant; the doctors had advised against it. Her body was too fragile, some of her organs irreparably damaged from the starvation. But she wasn't going to let the Nazis take everything from her. She was determined to have a family again."

Her words hang in the air above me. The imagery is overwhelming. The perils and obstacles Ilse faced at such a young age, about my age, confound me. My life seems so easy.

"She hoped to reinvent herself and start a new life in America."

"Is that her connection to *The Great Gatsby*?"

The wrinkles on her forehead push together. "Do you have the book with you?"

"Yes."

I open my bag and grab the novel, removing it from the protective Ziploc bag I had placed it in. I hand it over to her. The book's value to Gigi is now powerfully clear to me.

"Do you remember the year this novel was published?"

"1925."

"Correct. The book was a failure when originally released. It was then distributed to the soldiers on the front lines during World War II, and the story deeply resonated with them. Gatsby and Nick Carraway were former soldiers and survivors. The tale of the American spirit, the American dream, and unrequited love struck a chord with so many soldiers . . . especially Jack."

Her disposition lightens. "The author, F. Scott Fitzgerald, lived in Paris with his wife, Zelda, when *The Great Gatsby* was released. Fitzgerald had a deep connection to the city of love. Remember I told you our family was full of romantics? Jack scoured the city and found a first edition English version of the novel. He gave it to Ilse at their wedding."

My entire body twitches. The book I just read was a present from my great-grandfather to my great-grandmother in Paris, after the war, after she had survived Hitler and death. The book suddenly feels heavier. Sacred. Like the most important thing in my life.

"And the song?"

Gigi motions for me to follow her and opens a cabinet adjacent to the piano. She pulls out a stack of record albums and thumbs through them before handing one to me. "It was their song. George Gershwin wrote 'Embraceable You,' but Nat King Cole did a version in 1943 that was Jack's favorite."

"I've never heard of George Gershwin or Nat King Cole."

Gigi cocks her head at me. "I have so much to teach you. Do we even have enough time?"

That's a rhetorical question, right?

"George Gershwin was one of the greatest American composers of the twentieth century. His classics include songs like, 'Rhapsody in Blue,' 'Summertime,' 'An American in Paris,' 'I Got Rhythm,' and 'Someone to Watch Over Me.' You really haven't heard any of these songs?"

"Nope."

The cabinets hold a record player and some large wooden speakers. She carefully removes the record from its protective paper covering. I watch in fascination as she places the disc on the spindle, lifts the arm thing, and drops the needle gently on the record.

"Have you ever listened to an album on a record player?"

"Take a wild guess," I tease.

"I love playing albums, so let me give you a few pointers. You must line up the needle perfectly with the first groove of the record to start at the beginning of a song. If you want to jump ahead to a later song, you must determine precisely which groove the song begins on and drop the arm to the determined starting spot. The needle needs to have a soft landing." She winks at me. "There's an art and a science to playing a record."

As we listen to the song, my mind drifts to Jack and Ilse. The song ends and she places the record back in the sleeve. "I'm so sorry that you never knew your mother," I say.

Gigi exhales a labored breath. Her wrinkles are extra-crinkly, and she suddenly appears much older than her seventy-four years, but maybe it's the history aging both of us. She leans over, and the tips of her thumbs wipe my wet eyes. "I didn't share this story with you to make you feel sorry for me. I told you so you would know my history, *our* history."

"What happened to Jack?"

She lets out a long sigh. "There are no happy endings in this story. Losing Ilse, after losing so many friends from his combat unit, broke him wide open. All the death and devastation darkened his soul. We came to Texas, he left me with Nana, and he went on a warpath of vengeance."

"What does that mean? And why doesn't Mom know these stories? I don't understand why everything is a secret."

She rises and leaves the room, and I trail after her. Is she avoiding the questions? Did I say something wrong?

She's in the kitchen when I catch up to her. "Gigi, I'm sorry."

She busies herself with a few dishes, her back to me.

"Don't be sorry," she says, her hands quivering. "Our family history is complicated and exhausting for me to relive. I promise to give you answers to all your questions, but not today."

I tap her arm, tugging her into a hug. "I love you, Gigi."

Her chest heaves on mine, destroying my heart.

CHAPTER SEVEN

can't sleep.

I toss and turn, trying to get my brain to shut off, but Gigi's story plays on a loop in my head. I give up and kick off the covers. Flipping on my desk lamp, I sit down and power up my laptop. I type notes of everything Gigi shared and draft a family tree, trying to connect the dots of these mysterious figures. I want to help Gigi find her family.

Papa (unknown)—Nana (June)   Jack—Ilse

Gigi (Celeste)—Grandfather (unknown)

Mom—Dad

Hailey—Kyle

My family diagram isn't much. We only have Ilse's first name. A deep pain throbs inside me at the thought her identity may never be uncovered. I long to know more about her.

Her surname is probably something German like Schmidt or Wagner, and then I'm jolted that I failed to discuss with Gigi the big thing: we're Jewish.

Considering we come from a long line of hard-core Southern Baptists, this is a giant secret. Nana was super

Baptist. Gigi is a regular churchgoer but Mom less so. Our family rarely attends church, but we do join the masses for Christmas, Easter, and an occasional Mother's Day.

But now our religious heritage has been flipped upside down. My roots are Jewish. I think I read the Jewish lineage passes through the maternal line, so that means I'm legit. I make another chart:

Ilse—Gigi—Mom—Me

I chew on the end of my pencil. Oh, sweet Jesus! Oh, wait, maybe I shouldn't be saying "Jesus" now that I'm a Jew?

But being Jewish makes me think of one person.

Blake Alexander.

He's Jewish, too.

Blake's another piece of the puzzle. Why does he keep circling in my life? He's appeared out of nowhere, and we have all these strange connections.

I run my hand through my hair, yanking on the ends. Why am I thinking about Blake Alexander when I need to be thinking about Jack, Ilse, and Gigi?

I make a list of my questions for Gigi:

1. What happened to Jack?
2. Do you have a birth certificate from France?
3. Have you tried to find Ilse? Have you researched her name in historical records?
4. What other information do you know about her?

Maybe with the help of technology, I can find answers. Maybe I can solve the mysteries of our family for Gigi.

I wake up groggy, my head heavy with the past weighing on my mind. During my next visit to Gigi's, I plan to record every scrap of information she can recall. I know I'm chasing ghosts, but I can't shake the feeling Jack and Ilse's story isn't finished.

I wander downstairs, not even sure of the time. My first stop is to retrieve my phone. Mom and Dad make me keep it downstairs at night, an honor policy in place. I pick it up from the communal basket, and I have two messages.

From Blake Alexander!

Hey. I know it's early, but want to go for a run?

Then, eighteen minutes later.

I'm headed out. Another time.

Noooo!

It's 10:38 a.m. He texted at 7:55 am. Who would have thought he was an early riser?

I need to text him back. Do I throw out, How about tomorrow? Pacing back and forth, I debate the pros and cons in my head, and then silently scold myself. *Stop overthinking and get on with it!*

My fingers move at a feverish pace.

Sorry to have missed you. I'll be at my grandmother's tomorrow and my schedule's flexible. LMK!

I hit send and toss the phone to the counter, like it's on fire and searing my hands.

My phone immediately buzzes.

I'll stop by at 8.

I pump my fist and stomp my feet. I can't freaking believe my life!

Dad doesn't question me when I tell him I need to arrive at Gigi's by eight. He's in the middle of a busy week of depositions and was happy to head to the office early. I want to spend a few minutes with Gigi before taking off for the run with Blake. I know she'll be pleased about this development because Gigi is a hopeless romantic like me.

I'm decked out in my cutest Nike running outfit, and my hair is twisted in a braid, falling down my back like a thick rope. I've swished some mascara on my lashes and dashed some bronzer on my cheeks. When I arrive, I give Gigi a quick hug and tell her Blake is coming over. Gigi squeals and swivels her hips from side to side.

"It's not like that with us. He has a girlfriend," I say, playing it off. "He wants me to help improve his running."

Her eyes sparkle. "Uh, huh."

I ignore her comment but am pleased to hear that Gigi thinks Blake could like me. Even though I realize this is impossible because he has a girlfriend and he's out of my league, I appreciate the confidence boost.

The doorbell rings, and Gigi winks at me. "Go, get 'em, Tiger."

I would normally shudder if Mom or Dad said something so cringe-worthy, but coming from Gigi, I kind of love it and give her a wink back.

I open the door, and Blake Alexander stands in front of me. He's wearing Nike basketball shorts and a Dri-FIT tee; his thick brown hair curls on the ends.

"Hey, you ready?" he says.

I don't offer for Blake to come inside. I'm fully aware

Gigi might sabotage my laid-back approach. "Yeah, give me one sec."

I turn my head over my shoulder. "I'll be back in a half-hour or so," I say.

"Or so is fine!" cackles Gigi.

I hope Blake didn't hear that.

I step outside and we walk to the street. He winds his arms around like windmills and I pull my left quad back and then shake out my shoulders and arms. We stretch for a few more minutes and then I say, "Let's head out."

We start jogging, and I keep the pace easy. "How far can you comfortably run?"

"I don't know, about three miles."

Three miles is a good start. That distance will take less than thirty minutes. I feel slightly deflated that our time together will be short. "I'll control pace, and you let me know if you want to speed up or slow down. We'll aim for a nice and easy eight-minute mile, but then we'll kick it up for the last quarter mile. Sound good?"

He turns his head to me, a grin on his face. "Yes, boss lady."

We run a few strides in silence, passing an old man and a tiny dog, the pup yipping at our feet.

I steal a glance at his beautiful profile. I'm unsure what to say and whether he even wants to talk to me, but I decide to break the ice. "Do you like to talk when you run?"

"Yeah, sure."

"Cool," I say. "How's your summer going?"

He laughs. Why is that a funny question?

"It's going. Unofficial workouts for football have started, and we're already feeling the pressure, but it should be an exciting season."

"How's your summer going?" he then asks.

Do I tell him the truth? That I've had the most unexpected summer of my life since Gigi entered the picture?

"Better than I would have guessed. My parents asked me to help my grandmother out a few days a week, which I thought would totally blow, but it's actually been pretty fun." I point to the right. "Let's turn here and pick up our speed."

"Yeah, that car she has is sick. Do you get to drive it a lot?"

The car. God bless Betty.

"Gigi likes for me to drive her, but I was so intimidated at first."

"Her?"

A giggle escapes. "My grandmother is *interesting*, some might say *eccentric*, and well, the car is named Betty. She's also totally obsessed with The Beatles. She has a rule that their music must be playing while driving in Betty because she's concerned about my lack of Beatles knowledge."

His brows jump. "So that's why she put on 'Revolution' when we hopped in."

"You know that song?"

"Of course."

"And you like The Beatles?"

The excitement of this conversation causes me to add too much kick, and I can tell he's breathing hard now, so I slow us down a bit.

"Yeah. Doesn't everyone?"

"Does Bree?"

I can't believe I just asked that. I'm showing way too much interest in his personal life before we even know each other. Am I even supposed to act like I know he has a girlfriend?

"I don't know much about her these days. She broke up with me a few weeks ago."

Dad would be so proud of my poker face. Not even the faintest smile escapes my lips. But my heart pounds like a freaking bass drum. How did I not know about this breakup? Obviously, I'm way out of the loop with Livi gone.

I pretend to act supportive. "Oh, wow. I hadn't heard. Maybe it's just a summer breakup?"

"Yeah, she's traveling with her family a bunch and then at camp. I think she wanted to see other guys and not feel guilty. But you wouldn't know we were broken up by how much she texts me."

The air goes out of my balloon. Time for a new subject. "Where did you learn about The Beatles?"

"I don't know, my dad and . . ." He raises his arm to wipe his brow. "I play guitar. It's hard not to know The Beatles once you get into playing music."

Of course he plays guitar. Is there anything this guy can't do?

The sweat pours down my face, and I raise the bottom of my shirt and dab my cheeks. "Gigi made me these lists of her favorite Beatles songs, and I've listened to most of her recommendations. They are incredible songwriters."

Blake grabs the bottom of his shirt and lifts it toward his head.

What is going on? Is he really taking off his shirt?

Yep, his shirt is off. He folds it over and tucks it into the front of his athletic shorts. His lean chest is all muscle, his arms cut and toned. I tell myself to look away, eyes on the road.

"Lennon–McCartney is probably the greatest songwriting duo of all time," he says.

I smile on the inside. Gigi said the same thing. When I tell her that Blake Alexander likes The Beatles, she'll probably start planning our wedding.

We make another loop and reach the homestretch of our three miles. I don't want to stop chatting with Blake, but I can tell he's tiring. "Let's go hard these last two hundred yards."

We take off at a full sprint, and he blazes by me.

I catch up and bend over, gasping large breaths. "Dude, you're really fast."

His gorgeous single-dimpled smile spreads across his face. He raises his hand, and we share a hard high-five.

"That was good stuff. You're the fast one. I was struggling to keep up with you."

"You aren't the first guy to tell me that," I sass back.

Where did that just come from? Am I flirting with Blake Alexander?

He runs his shirt over his sweaty, beautiful hair. "We'll have to make this a regular thing so I can catch you."

His words set my chest on fire. Did he just say he wants to "catch me?"

After using Gigi's shower, I change into my jean cutoffs and favorite H&M tee. They ran a series last spring of famous artworks silkscreen-printed on T-shirts, and I scooped up a few. Today I'm wearing Magritte's *The Son of Man* painting where a guy's face is covered by a green apple. I love this painting, something about how we always want to see what is hidden from us, like everything we see hides something else. Like when I'm staring at Gigi in her sunglasses, and she takes them off to reveal her stunning green eyes. There is so much more behind those eyes I can't see, but I'm desperate to discover.

Gigi and I run a few errands and take Betty. Of course, we're listening to The Beatles. We both sing along passionately to "Eleanor Rigby." The song is haunting, and I relate to all the lonely people.

"It sounds like the musicians are attacking the violins with their bows," I say.

"That's a musical technique called staccato and used frequently in classical compositions," she replies.

Gigi knows so much about music.

"This is the only Beatles song that Ringo, John, Paul, and George don't play instruments on. Paul sings lead, and George and John provide vocals on the background melodies. They are backed by a group of violins, cellos, and violas."

"Do you have some Beatles fact book you study at night?"

She flits her eyes at me. "No."

"Then how do you know about the instruments and voices?"

"I can hear it."

We're cruising through the neighborhood, the top is down, a warm breeze blows through our hair, and the tunes blare loudly from the eight-track. I gaze over at Gigi, and she is so happy in this car. I giggle at her giant sunglasses that make her look bug-eyed and she catches me.

"What's so funny?"

I stop laughing, but then another giggle spills out. "Those sunglasses are too big for your face. You look like you have alien eyes."

She scowls at me. "These are Jackie O sunglasses. They are classic and chic like their namesake."

"Who's Jackie O?" I ask.

"*What?*" Gigi says, her voice shooting up an octave. "You don't know who Jaqueline Kennedy Onassis is? I wasn't entirely shocked by your lack of familiarity with George Gershwin or Nat King Cole. But Jackie Kennedy? Do they not teach you young people anything in school?"

I can recover a little ground with her on this one. "I know Jackie Kennedy, but I didn't know she was also Jackie O."

"Jackie O is how the masses, her ardent fans, affectionately refer to her. She remarried after President Kennedy was assassinated. Her second husband was Aristotle Onassis, a Greek shipping magnate. By the way, he was quite the downgrade from Jack.

"You know, I saw her in person once. I'll never forget that day," she says, her voice shaky, the emotion bubbling out of her.

We've reached her house, and I drive Betty into the back driveway. I know the day she means. Most everyone who's grown up in Dallas has been to the grassy knoll and learned the awful details of the car parade through downtown.

"The day President Kennedy was killed."

We remain seated in the car, even though I have cut the engine and parked her in the small one-car garage. "You were at the parade, right? I think I remember Mom telling me that story."

She removes her sunglasses and places them in their giant case. A frown pushes her brows together. "Yes. It was a Friday. I went downtown with friends to watch the parade. It was a big deal to have the President in Dallas. The motorcade had just passed us, and we were all commenting on Jackie's beautiful pink suit and how glamorous and perfect she looked.

"We were in the process of dispersing when we heard frantic screaming. Then pandemonium broke out. People were shouting, 'The President's been shot! The President's been shot!' It was terrifying and chaotic. We all hurried home as fast as we could."

She shakes her head. "The world was never the same. Our voices and spirits drowned that day."

Gigi has really lived through so much history. I guess that's what happens when you've been on this planet for close to seventy-five years.

"They just don't make them like her anymore," she says. "A bygone era of elegance and grace."

That is exactly what I've been thinking about Gigi. She and Jackie O have a lot in common.

We finish lunch and move into the living room. Gigi hasn't brought up Jack and Ilse, but I can't wait any longer.

I clear my throat, and she raises her eyes from the crossword. "Yes?"

"I have some questions for you."

"About what?"

She must know what I'm referring to. Is this a game or is she starting to become senile? I've heard these kinds of memory glitches happen to old people. One day they're here, and the next day they can't remember their name. It reinforces that I need to get facts from her and fast.

"About Jack and Ilse and why this is such a big secret."

She places her puzzle book on her lap. "You might not like everything you hear. Are you prepared to be disappointed?"

"I don't understand. How would I be disappointed?"

"In the end of Jack's story. What happened to him. What happened with me and Nana . . . and your mother."

And there it is. I knew Mom must have a reason for her coldness to Gigi. But I never would have guessed it looped back to Jack and Ilse. "I want to hear it all. I've brought my phone to record your stories and preserve our history. I want to help you find the answers about your parents."

Her green eyes darken; a sadness hangs in the deepening of her wrinkles. But then she smiles, and her face softens. "We should start at the beginning. I would like to go back to where it all started, retrace Jack's steps, teach you what I know, and take the journey together."

Journey? What does that mean?

"Betty, you, and me," she says. "Let's leave tomorrow morning. A simple day trip, but we'll be gone from sunup to sundown."

A road trip with Gigi to uncover family secrets. This is more than I could have asked for! "I'm in. But where are we going?"

"Malone, Texas."

"I've never heard of it."

"Not many people have."

My curiosity rivals a cat's. "What's in Malone?"

"Your family history."

She's clearly not giving me any scoop, but I want to confirm this road trip is happening. "We'll leave tomorrow?"

"Yes, tomorrow. And why don't you spend the night in case we arrive back a little late. Now let's go take Betty for some ice cream. I want us to hit the trinity again today."

I give a half-smile. "Good book. Great song. Cool car."

Her eyes flicker with golden flecks, like tiny sparkles of fire. "You're catching on."

It's another steamy afternoon, but clouds drip across the sky, so we keep the top down. Gigi's playing *Magical Mystery Tour*, and I think that might be my favorite Beatles album. It's only a short drive over to the neighborhood ice cream shop, and we finish up a rousing singalong of "Penny Lane" as I turn Betty into a parking spot.

We open the store door, and Gigi and I are energized from the joy that Betty and The Beatles bring us. But my mood shifts fast. Bree's posse of popular girls are huddled around three tables in the center of the store. Several football players hover around them. I avoid eye contact, staring at the flavors listed on the wall.

"Hey, hey, hey. It's our new friend with the cool car," says a voice from that group.

DeMarcus.

I glance in their direction and DeMarcus wears a big smile and seems genuine in his friendliness, but the sneers from the girls next to him make me suspect. They type on their phones, and I know they're texting each other about me.

And he's here with them.

Blake.

"It's Hailey," he says.

He jumps up and walks over to greet Gigi and me. DeMarcus soon follows and wraps his arms around me. Does he always hug strangers? Not that I mind. As DeMarcus makes flavor recommendations to me and Gigi, the girls' rude chatter is loud enough to reach us.

"She's here with her grandmother. Like, does she not have any friends?"

"Oh my God, I would die if I were her. It's so embarrassing."

I ignore them and focus on studying the menu, but I've lost my appetite. DeMarcus whips his head around to face the girls. "Y'all need to stop being disrespectful. What? Are you too cool to hang with your grandma? What have any of y'all done today besides stare at your phones?"

I bite my lip to hold in a chuckle.

One of the girls, Lainey, glares at him. "You're one to talk. What have you done today?"

His brown eyes bulge big; his eyebrows arch so high they pass over his forehead and into his hairline. I'm guessing he's not used to back talk. I mean, he is DeMarcus Thomas.

"What did *I* do?" he says, his deep voice hitting a high note. "Did you just ask, 'What did DeMarcus do today?' I'll tell you what I did. I got up at seven and went for a run. Next, I went to the gym and lifted weights. After that, I came home and watched some film with Blake and Cody. We then had an unofficial workout. And *then* I made the mistake of coming to meet you fools."

He throws his arm around my shoulder and leans into my ear. "I love my grandmama. She's my favorite person in the whole world, and I hang out with her all the time. Don't let those witches bother you."

He walks back to the group, pointing his finger at each girl, shaming them into silence.

Gigi gives a closed-mouth smile.

Blake stands beside me. "DeMarcus is a good guy. And now you're on his list, so you'll be golden as well."

"His list?"

"He has a mental checklist of people he likes and doesn't like, and he never changes his mind. But you're most definitely on the like list. He's a sucker for anything related to grandmothers."

I laugh and can't help but think of my good fortune of being forced to spend time with Gigi.

We stare at each for a moment before he steps back. "See you around."

I join Gigi at the counter, and we place our orders. We both go for double scoops of coffee caramel crunch in waffle cones. I take the seat that places my back to the power group. I hope they leave soon.

My wish is granted as metal chairs scrape the floor, a signal that the herd is exiting. I've caught Gigi eyeing them discreetly several times. I know she's going to have some astute observations on that crew. Before I can ask her, she waves in the direction of the cool kids.

I lean across the table. "Gigi, what are you doing?" I whisper.

Her face contorts in confusion. "What did you say?"

I inch in closer. "What are you doing?" I whisper again.

She shakes her head and points at her ears. "I can't hear you."

I try one more time, slowly mouthing out each word.

She takes a bite of ice cream, ignoring my pleas. The bell rings, and I know they're gone.

"I was waving to DeMarcus and Blake."

Of course, she was waving to the boys.

Because Gigi is a big, fat flirt.

CHAPTER EIGHT

I need to ask Mom and Dad for permission to spend the night with Gigi while avoiding mention of our road trip plans. There's no way my parents would let me drive Betty on the interstate when I don't have my license yet.

I decide to broach the subject during family dinner. Dad has picked up food on the way home from work and tonight's fare is Chinese. Dad loves to try out new places. He's always on a mission to discover the latest and greatest taco stand, Chinese takeout, Indian curry, or slice of pizza. He's not a connoisseur of fine food; he's a connoisseur of the dirty, good stuff. He'll drive an hour away if he's read a good review of a place, preferably a hole-in-the-wall joint, and as we eat, he loves to talk about the pros and cons of each item we order. Kyle digs it as well, but Mom and I both go along to make him happy.

As we sit and debate the egg rolls and pot stickers of his latest discovery, The Golden Dragon, I plot my move. Mom is distracted by work; she flips her phone over every time it buzzes, even though we have a family rule about phones at the dinner table. Apparently, the rules apply to everyone except her.

Kyle currently has plum sauce dripping down his chin, and I want to lash at him to wipe his mouth. He's disgusting and doesn't care, but that might set Mom off, which will work against me. After spending time with Gigi, I'm shocked Mom continues to let Kyle be a caveman at the table.

Mom puts her phone down. "How was your day?" she asks.

I finish chewing my food before answering. "Good. Gigi has me reorganizing her closets."

This is a lie but a plausible explanation of how we spend our time. I add a few more details to solidify my alibi for the next forty-eight hours. "Her closets are jammed full. She's such a pack rat! We have both guest room closets to wade through and then her master closet. She asked if I could spend the night tomorrow evening, so we can plow through it all."

Mom's face changes slightly, not a look of deep suspicion, but a curious gaze. "And that works for you? To spend the night working long hours cleaning out closets? I find this interesting because I can't get you to pick up your room."

Dad lets out a laugh, and I'm relieved for the interruption. "Well, I'm proud of you for being so generous with your time. Maybe all that organization will spill over into your personal life."

I give them my sweet, sugary, daughter smile. "It feels nice to help her out, and she's so appreciative of everything I do."

I'm nervous Mom might interpret my last sentence the wrong way, but thankfully no one says another word. I add, "We're going to throw in some fun. There's a two-part George Harrison documentary on Netflix Gigi hasn't seen, so we're going to binge it."

Mom coughs—an uncomfortable, scratchy, throat-clearing noise—like she's choking on her wine. She grabs her glass of water and gulps a few sips down. "You're listening to The Beatles with Gigi?" she says.

I meet her eyes. "Yeah. She's a big fan."

She stares at me, and I wait for her to ask another question, but she remains silent, her face emotionless. I catch the way her eyes have moved over to Dad and are drilling into him. I know this look. It's their way of communicating with each other when one is worried about something Kyle or I have said. It says, "We need to huddle after dinner and hash this out," and then one or the other, but never both, will drop by my room afterward to share the parental consensus.

Dad jabbers about Kung Pao Chicken versus General Tso Chicken. I figure this means I'm in the clear for my stealth mission with Gigi.

I retreat to my room after dinner to pack my bag and prepare for our big getaway. Texas weather can be unpredictable in summer, and powerful storms can roll in quickly, especially in the open plains, which is where I think we're headed. I pitch into my bag a raincoat, rain boots, my favorite pair of jeans, pajamas, and my Nikes. I figure I want sturdy shoes in case I'm scaling fences or racing away from danger. But I'm not sure where Gigi is in that scenario. Driving the getaway car? Clearly, I have an active imagination but isn't there some saying, "Hope for the best, prepare for the worst?"

I poke around my nail polish collection, tossing in a few colors I think Gigi might like. If we have some downtime, I can always give her a manicure. I throw in my Polaroid camera for instant photos; Gigi might appreciate me kicking it old school with that thing. The photo quality is terrible, but it's way too much work to print pictures off my phone.

I make sure to pack Jack and Ilse's copy of *The Great Gatsby*, our unofficial guidebook to the past. My gaze travels around my room—from bed to bookshelves to bulletin boards—trying to see if there is anything I'm missing. My phone buzzes, breaking my concentration.

I have a notification from Instagram.

blakea05 requested to follow you.

My jaw dangles down in disbelief. I swipe my screen and jump over to my Insta app. Can I reply "Hell, yes!" to his request?

I hit confirm and request to follow back. Or am I supposed to wait a bit before asking to follow him? Was I too quick on the trigger?

A notification.

blakea05 started following you.

And then more alerts pop up.

blakea05 accepted your follow request.
dmac22 requested to follow you.

dmac22?

DeMarcus. He wears number twenty-two, the same number as the greatest Dallas Cowboys running back of all time, Emmitt Smith. Duh.

I hit confirm and follow him back.

dmac22 started following you.

Having DeMarcus Thomas follow you is a gamechanger. He has 10,000 followers but only follows around 250 people. And I'm one of them. My social status just shot up to an entire new level. Where is Livi when I need her!

A notification flashes across my phone. A direct message on Instagram from Blake.

What is going on? Is this when he tells me it was a mistake? I open the message.

Want to run tomorrow?

Shoot. I'm leaving with Gigi tomorrow. This is a serious dilemma. Do I cancel on Gigi? No way. As my mind battles what to do, I remember Gigi and her flirty ways. She would kill me for turning Blake down. I think I have a solution.

Sure, but I need to run early. 7:30?

If he agrees, we can run a fast thirty-minute route, I can hop in Gigi's shower, and then we can hit the road before nine.

I throw my phone on my bed and collapse into my pillows in a joyful free fall, my arm stretched above my head. Tomorrow might be the greatest day of my fifteen years. A morning run with Blake Alexander followed by a day spent in Betty, learning the mystery of Jack and Ilse.

And Gigi.

My legs shake and my stomach churns as Dad drives me over to Gigi's. We're cutting it close on time, and I worry Dad will catch sight of my new running friend and realize he's been replaced by a much younger guy. It's not like he can run with me on weekdays, but I don't want to wound him before work.

Thankfully Dad drives off before a Blake sighting. I grab the secret key and I let myself in. Pitching my bag onto Gigi's living room sofa, I then tiptoe around the house to see if she is awake. I find her in the kitchen, standing in front of her coffeemaker. "Well, you're here early. It looks like you're ready for a run."

She places her mug down, outstretches her arms, and motions me over for a hug. I fall into her embrace, the security blanket of love she always wraps around me. "Is there a certain young man joining you this morning?"

I give a tight squeeze before stepping back. "Yes. But I promise I'll be showered and ready to head out on schedule."

She takes a long sip of her coffee, before flashing a bright smile. "Have a nice run and take your time."

I walk outside and Blake stands on the sidewalk, one calf pulled behind him, stretching his quad. I join him and do the same. He wears a Dallas Cowboys T-shirt with silver Nike shorts, and I immediately zone in on the new running shoes. He's taking our training seriously.

He smiles at me, and I tingle all over.

We jog for a few strides in silence. It's early, so I don't expect him to be chatty.

"Why did we need to run early today?" he asks.

His question surprises me. Is he curious about my life?

"Oh, well, um . . . it's complicated."

"What does that mean?"

Do I tell him about me and Gigi? I've been dying for someone to confide in, but I hardly know Blake.

I gaze over at him, and he must feel my stare because he turns to me, his eyes kind and warm, like an open doorway inviting me in.

"If I share some things with you, can it stay between us?"

"Yeah, of course."

"With Livi cut-off from me for the summer, I have no one to bounce stuff off. A lot is going on and trying to figure it out on my own has my head spinning."

"I heard she was banished. Rough."

"Yeah, it's been tough."

He laughs. "I meant for her."

"Oh, yeah, of course. I miss her so much and worry about how she's coping. I'm not even allowed to write her letters. But I have no one to talk to now."

He gives a half-smile. "Well, now you have me."

I almost stop breathing. Like I might faint from the full-on swoon overtaking my body. This guy is good.

I gather myself and decide to trust him and share with him a little of Gigi's story. "Before this summer, I never really knew my grandmother. Mom's an only child and her dad walked out when she was young, so we've always been a small family. Gigi would pop in and out through the years, but I don't remember much. Turns out she's this really interesting person who has shared with me some family history that no one else knows."

I guide us left at the stop sign.

"Gigi and I are leaving today on a road trip to try to solve a few family mysteries. But I can't figure out why everything with her is so secretive. I also can't figure out why Mom gives off these bad vibes toward Gigi when Gigi shows no signs of animosity toward Mom."

"Like what sort of secrets?" he asks.

I decide to lay it on him. "Like we're really Jewish."

He looks at me. "You know I'm Jewish?"

I let out a laugh. "*I know.*"

"Why is that funny?"

Now's probably not the time to admit that I know a lot more about him than he realizes. "Your bar mitzvah was a big deal in seventh grade. Every kid was trying to score an invite to that party. I didn't make the cut, but that's how I know you're Jewish."

He raises his shirt to wipe the sweat from his brow. "If it

makes you feel better, I didn't even care to have girls there, but my mom forced me to invite them."

I don't show any reaction, but that does make me feel better.

He reaches over and playfully jabs me in the ribs. "Welcome to the tribe. But why is being Jewish a secret?"

I shrug. "I don't know. It's this heart-wrenching story about my great-grandmother being a Holocaust survivor who was saved by my great-grandfather, an American G.I. They fell in love and had my Gigi in Paris."

I take a few deep breaths before continuing. "But then my great-grandmother died, and Gigi was brought to America and raised by her aunt, my nana. Gigi thought Nana was her mom until Jack told her he was actually her father, but then he left."

"Holy shit."

"Right? I'm hoping our trip today will help resolve some unanswered questions."

We near the end of our run, and I start to worry I've shared too much. I redirect conversation, "Let's kick it hard these last two minutes."

I set my watch timer and we run fast the first sixty seconds and then full-on sprint the last sixty. Blake beats me again.

We start a cool down walk, lifting our hands above our heads as our breathing and heart rates settle. We circle back to Gigi's house.

"Y'all are leaving now?" he asks.

"Yep."

His eyes lock on mine for a few seconds, but it feels like an eternity. I break contact, dropping my gaze to my feet. He taps my arm and I look up. "Listen, I'm not Livi, and I probably don't have the correct expert insight, but you can always talk to me. I promise I won't share anything you tell me. I'm curious to hear what you learn on your trip. DM me when you get back and fill me in."

I'm tingling all over again.

As he walks down the street toward his house, he suddenly swings back around, a perfect dimpled smile on his face. "That's really a wild story about your family!" he shouts.

"I know!" I yell back.

But somehow it feels like the tip of the iceberg.

CHAPTER NINE

We load Betty with supplies and goodies. Gigi packs us sandwiches and freshly baked chocolate chip cookies for the trip. I made sure to grab a few Dr Peppers from my house to bring with us. Subtlety is the best way to let Gigi know my drink preferences.

We hop into Betty and get on the road. I'm the driver and Gigi's riding shotgun. I still can't believe she's letting me drive on the interstate. If Mom knew I had Betty out on I-35, she would lose her mind, and she'd lose it on Gigi. I try to tie up a few loose ends to make sure we don't get caught.

"Did you bring your cell phone?"

She lifts her handbag up from the car floor and digs through its contents. Pulling the flip phone out, she then waves it in the air. "Yes. But I never use this thing."

"Is it turned on?"

"No."

"Well, we should turn it on because I forgot my phone."

Pangs of guilt course through me at giving Gigi such a fat lie. I would never "forget" my phone; panic overtakes me when it's not in my line of sight. But I wasn't going to let Mom thwart our plans.

I purposefully left my phone at Gigi's house so Mom can't track me and find my location. She routinely checks where I am because I get annoying text messages from her if I'm not where I said I would be. Do I really need to send a text when my friends and I decide to hit up Chick-fil-A instead of Wendy's? Mom loves to be all up in my business. Doesn't she have anything better to do?

"But I didn't bring a charger," replies Gigi.

Who doesn't bring a charger for their phone on a road trip? Sometimes I think I have more to teach Gigi than I have to learn from her.

"Okay, leave your cell off, but let's turn it on when we get to Malone and check your messages to make sure Mom or Dad haven't called."

She nods, seeming satisfied with that answer.

As we pull onto the highway, I ask her for directions. Gigi studies the giant road map sitting on her lap. I've never seen anyone use a paper map, but I guess it's necessary when you don't have a smartphone and drive a classic car with no GPS. This technology-free adventure makes me nervous. I have no cell phone and no British lady telling me which direction to go. What are we supposed to do if we get lost?

Gigi wears her reading glasses, intently studying the details of our trip. "It's as the crow flies. A straight shot down the interstate and then we exit at Milford. We'll pass through a few small towns before arriving at Malone. Once we arrive, we'll get a feel for what it was like when Jack and Nana lived there. Malone is a small place and not much has changed in a hundred years."

A hundred years and not much progress? What in the world kind of place is Malone?

She closes the map, tossing it on the back seat.

We cruise along, approaching downtown Dallas and its many skyscrapers. As we loop around the city, traffic intensifies, and the road signs confuse me. Cars whiz by us, weaving in and out of lanes like this is a game of Pole Position at the arcade.

I'm at a code red with anxiety as I death-grip the steering wheel. "Gigi, which exit? Which lane?"

"Just stay to the left," she says, her voice calm and steady. "Almost there."

We make the turn onto I- 35, and we soon pass through the south suburbs of Dallas. Leaving concrete and congestion behind us, my shoulders relax, and I release a big sigh. Now I know why Mom and Dad never let me drive downtown.

The sun is bright and reflects off the endless farmland while we cruise the open road. Gigi's wearing her Jackie O sunglasses while I flex my Target Ray-Ban wannabes.

We're listening to The Beatles' *Rubber Soul* album. When "I'm Looking through You" comes on, with its tambourine and happy beat, we both let loose—me jamming on the steering wheel and Gigi doing her rhythmic clap move. The song is confusing because it's a total rocking dance song, but the lyrics are brutal, like the perfect song for when someone betrays you. It reminds me of Taylor's, "We Are Never Ever Getting Back Together," a song that compels you to move and sing along passionately while you're screaming about being pissed off!

"You have a lovely singing voice. You sang that harmony perfectly," Gigi says. She wags her finger at me. "I suspect you get that from me and Jack."

Another nugget from Gigi about the past. "Jack was musical?"

"Extremely. He played piano and guitar. Really, any instrument he picked up. He played by ear, like me. Nana was musical as well, but she read music. She loved to play the piano."

She's back to singing along to the music.

As we drive along, we work our way through the album. I've noticed that The Beatles make conversation unnecessary. It's like we're having an interesting discussion just listening to their songs.

"In My Life" comes on and Gigi passionately sings the verses. Turning the volume down as the song ends, she reaches over and touches my arm. "Can you promise me something?"

I glance at her, my answer obvious. "Of course."

"When I die, can you play this song as they lower me into the ground?"

"Gigi!"

Why are we back to talking about death again?

"I'm serious. This song has carried me through so many dark moments. I want it to carry me to the light when it all ends."

Another deep and thoughtful insight from Gigi. She's like a walking philosopher. Mom and Dad really need to step up their game.

"Okay, I mean, yes, I'll make sure of it. But I don't even want to think about a time when you're not in my life."

And I mean it.

She touches my hair, running her fingers through a curl.

"Run for Your Life" is on and the upbeat tempo has us smiling and laughing again. Gigi taps my leg. "Want to play a game? How about the billboard game?"

Dad loves car ride games whereas Mom's always buried in her phone, scrolling through Instagram, or researching our intended destination. "I have a better idea. Let's play a game Dad and I love. We do it with movie lines, but let's do it with Beatles songs. We have to make a coherent conversation, but you can only use Beatles song titles."

Gigi claps her hands. "Oohh, I love it. I'm going to win this one!"

I give her a side glance, making sure to not take my hands off the wheel. "You shouldn't be so confident. I've been listening to The Beatles nonstop, and I think my youth gives me the advantage on this one."

Her high-pitched, infectious laugh spills from her lips. "We'll see about that. I'll start us off."

She clears her throat, then pivots her shoulders toward me. "Oh, Darling."

That wasn't much of a kick-off. I'm a little disappointed, but I'm betting she's saving the good stuff to beat me. "Good Day, Sunshine," I say.

"Good Morning, Good Morning."

"Here Comes the Sun," I reply.

"Do You Want to Know a Secret?"

Hmmm, what secret do I want to know? "Every Little Thing."

"You're Going to Lose That Girl."

Gigi is so fast at this game. I need a good comeback. "Tell Me Why," I say.

"She's Leaving Home."

"Because?"

"Let It Be," Gigi says.

I draw a blank. I playfully pound the steering wheel. "I have songs in my head, but none that make sense for why a girl is leaving home!"

Gigi slaps her thighs. "I win!"

We both fall into laughter.

She grabs the road map from the backseat. "We're getting close. Take the next exit."

I turn off the interstate, and we weave through the small town of Milford. Silos and cornfields line the road and a couple of ranch houses dot the open land. Shiny pickup trucks sit in driveways and Texas flags flap in the wind.

"Everything is burnt up now, but in springtime, these hills are covered in wildflowers—a sea of bluebonnets and Indian paintbrush, sometimes Queen Anne's lace sprinkled in," says Gigi. "It's simply majestic out here when these flowers are blooming. Shades of red and orange, blue and purple, all blending with the green grass. It's as if God painted the land. Have your parents ever taken you on a trip to see the bluebonnets?" she asks.

"Never."

"Well, that's a shame. You and I will have to come back here together next spring so you can see it first-hand. I'll show you my favorite spots."

I gaze over at her and she's smiling at me, her big sunglasses covering what I know is some major eye twinkling. "Our next road trip," I say.

We pass signs that tell us we're in Irene and Mertens, but there isn't even a gas station or grocery. These places are tiny! Irene: population 160; Mertens: population 125. One-stoplight towns and then nothing but land.

We continue to wind deeper into the country, passing endless rows of crops. "What are they growing out here?"

"Corn and cotton," says Gigi. We pass a herd of cattle, and she says, "And those are Charolais. They're some of the finest beef cows in the world."

How does she know all this stuff?

We drive through more farmland and then we're here. Malone, Texas. Population: 305.

We turn onto what appears to be the main drag of Malone, a street called Live Oak. The road is dusty, and the town center consists of two blocks of storefronts. Malone isn't abandoned, but it's most definitely seen better days. I almost expect tumbleweeds to blow down the street, like in a ghost town from the Wild West. The restaurant we passed on the way in was called a "saloon," so my imagination isn't that far off.

I park on the street across from a motor motel and we both step out.

"This way," Gigi says. "The heart of the town used to be on Pecan Street."

We cross over to a dilapidated block of buildings and survey this relic of a town: a post office, fire department, city administrative building, and restaurant.

"Where do we begin?" I ask.

She sighs. "At the beginning."

She removes her sunglasses and places them on top of her head. "There used to be a bank on that corner and a dry cleaner across the street." She motions toward the restaurant. "Let's go inside."

We enter the small and poorly lit space. Patrons fill two-thirds of it, a larger crowd than I expected. We're directed to choose our own seat, and we select a table in the corner. Our waitress chats with the group next to us, a discussion amongst friends. Nobody seems to be in a rush around here, including Gigi. Don't we need to be exploring? Eventually, the waitress twirls around, greeting us with a twangy, "Hey, y'all." Gigi orders a coffee, and I ask for a Dr Pepper.

Gigi pours cream and sugar in her mug, taking her time to stir the contents thoroughly. I watch her, waiting for her to reveal the family secrets. I drain my Dr Pepper through the straw, my eyes not moving from Gigi. She sips her coffee slowly.

"This is good coffee."

"And this is a good Dr Pepper."

She smiles at me, but her hands shake slightly, although that could be old age or the caffeine. "I thought I would share with you what I know, and then we can retrace Jack's steps."

I lean in. She's got my full attention.

"Jack and Nana were born and raised in this town. Their father, Otto, was a German immigrant. He was a teenager when he arrived in central Texas at the turn of the century, around 1900. He was smart and tenacious, mastering English and marrying my grandmother, Clara. They came to Malone to open a general store. Malone was bigger than it is today but still less than a thousand people. The local farmers would arrive on Saturdays to sell their crops and purchase supplies at the town's general stores. For Otto and Clara, money was tight, and they were poor, but most people were back then."

She takes another sip of her coffee. "Clara had three kids in four years and died in childbirth while having Jack in 1918. Otto found himself a widower with three babies to raise during an already tumultuous time for the family, having been accused of being German sympathizers during The Great War."

"The Great War?" I ask, interrupting her.

"World War I. It was called 'The Great War.' Many Germans in America were treated terribly, especially in small towns. Otto spoke German with the kids and had a thick accent, so people were suspicious."

Wow. I had no idea this happened to German Americans in this country. We studied World War I in world history this year, but when you're blowing through a thousand years in ten months, things get glossed over.

"Jack spoke German?"

"Yes."

I'm impressed. I'm in my third year of Spanish, and rolling my R's and asking, "*¿Dónde está el baño?*" is about all I've mastered.

She continues, "Otto's store was raided and searched. They accused him of hoarding rationed goods and supplies. Of course, they found nothing, but it was a great humiliation. The locals stopped shopping at his store and then Clara died."

My family is full of sad stories.

"Otto remarried a woman who turned out to be unkind and resentful of the children. Billy, Jack, and Nana had an unhappy childhood, with a monster of a stepmother. Otto had turned to drinking, so he was mostly useless."

"Who's Billy?"

"The oldest brother. He was a year above Nana."

"You've never mentioned him before."

"He was killed in a car accident when he was twenty-five. I'll get to him later."

I'm starting to feel like Mom's side of the family is cursed. Maybe it's not so bad that I take after Dad.

"Things picked up for Otto's store in the 1920s, but then the Great Depression hit, and they were back to barely surviving."

"The Great Depression was in the 1930s?"

"Yes. It started when the Stock Market crashed in 1929 and lasted until about 1933. Times were hard, and Otto hadn't forgiven the local government and authorities for raiding his store and treating him like a traitor to a country he loved. And he was fearful that with the Depression they would come after him again and accuse him of hoarding food and supplies."

She takes another long sip. Can she stop drinking coffee? I chomp on my straw.

"This is where the story that Nana told me takes a bad turn. During the Great Depression, lawlessness was on the rise. Famous gangs roamed Texas towns, robbing banks, and engaging in other criminal activity."

Her eyes twinkle. This is going to be one good story. "Otto was returning to Malone one evening after visiting a cousin in Corsicana when he saw a car on the side of the road. The sun was setting, and the car was broken down, so Otto offered the man a ride and to put him up for the night.

"He and the man stayed up the entire night talking and drinking whiskey, which was always Otto's downfall. Otto and this gentleman commiserated about their hatred of government and authority. Otto told the man his troubles with the town and local sheriff. This man said he was looking for help with his business that also had problems with cops."

Huh? Otto was a criminal?

"He gave Otto money to buy land. It was to be a hideout for this man's gang."

"Who was this guy?"

She leans in, and I do the same. "Clyde Barrow," she says, her voice barely above a whisper.

I stare at her. "Gigi, you know the routine with me and historical figures. Who's Clyde Barrow?"

She looks over her shoulder, before inching back toward me. "Clyde Barrow of Bonnie and Clyde? Two of the most famous bank robbers in Texas history! They murdered many people, robbed many banks, and were killed in a shootout with police."

"Otto was part of his gang?" I ask, my voice raising up an octave.

Gigi shakes her head, bringing her finger to her lips for me to quiet down. "Gosh, no. He just bought the land for Barrow and took a kickback for doing it. But the land remained in our family. Jack and Nana were at the property shortly after the shootout, and Nana remembers seeing a car in a barn with guns in the back seat. But that was her only memory of the hideout and the last she heard of any connection to Bonnie and Clyde."

This is a fun story, but what does it have to do with Jack and Ilse? "What about Jack?"

"I'm getting there." She leans back into the booth. "I want you to understand that you come from a long line of adventurous, reckless, passionate fools. Some might even call us troublemakers. This runs through my grandfather, my father, and me. I think you and your mother may have a little of it. Why do you think your mom moves so frequently? She doesn't know her past to understand we come from restless souls."

I never did understand Mom and the moving.

"Jack finished school at sixteen, around 1934. He took up with some nefarious figures and engaged in petty theft, but there were no jobs and people were starving. He worked odd jobs in and around Hill County, relocating to Hillsboro for a bit.

"Nana had gone to Waco to attend Baylor University a year ahead of him. She studied to be a teacher and was married to Papa and teaching school by the time she was twenty. Nana was always different; she knew she wanted stability and found both that and a deep love with Papa."

She takes a deep breath. "I don't have many details about what Jack was doing until we fast forward to World War II. Pearl Harbor was bombed, and every young, able-bodied American man enlisted. Including Jack. I've told you about Ilse and Jack and how they met. But I didn't tell you everything."

I hope what's left to share are the good parts. More of the love story, more about my great-grandmother and who she was and where she came from.

"They had a couple of years together in Paris. They were in love in the city of love, but they were both haunted by the ghosts of war. Ilse had suffered terribly in the concentration camp, contracting TB and starvation sickness."

My stomach tightens. "What are those?"

"Tuberculosis is a bacterial infection that attacks the lungs and makes breathing difficult. Starvation sickness is when the body goes into failure from lack of food, causing swollen legs, horrible digestive issues, hearing and vision problems, and memory and mental problems. It's truly a miracle that she was able to have me. Her body was ravaged by so many years of abuse."

Tears prick my eyes, and I brush them away with my thumbs.

"I was born, and Ilse died." She looks away, a quiver on her lips.

I feel connected to her with my entire being. "Jack brought me to Nana and then he left."

I touch her hand across the table. "I'm so sorry. For all of it. Where did he go?"

She shifts her body in her seat, looking over her shoulder again. "Well, our people aren't just restless adventurers; the family also has a vengeance streak. No one wrongs us without paying a price. Otto was going to stick it to the government and Jack was going to stick it to the Nazis."

Is this for real?

"He went to Galveston and hopped on a freighter to South America."

"Why South America?"

"Because that is supposedly where all the Nazis who had survived the war had gone."

"Wait, *what*? He went looking for Nazis?"

"Exactly. He crisscrossed the South American continent but was mostly in Argentina, a country with a large German population that became a haven for Nazis. The government refused to admit war criminals lived among them, and some happily took bribes to protect them. Jack searched out former Nazis, raided their homes, took things back, and exacted his revenge."

My mouth hangs open. "What things?"

"Artwork. Jewelry. Money. Anything he could find that he knew was stolen from Jews. Ilse had mentioned a specific painting of a young woman in white taken from their home and several family heirlooms like silver candlesticks and a gold watch."

I'm stunned, unable to string two words together.

She leans in again. "Remember, my conversation with Jack when I was a little girl, and he told me his story? He said there was a collection of loot that he had stowed away at the hideout."

The hideout?

"Bonnie and Clyde's hideout on the land that Otto owned," she whispers. "But then Jack died, and Nana never mentioned it. Many years later, I asked her about the hide-out, but she couldn't recall any details other than the place was somewhere around Malone. And she gave no hint of knowing this story. The only thing Jack ever asked of her was to make sure I got the book. He told her that the novel binds our lives together."

The novel.

It all circles back to the copy of *The Great Gatsby* in my bag.

"I came down here years ago, asking around about our family, but no one remembered the Webers."

Weber. The family name. How did I not think to ask this vital fact? My head flip-flops from Gigi's revelations.

"Wait, how did Jack die?"

She takes a long sip of her coffee, her eyes darkening. "Jack had gone down the rabbit hole, letting anger and vengeance eat away all the good in him. He sold some of what he recovered and was busted by police. He went to jail but was there only a week when he got into a brawl with another inmate and was killed."

I take a moment to let this settle. Jack died a criminal, not a hero.

But he was a hero. He saved my great-grandmother. He fought Nazis in Europe and after. I turn up my palms, studying each lifeline, wondering if they show signs of adventure or trouble like Jack. Then I remember I take after Dad. Why does this now disappoint me?

"I told you there are no happy endings for Jack," she says.

The characters swirl in my mind. Otto and Clara. Bonnie and Clyde. Gatsby and Daisy. Nazi hunters. Billy. Nana. Jack and Ilse. I'm back to the most lingering question. "Why are these stories a secret? Why doesn't Mom know the truth about your parents?"

Gigi calls the waitress over and asks for the bill. We sit silently as I wait for her to answer. She avoids my eyes, releasing a deep exhale. She pays in cash, and we leave the money and my unanswered questions on the table.

We walk back to Betty. "I want to show you the house Jack and Nana grew up in," says Gigi.

Gigi directs me down the street. We drive past run-down houses with front yards full of junk, juxtaposed with white-picket-fence perfection next door. This town is a hodgepodge of old and new, the past and the present colliding. We make two right turns, and she tells me to stop. "This is the old family home. It's not much, is it?"

The house looks like it's been in a fight, battered and bruised by weather and time. Busted windows, a broken screen door, the exterior paint chipping and flaking, and the roof patched with mismatching tiles. Maybe it was lovely years ago? Maybe it wasn't so bad when Jack and Nana lived there?

"Do you want me to take a picture?"

She frowns, her brows pinching together. "Goodness, no. Nana hated this house because of her stepmother. She moved out as soon as she was old enough to live on her own."

We take another moment to peer at the house. I study it, thinking about how Otto, Jack, and Nana lived here, a lifetime ago, and yet the structure is still here. Maybe other pieces of the past have survived?

"What about the hideout? Where do you think it is?"

She shakes her head, biting her lower lip. "I have no idea. I've told you everything I know."

"There must be clues here in Malone. What else can you remember?"

She points across the street. "See that church? It used to be the old schoolhouse. Thirty kids in a one-room house, ages five to sixteen. Nana, Billy, and Jack attended school there. Nana loved her teacher. She was the mother-figure she always longed for, and the reason Nana entered the teaching profession."

"Nana wasn't an adventurer or wild like Jack?"

"No. Nana was kind and gentle. She loved her brother and did whatever he asked of her, including raising me."

I realize a fact we glossed over from before. "Can you tell me about Billy?"

She removes her sunglasses and wipes off the condensation building from the humidity seeping in through the rolled-down window. "Nana and Jack had an older brother, William, but everyone called him Billy. He was gorgeous and charming, wild and reckless, and a drunk like Otto."

"There is so much tragedy in our family."

She remains quiet for a moment. "Nana loved her brother fiercely, and Otto never recovered from his death."

Gigi rolls the window up, gazing forward. She's ready to move on.

CHAPTER TEN

I put Betty in drive. "We need to visit every single place that has a connection to Jack."

Gigi has the roadmap on her lap. "The only thing left is the cemetery where they're buried."

I'm not sure how this will be helpful, but it's worth a shot. "How far?"

"Just a few miles. It's between here and Hubbard, along the old road to Dallas."

We drive for about ten minutes along a two-lane gravel road, passing pastures with grazing cows and aimless horses. As we weave farther into the country, the road undulates until we descend into a flat stretch of land. We arrive at the cemetery, but a chain-link fence blocks the entrance. Gigi steps out of the car, unties the gate, and pushes it open. She motions for me to drive ahead.

I pull Betty inside. The cemetery is small, with only a single loop to view all the plots. Gigi points to the left side of the dirt road. "Here is good."

We both step out of the car, and I wait for Gigi's instruction. She raises her hand to her forehead, shielding the sun, even though her sunglasses cover her eyes. "If I remember correctly, they're buried up this way a bit."

She walks along the dirt path, and I follow. "There is etiquette when traversing a cemetery," she says. "We must be respectful, so try not to cross over any graves unless absolutely necessary."

As we walk along the road, I glance at the names and dates on headstones. Almost everyone here died before 1970, and some stones are difficult to read. Nature has taken over this forgotten place; overgrown grass crawls up and around the markers, and weeds run amok. Aren't cemeteries supposed to have caretakers? They always do in the movies, even if the old guys are creepy and missing teeth.

This place is so different from where Granny is buried. Granny, my dad's mom, is at this well-groomed place in Dallas with fancy buildings and intricate headstones and miles of roads that loop in circles. It's so big that you need a map to find a loved one. She's basically staying at The Ritz of cemeteries.

I never met Granny. She died from breast cancer when Dad was in college, and he doesn't talk about her much. Whenever he does share a story, he tears up. Of course seeing my father cry turns me into a blubbery mess. Then he asks why I'm crying, and I say because he's crying and then he makes a bad joke. We're then laughing and crying at the same time, and I hug him, and he holds me so tight I struggle to catch my breath.

"Here," says Gigi. She kneels to the ground, her linen pants touching the tips of the grass. Out of caution I stand behind her, worried she may tumble over. But Gigi's limber for her age, squatting without the slightest shake. Good knees must run in our family, which is great news for me.

She slowly moves her hand over the raised letters on each tombstone.

CLARA MARIE
THOMAS WEBER
1895-1918

OTTO FRANZ
WEBER
1880-1948

WILLIAM "BILLY" DAVIS WEBER
1915-1940

JOHN "JACK" SAMUEL WEBER
1918-1959

Tears fills my eyes as I watch her. We're staring at the names of her grandparents, her uncle, and her father. People she never really knew. Strangers but family. A strong gust of wind eerily passes over us, like ghosts whizzing by.

Gigi swipes the corners of her eyes before tapping the ground beside her. I lower my body and place my backpack in my lap.

She picks up my hand and raises it toward the gravestones. "Everyone, I want to introduce you to my granddaughter, Hailey Jane."

Is she really talking to dead people?

"Hailey is one magnetic young woman. Smart, clever, and resourceful. A little rebel hiding within her. She is most definitely a Weber."

She squeezes my hand and although this is completely crazy, I swell from her words.

She pats my leg. "Your turn."

What in the world do I say?

I have an idea. I open my bag and pull out the novel. "Hello, everyone. Let me say I've never spoken to the dead before, so my apologies if I don't get this quite right."

Oh, man, do I sound ridiculous or what?

"I never knew about any of you or your stories until this summer. In my defense, y'all died before I entered the world. I never even met Nana."

I stop and tug on Gigi's sleeve. "Wait, why isn't Nana here?"

"She and Papa are buried together in Waco with his family," she says.

Her answer makes sense. I return to addressing the dearly departed. "Anyway, I want my great-grandfather, Jack, to know that Gigi has given me Ilse's copy of *The Great Gatsby*. I will guard it with my life and treasure it always. I will make sure your story stays alive in our family. I think that's all I have to say." I tuck a loose hair behind my ear. "Oh, one more thing. I plan to come back and see you again someday now that I know y'all are here. You are not forgotten."

I reach over and touch Jack's tombstone, running my fingers over his name. Why does sitting with the dead make life seem more precious?

Gigi leans over and kisses my cheek, her tears mixing with mine.

I take out my Polaroid from my bag and snap two photos of the headstones. I then aim the camera toward Gigi and take her picture.

"What are you doing?"

"Just documenting that we were here."

I wave the pictures in the air, and like the miracle that is instant film, the images begin to appear.

The wind has died, and the sun beats down on us. I can feel sweat at the base of my back and under my knees. But I don't move; I'm waiting for Gigi's cue.

She rises slowly, using her hands to thrust her body off the ground. I simply hop up to a standing position. She wraps her arm around me as we walk toward the car. I think about Jack. He took so much to the grave with him. So many of the answers we seek are buried six feet down.

We begin the ride home in silence. Luckily, I take after Dad and have a keen sense of direction. I remember how we came and guide us back to the interstate. Before we turn on to I-35, I say, "Last chance. Any other places we need to check out before heading home?"

Her cheek presses against the window. "That's it. You've seen it all. It's not much, but at the same time, it's everything."

Is she talking about family or Malone?

I turn Betty onto the highway, and the small towns disappear behind us. Gigi takes the *Help!* cassette from the glovebox and puts on "Yesterday," a soothing song, reflective of the past and perfect for our somber mood. Past troubles definitely hang all around us.

Then it hits me. "Wait, we should go search the county records. We could look for property deeds."

Gigi shakes her head. "No, I did that years ago. I went to the courthouse in the county seat of Hillsboro and even stopped at the library and searched old newspapers for any mention of Otto or Jack."

"When was this?"

"Oh, gosh, forever ago. I think it was around 1995?"

1995. That was ten years before I was born and twenty-five years ago. I pound the steering wheel in excitement. "Gigi, that was before the Internet!"

"Yes."

She's not following. She clearly doesn't watch a lot of crime shows about cold cases. "There might be so much stuff that we can find now using Google or other record searches. What if the file clerk didn't look in all the right years or in the wrong files? Or what if the data entered in 1995 wasn't complete? I read an article for school once about old paper records. It said that since the Internet, counties and states have scanned and uploaded all their old documents into databases."

She straightens her back, her mood perking up. "I guess that's possible."

I think I might be onto something here. "What if something was entered incorrectly? I noticed on the tombstones Weber was spelled with one 'b,' where so often it's spelled with two in English. And did Jack always call himself 'Jack'? Did he sometimes use 'John'? We can search all the different ways he might have filled out forms. There has to be a way for us to find the hideout and learn more about Jack."

Her eyes glimmer. "I love your youth and enthusiasm. You're the shot in the arm this old lady needed."

It's dusk by the time we arrive back to her house. We sit in the kitchen and share a few scoops of ice cream. The entire day plays through my mind. How can I help Gigi find the hideout and learn more about her parents?

"Do you have any possessions of Jack's?" I ask. "Anything that might help us understand him."

She removes the spoon from her mouth and sets it delicately inside her bowl. "Nana had a small box of his things. A uniform, a few pictures, and a couple of letters he wrote from the front to her and Otto, but I couldn't find them when she passed. I have just one thing, other than the novel."

Gigi opens the pantry door. She perches on the tips of her toes and reaches her arms up to a high shelf. Returning to the table, she holds a coffee container. "It's a fake can," she says. "It hides some of my best jewelry."

Her hand moves in the can, before she raises it to eye-level to peek inside. "Aha! There it is." She pulls out a medal. "Jack was awarded the Medal of Honor for his service in the war."

She passes it over to me. A five-point star hangs off a blue ribbon. The word "valor" is written below an eagle. I stare at the medal in awe. "What does valor mean?" I ask.

"Valor is great courage in the face of danger. The Medal of Honor is the highest military award given to soldiers."

"The highest? Wow. That's a big deal. What did he do to receive such an honor?"

A sadness circles her eyes. "I don't know. It was such a different time back then. No one talked about the war. And I didn't ask questions. With Jack and the war, I sensed these were things best left alone. I'm sure Nana knew but I think she felt it was in my best interest to not learn about the past." She releases a deep sigh. "There are so many things we will simply never know."

But I want to know more about Jack. There's got to be something out there.

I'm awake early the next morning so I'm ready when Mom arrives. I don't want to tick her off by making her wait. I'm sitting in the wingback chair with my phone on my lap. Gigi sits across from me, sipping her coffee and reading the newspaper.

My phone buzzes, and I stand to leave. "She's here."

I lean over and kiss her cheek. She grabs my hand, giving it a squeeze. "Thank you for helping me. I needed to get back down there. I couldn't have made the trip without you."

"It was super cool to see Malone. And we'll return in the spring so you can show me the bluebonnets?"

The green of her eyes sparkle. "It's a date."

I walk outside and the sun shines brightly. Pulling out my sunglasses from my bag, I put them on before sliding into the front seat. Mom smiles at me. "How was your sleepover?"

I'm glad these shades cover my eyes while I lie. "It was good. We got most of the closets cleaned out."

The car slowly moves forward. "Since it was such a success, it would be nice if you took a stab at organizing your room."

"I'll think about it."

We drive along in silence. No grilling from Mom. I think my ruse worked. I decide to ask her the question that has been nagging at me. "Why don't you ever come in and visit with Gigi?"

"We're always on a tight schedule," she says, her eyes focused on the road, but her voice sounds pitchy, like she's not sure of her answer. "Work is really busy, so afternoons are tough. I do call and check-in on her every now and then." She touches my hand. "That's why it's nice for you to be spending time with her."

I don't buy that answer but leave it alone. She's confirmed for me she doesn't like Gigi. Who doesn't visit their mother?

I'm at home in my room, trying to process all the discoveries of our trip. Sitting at my desk, I open my laptop and my family tree, adding details learned in Malone about Great-Uncle Billy, Otto, Clara, and the family name. The Polaroid photo of the headstones lies next to my computer, and I double-check that names are spelled correctly and birth and death dates match exactly.

I jump over to Google and search for record sources. Maybe Dad can help me? He's an attorney, and I know has access to government records and stuff. But what do I tell him?

My phone buzzes. I have a message on Instagram. I quickly swipe the app.

How was the road trip? Are you back?

Blake.

He's asking about me. He's not asking for something from me but about me. Even I can see the difference here.

But where do I begin?

It was good. I have so much to tell you. Too long for a DM.

The screen bubbles.

Want to go for a run tomorrow and fill me in?

Crap. Mom has me on Kyle duty tomorrow.

Sorry, I can't tomorrow. Babysitting my little brother.

Did I really turn him down?

Day after?

My heart balloons. Am I that good of a runner? Or could it be something else?

That works! You pick the time.

9?

I quickly fire back my response.

I cover my mouth with my hand. I think he wants to spend time with me.

CHAPTER ELEVEN

I'm waiting on Gigi's front lawn for Blake. I spy him walking my way, his face tilted down at his phone. He looks up and our eyes meet. He smiles, his dimple popping out, and I maintain my outward composure as my insides turn to jelly.

I motion my head toward the street. "Let's go."

We start off with an easy jog. As we pass a yard crew, the whirring of the lawnmower pulses in my ears and scents of cut grass hang in the air. "Should we go four miles today?" I ask. "Or you want to pick up the pace on three?"

"Let's do both and then still sprint to the finish."

I nod and increase our speed. He's doing a better job at keeping up. "Your running's improving."

His arm swipes mine. "I have the best coach."

Coach. That's what I am to Blake. Meh.

"Hey, so tell me about the road trip."

I steady my breathing to be able to talk smoothly. "It was good. We went to this small town my great-grandfather was born and raised in. This place is tiny, like it almost feels forgotten. It was sort of surreal to imagine what life was like for him growing up there. We visited the cemetery where he's buried, alongside my great-great grandparents and great-uncle."

I ask Blake the question weighing on my mind since returning from Malone. "What do you think happens when we die?"

"Are we talking about the physical part of dying, or do I believe in an afterlife?"

"The second part."

He wipes his brow with his hand, flicking sweat to the side. "I definitely believe in God, but I haven't given much thought beyond that. We have a long time until we have to figure it out."

I felt the same way until I started talking to dead people. "Yeah, I believe in God. I believe in ghosts and spirits as well, and I don't think it's over when we leave the physical body, but I'm not sure what's next. Gigi believes in reincarnation."

"That's one theory."

"You don't?"

"That our souls are reborn and come back as an animal or another human? Nah, I don't buy into that one."

We are at a stop sign, and I guide us to the right. "I need to read more about it. Gigi told me she hopes to come back as a bird because they have beautiful singing voices and soar through the clouds. She went on about dipping in and out of the sky and being a part of nature. She makes it all seem so romantic. But Gigi has a lot of kooky ideas. I mean, she's requested we play 'In My Life' at her funeral as she's lowered into the ground!"

He laughs. "Your grandmother is definitely built different. Any big bombshells like you were hoping for?"

"Yeah."

"Like what?"

Should I tell him everything? I've already told him so much that I might as well share the entire story. "You promise this doesn't ever go beyond you and me?"

"Yeah, of course."

I turn my head so I can watch his reaction to this one. "My great-grandfather became broken after the war when my great-grandmother died and . . ."

Do I just spit it out?

"He went all rogue and became set on avenging her death. He went to South America to hunt down Nazis."

Blake stops running, like dead in his tracks in the middle of the street. "Are you freaking serious?"

I stop as well. I lift my shoulders, holding them up for a second before releasing them. "Yeah, I think so. He went to recover stuff stolen from Jews. Or maybe he was just robbing Germans and possibly murdering them. It's all a little unclear."

His smile spreads all the way to his eyes. "Your family is so cool."

I feel the same way. Is it weird I'm proud of a man who was a criminal? "He supposedly brought a lot of stuff back and stashed it in a hideout somewhere near that town we went to, but Gigi doesn't know the location. She's scoured what's left of Jack, trying to pinpoint where the hideout might be, but she's never found anything. I left out one other part. Apparently, he went all Darth Vader, pushed to the dark side by all the evil and death. Even though he was stealing stuff back, he was selling some recovered items as well. He was arrested and went to jail. He died in prison."

I tug on his arm. "Come on, let's keep running."

"So what happens now?" he asks.

"I'm going to help Gigi look for the hideout and find details about Jack. Gigi did some county record searches for the land, but it was years ago. My plan is to spend the rest of the day at her house, searching on the Internet to see what I can uncover."

"I bet there are military records from his time in the service. You should be able to find him in census records and a death certificate," Blake says. "Does your grandmother have any of that stuff?"

"Nope."

"I can help you today," he says, giving a half-grin. "We could tag team and work together. Two heads are better than one, right?"

It wasn't my intention to suck him into this research project, but of course my heart flutters at the suggestion. "Really? That would be amazing to have your help. As you know, Gigi is clueless with technology."

"I'll shower after our run and then swing by."

I'm tingling again.

"Let's go hard this last quarter mile," I say, my adrenaline rocketing through my body as I take off at full speed.

I'm pushing him, but he doesn't give up as we sprint to the finish. I eke out slightly ahead. He shakes his head as he catches up to me. "You might be the fastest girl I know."

He walks off toward his house and my eyes linger on the back of him. I'm not entirely sure what's going on between us, but whatever it is, I'm happy Blake Alexander is in my life.

I quickly shower and am thankful I brought a decent outfit with me. I change into cut-off jean shorts and a University of Texas tee. My unruly hair is not cooperating, so I weave it into a mermaid tail braid. I've become a master braider by watching YouTube videos. I gotta say, my skills are strong.

The doorbell rings and I scurry over. I fight a smile, trying to look relaxed and unaffected by Blake's arrival. My gaze discreetly rakes over him, taking him all in.

He wears a slightly different version of his earlier outfit. Instead of Dallas Cowboys plastered across his chest, this tee is simply a big star logo in a blue inset on heather gray. His hair is damp from the shower, and he smells fresh and clean. I'm picking up a hint of evergreen; it's a little intoxicating. He gives a closed-mouth grin, and my heart skips a beat.

His computer bag hangs over his shoulder, his hand resting on the bag's handle. He's one step ahead of me already. "Come in. I was thinking we'd set up home base in Gigi's office since her computer's in there."

He follows me and we bump into Gigi in the kitchen. Her brows jump at the sight of Blake. "Hello, Blake. It's lovely to see you. To what do we owe the pleasure of your company?"

Gigi is so formal and funny. What in the world was that last sentence? I answer for him. "Blake's great with computers, so he's going to help me with a few things this afternoon."

"That's so nice of you," replies Gigi.

We keep moving and enter her office. I don't shut the door; Gigi might get the wrong idea. I close the door about three-quarters of the way. "Gigi doesn't know I told you our family history, so let's try to keep our voices down," I whisper to Blake. "And she has a hard time hearing soooo . . ."

He lets out a laugh. "No problem."

He sits down on the sofa, and I plop down at Gigi's desk across from him. I glide the wheeled chair over to him, a pen and paper in my lap. "So, I'm thinking we divide and conquer. What if you tackle the National Archives research, things like military and immigration records, and I'll play around on ancestry.com? I'll dig for birth certificates, death certificates, census records, and see if he or Otto pop up on someone else's family tree."

He unzips his computer bag and pulls out his laptop. "Sounds good. Do you know his years of service and any specifics of his combat unit?"

I frown. "I only know he was in the army, and he enlisted in response to Pearl Harbor. It was bombed on December 7, 1941, so I assume he was shipped out sometime in 1942. Let me text you the picture of his headstone so you have birth and death dates and the exact spelling of his name."

I swivel around and scoot my chair back over to Gigi's desktop. We both work diligently. I'm thrilled when I find a death certificate and it confirms Gigi's story. I quickly print it out. Place of death is listed as Huntsville prison and date of death is February 18, 1959. Cause of death: knife wounds to the abdomen, chest, and back.

My eyes mist, and my heart tightens. I push my chair away from the computer, taking in a deep breath. What a terrible way to die. Jack was stabbed in prison with no loved ones nearby to comfort him in his last moments. Dying alone and dying a senseless death.

"You okay?"

I brush my pinky finger across the corner of each eye. Moving my chair to face him, I then toss the printed death certificate on the sofa. "Yeah, I just read Jack's death certificate. The good news is that it confirms Gigi's story that he died in prison, but it's difficult to read that my great-grandfather's life ended in such a horrible way."

He examines the document before handing it back to me. "I'm sorry."

I nod, exhaling the breath I had been holding. "Have you made any progress?" I ask.

"It's taken me awhile to locate the correct records, but I think I found his enlistment record on the National Archives database. Let me print it for you to take a look."

A few seconds later the printer buzzes, and I pick up Jack's enlistment information.

FIELD TITLE	VALUE	MEETING
ARMY SERIAL NUMBER	38240159	38240159
NAME	WEBER#JOHN########	WEBER#JOHN#S########
RESIDENCE: STATE	85	TEXAS
RESIDENCE: COUNTY	201	HILL
PLACE OF ENLISTMENT	8567	DALLAS, TEXAS
DATE OF ENLISTMENT DAY	19	19
DATE OF ENLISTMENT MONTH	03	03
DATE OF ENLISTMENT YEAR	42	42
GRADE: ALPHA DESIGNATION	PVT#	Private
GRADE: CODE	8	Private
TERM OF ENLISTMENT	5	Enlistment for the duration of the war or other emergency, plus six months, subject to the discretion of the President
LONGEVITY	###	###
SOURCE OF ARMY PERSONNEL	0	Civil life
NATIVITY	85	TEXAS
YEAR OF BIRTH	18	18
RACE AND CITIZENSHIP	1	White, citizen
EDUCATION	4	4 years of high school
CIVILIAN OCCUPATION	170	Sales clerk, laborer
MARITAL STATUS	1	Single

I peruse the details. "This is great to have in our file. It confirms he was single when he enlisted, but unfortunately doesn't provide any new information."

"I know. We need a few more details to dig deeper. Can you tell me again everything you know about his service during the war?"

"Gigi said he fought in the Battle of the Bulge."

"With pretty much half the US forces."

Clearly that isn't helpful. I chew my thumbnail, trying to remember other details of Jack's service. "He helped liberate the Dachau concentration camp."

Blake taps his fingers on his laptop. "Let me try to track down specifically what units were at Dachau on Liberation Day."

He is busy at work, and I turn back to ancestry.com. I've gathered some census records, but there are more Webers in Texas than I would have ever imagined. I'm slowly slogging my way through when there's a knock at the door.

"Hello? Am I interrupting?"

Gigi.

Blake pulls his laptop screen down toward his chest to obstruct the view, and I minimize my search tabs. "Come on in."

She steps inside the office. "I wanted to check on you two to see if anyone is hungry. It's lunchtime, so I thought I would make us sandwiches."

I stay quiet, letting Blake make the decision. "Sure. Sounds good to me," he says.

She claps her hands together. "Wonderful. I'll prepare turkey and ham sandwiches. Let's reconvene in fifteen minutes."

Who knew lunch could be so exciting?

We join Gigi at the kitchen table where she has laid out quite a spread for us: an array of deli meats, cheeses, bread choices, toppings, and condiments. I study Blake intently. Our friendship has hit its first real test. Please don't let him pick up the mayonnaise. It's one of the most disgusting inventions of modern civilization. Even the sound of the word—*mayonnaise*—makes me want to vomit. If either of them squirts any from the bottle, I might hurl. He picks up his sandwich and takes a bite. He's not added a single condiment. We're in the clear.

Gigi chatters away with Blake about the Texas Rangers' last game. Here's another quirk of Gigi: she loves baseball. Most people in Texas love football, but her heart is with the most boring sport on earth. Kyle plays baseball, and I refuse to go to the games because they're so long and dull. Plus, he plays the outfield and bats like eighth, but I know better than to point out these facts.

I eat my food, not really listening to discussions of weak bullpens and the yips and low batting averages. My mind wanders back to Jack. I think we need to focus on property record searches to find the old hideout.

When Gigi says my name, I snap out of it. "I'm sorry, can you repeat that?"

"I was asking if you had plans for the big holiday," she says.

I'm not following. She lifts her brows. "The Fourth of July is this week."

I take a sip of water to have a second to prepare my response. The Fourth of July is a big party night, but with Livi gone, I'm out of the loop. It's not my scene anyway. "No, I haven't given it much thought."

"What about you, Blake?"

"I'm going over to our club with some friends. They have fireworks, a DJ, and a big buffet."

So that's what the popular crowd is doing for the Fourth.

"You should come with us," he says.

A smile slips from Gigi's lips. She set this up. God, she's good.

But I'm not sure I want to sign on for an evening with that group, even if it means being near Blake. "Really? Gigi, I'm supposed to be at your house that day helping."

"You could come here for the morning and then meet up with Blake in the afternoon."

"Yeah, we have another unofficial practice that morning, so we'll go later. I can swing by and pick you up around four if that works?"

My gaze moves from Gigi to Blake. I feel like I'm the only one not on board with these plans. I noticed he said, "We'll" but I don't know who that means. What if Bree is back in town? Even though my gut is telling me this is a bad idea, I'm too curious to say no. "Okay, cool."

I hope I'm not crashing some party I wasn't ever meant to be at because of one meddling old lady.

We finish lunch and Blake and I stand and take our plates to the sink.

"Ready to get back to work?" I ask.

"I actually need to run," he replies. "I promised my mom I would help her with a few things at the house."

I feel a sting of rejection, and I don't even know why. "Of course. Let me help you get your laptop."

We move into the office, and he closes the door behind us. We stand a few feet apart. "I'll keep working at home and DM you any good info I find," he says in hushed tones.

I wave him off. "Seriously, you don't have to do that."

"I want to help. This is so interesting."

I run my hand over my braid and dart my eyes away before settling back on his gorgeous face. "Hey, that was so awkward with Gigi bringing up the Fourth of July. You didn't need to invite me to join your group. So please know we're cool and can just keep running and working on this stuff."

He crosses his arms, a grin hanging on his lips. "It'll be a fun night, and you should come with us. No pressure, though."

He seems sincere and genuine, and I can't help but smile. "I'll see you at four on the Fourth."

Raising the computer bag strap over his shoulder, he lifts his chin toward me. "See you then."

He exits the room and I collapse into the swivel chair, spinning it round and round.

CHAPTER TWELVE

We're at family dinner when I decide to throw out to the table that I've got plans on the Fourth of July. I'm bracing for some pushback, because we've watched the fireworks together as a family every year since I can remember.

I repeatedly clear my throat, signaling I would like to take the floor. Dad stops jabbering about thick crust versus thin crust and silence envelops us. I'm still plotting my first move in this parent/child chess game when I lurch forward, announcing, "I have some plans with friends for the Fourth. I think it's easier if I spend the night at Gigi's since she lives near the club we're going to." I pause and then say, "If that's okay with y'all?"

"What friends? Is Livi back?" Mom asks.

"No, some new friends."

I know this answer is not satisfactory, but I'm not sure how she will react to my "new" friends being boys.

"And their names?"

Here we go.

"Blake and DeMarcus."

Mom's jaw falls open. "DeMarcus Thomas? The running back?"

I'm working hard to hold my innocent gaze. "Yep."

Dad smiles. "Your new buddies from the parking lot."

Mom glares at us, and I want to scream at him, "Rookie mistake, big fella!"

She places her wine glass down, leaning forward. "Looks like I've been left out of the mix. What parking lot buddies?"

I've got to salvage my Fourth plans and clean up Dad's mess. "Oh, Gigi and I were running errands and we bumped into some football guys, and it ends up Blake lives down the street from Gigi and they know each other, and well . . ."

Do I keep this going? She seems intrigued, so I continue telling half-truths. "And, yeah, um, we've hung out a few times at Gigi's, I mean, with Gigi. He's a nice guy and their group is going over to his country club by Gigi's house, and he invited me to join."

"Sounds fun," Dad says, as he picks up another slice of pizza from the box.

Mom taps the rim of her wine glass. "Is this the popular crowd? Aren't these the wild kids?"

She's clearly not convinced. I need to get this night back on track. "Yeah, they're popular, but I don't think they drink. That is what you're asking, right? These guys are so focused on football that there's no way they would do anything to risk missing a game."

Solid answer, even though probably not true.

She stews on my words, but I don't think any red flags have shot up. "But how will I know you haven't broken curfew?"

I stare at her, trying not to blink. "Because I wouldn't break curfew."

Now I'm lying. I would totally break curfew, but just not at Gigi's. That's not cool to do to a nice old lady.

"I don't plan to stay out late anyway because of Gigi. The fireworks will be around nine, and then I'll head home. I'll text you when I get to her house if that makes you feel better."

I don't add in the obvious, which is I know she'll be tracking me all night and will know exactly where I am.

Her scowl fades. "Fine. But not a minute past ten o'clock."

I give a military salute and Kyle laughs.

"Hey, if anything starts happening that you're not comfortable with, text me and I'll come pick you up. No questions asked," chimes in Dad.

This exchange is a perfect example of why Dad is my person in the family. He gives me space but is always looking out for me.

"Of course."

"Thanks for letting me go," I add.

Mom sips her wine and purses her lips.

I've brought a few different outfit choices over to Gigi's, and she insists I try them all on. We intently study my appearance in her bathroom's full-length mirror as I twist from side to side. We both agree my red romper with my white, slip-on Converse Chuck Taylors look best. The outfit is casual yet feels a tad dressier than jeans shorts and a tee. I'm wearing a bit of red, white, and blue, but not in a cheesy, "God Bless the USA" way—more subtle, like I'm out on a boat in Nantucket, living the Americana lifestyle.

Gigi and I spend the early afternoon painting our nails. I go with sapphire blue for my toes but leave my fingers a light shade of pink. I paint Gigi's long and slender fingers a fire-engine red. Gigi then helps me with my makeup, picking out a bold lipstick shade that complements the red I'm wearing. She also pencils in my eyebrows and, I must admit, they make my eyes pop.

I flat iron my hair, which is a massive undertaking. It takes me over an hour to run my strands through the wand, trying to calm my hair from its natural corkscrew state. I exit the bathroom with my hair and makeup set, and Gigi's mouth breaks into a ridiculous grin. She pushes off the bed and wags her finger at me. "You're missing one thing."

She steps toward her vanity and returns with her Chanel No. 5 bottle. I smile, touched by her thoughtfulness, but I don't want to smell like an old lady tonight. Plus, that scent is not subtle.

"Gigi, you're so sweet, but I don't want to come on too strong, if you know what I mean," I say.

She flips my palms over. "Just a dab on the inside of your wrists and then raise your hands and swipe behind the ears. Trust me, a tiny bit is all you need. You want to stimulate *all* of a man's senses."

I hold in the laughter, but I'm busting a gut. She is so old school, as if getting a man is the goal. I'm more concerned with holding my own with Bree's squad and looking like I belong than having Blake fall for me. Although, who am I kidding? I'd happily take both.

I allow her to lightly dot the inside of each wrist. Raising my arm to my nose, I take a whiff. It smells a little different on me, but it's still sweet with a hint of vanilla and definitely has a little sparkle to it.

When the doorbell rings, she squeezes my hand. "Let me answer it and then you can make your grand entrance."

Oh, good Lord, this lady is over the top. "Thanks, Gigi, but this isn't a date. It's just a friend hangout, so I think it's best if I greet him."

I hurry out of the bedroom but can feel Gigi on my heels. Before she can reach the handle, I swing the door open to Blake and his killer smile.

He's dressed in a navy polo and drawstring khaki shorts, with flip-flops on his feet. His thick hair is swept to the side, held in place with a dollop of hair gel. "Wow. You look great."

I'm hoping great means pretty. I turn back to Gigi, who gives me a wink.

"Hello, Mrs. Turner."

Gigi waves. "Hello, Blake." She peeks her head out the door. "Is that the car you're driving my granddaughter in tonight?"

Blake's pickup truck sits in front of Gigi's house with DeMarcus in the front seat. She waves. "Hello, DeMarcus!"

He sees her and steps out of the car. So much for my quick exit.

DeMarcus is dressed in a button-down shirt with the sleeves rolled to his elbows, his shirttail hanging loosely in front. His biceps bulge in the cotton shirt, his legs one swath of muscle definition. With navy shorts and boat shoes, he looks like a J. Crew model.

"Hello, Mrs. Turner," he says, the charm dripping off him.

He raises a hand at me. "Hey, Hailey."

I slap his firmly. "Hey."

"Can y'all fit in the truck?" Gigi asks. "Is there enough room?"

"Yes, ma'am. It sits three across," Blake replies.

Gigi steps outside, walking over to the car and the three of us trail after her. She opens the passenger side door and inspects the inside of the cab.

"Girl, you look good," DeMarcus whispers in my ear. "You're bringing your A-game tonight."

I playfully jab him in the ribs as I fight a smile. "You, too."

Gigi closes the truck's door. "It's a little tight for three people."

Is she going to not let me go? Did Mom call her and give instructions to sabotage my night?

"Why don't you take Betty? You'll have a lot more room and evenings are the best time to have the top down."

I cover my mouth. The guys look excited, but then I

remember I don't have my driver's license. "Gigi, I only have my permit, so we need an adult in the car for me to drive her."

"Blake can drive her then."

I'm gobsmacked by the suggestion. "Are you sure?"

"Yes, are you sure, Mrs. Turner?" Blake echoes.

"I trust you both. And you, as well, DeMarcus."

DeMarcus throws an arm around Gigi's shoulders.

"Well, let's go have Blake test her out."

We loop around to the garage and Blake, DeMarcus, and I climb in Betty. I'm in the front passenger side and DeMarcus is spread out in back, reclining the length of the seat. "This car is so much better than that stanky, nasty truck. Thank you, Mrs. Turner."

Blake places the key in the ignition, bringing her to life. Betty's engine hums loudly. "I'll take good care of her," he says.

Gigi stands next to the driver's side door and gently touches his arm. "I hope you're talking about my grand-daughter and not the car. She's much more valuable to me."

Gigi, tone it down! I'm sure my cheeks look like a tomato. I glance over to Blake, who is also flushed pink. "Of course, ma'am."

"They're both safe with us," chimes in DeMarcus from the backseat.

Gigi gives an approving nod. "Hailey, you know what song to play off *Rubber Soul*, right?"

I laugh because I can read her mind and was waiting for it. "Yep."

Rustling through the glovebox, I grab *Rubber Soul*, and insert the cassette in the eight-track. As the first few riffs of "Drive My Car" play, Gigi sticks her thumbs up, and Blake turns Betty into the alley.

I've spent the last hour avoiding the group of girls that scare me. I've made small talk with Blake, DeMarcus, and a few other guys but mostly sat around listening to conversations and hiding behind my sunglasses.

We've moved over to the 17th green for the big fireworks show. We're the only ones out here, and I'm not sure if this is even allowed. I can't imagine this fancy country club wants us sitting on their prized green with soda cans and a few other dubious cans tipped over.

I'm sprawled out, knocking back my third Dr Pepper of the night, when Blake squats down beside me. He stretches his legs out, resting on his palms behind him. "How has your night been?"

I take a sip, before leaning in toward him. "I've dodged Bree's friends, so I think it's a success."

He laughs, looking over his shoulder and giving them a wave. "You don't need to worry about those girls."

"I wouldn't exactly say that."

"They won't give you trouble with me and D around."

I hope he's right. "Do you come to this club a lot? It's super nice."

"Not really. My family used to live at the pool in summers, but now I'm too busy with football. I play golf occasionally with my dad. In the evenings, D and I sometimes sneak over and go fishing. The pond on the 8th green is massive and has a lot of catfish."

"You like to fish?"

His eyes lock on mine. "I do. It's chill and a nice break from the intensity of football. We have good talks while waiting for a bite. D's a deep thinker like me. We both like to read books on things like sports psychology, diet, and mind/body balance, and fishing is where we sort it all out."

He's so out of my league.

"What about you? What are you into besides running?" he asks.

"Well, don't laugh, but Livi and I like to paint our nails. It's like fishing with DeMarcus. It's just chill time, and although I wouldn't call our conversations deep, we discuss stuff—school, family, her love life."

"So that's why your fingers are a different color every time I see you."

He noticed. Maybe he does see me? "But I do other things, obviously. I like to read and watch movies. My family spends a lot of time together—bike rides and hikes on the weekends, dinners out, and we've been having lots of family game nights this summer. Cards, Scrabble, and thousand-piece puzzles are my jam."

He smiles and nudges his shoulder into mine. "Same with my family. My grandparents taught me nickel and gin rummy when I was little and we still play every visit. My dad and I have epic chess battles and family ping-pong matches at my house are *intense*. And you don't want to be over when *Jeopardy* is on."

"I love *Jeopardy*!"

"Right?"

We're both laughing and smiling. Why is it so easy to talk to him?

And then he does it. He touches my hand, covering it completely. I gaze into his eyes, and he's staring into mine. Our faces are inches apart. Is he going to kiss me? If he does, do I kiss him back? My heart thumps in my throat.

Suddenly, DeMarcus pops his head down between us. Our romantic moment is foiled. "Yo, we have a situation. Caroline has been overserved, and she's puking. Come on. I need your help."

We both stand and follow DeMarcus to the hole's water hazard, the edges now soiled with a heavy yellow color.

Caroline Chase has been gorgeous since birth. I'm sure she left the womb a perfect cherub while the rest of us were squished-up globs of goo. Long hair, long legs, and long eyelashes are just a few of her winning attributes.

She's popular and smart, and we used to be friends. She's always been nice to me, but I stopped getting invited to birthday parties and other social events in middle school. It's definitely shocking to see her beautiful blond hair doused in her own vomit. I haven't tried alcohol yet, choosing to live vicariously through Livi's stories. Watching Caroline is making me more confident in my abstinence decision. Barfing all over yourself is not a good look.

DeMarcus and Blake talk to her while I stand a few steps back. Why aren't her best friends helping her? I look around the golf course, and I see two of her friends drinking and flirting with QB Cody. Thank goodness these guys are helping her.

I dig through my bag, pull out a few tissues, and hand them to Blake to help clean up her face. "Someone needs to get her home," I say.

Caroline is propped against DeMarcus, while Blake helps her drink a cup of water.

"I can't go home. I need to sober up," she gargles out.

DeMarcus and Blake look back and forth from one another. We need a plan. "Y'all go find some food, and I'll stay here and make sure she doesn't pass out."

"Are you sure?" Blake says.

"Yes. We need to get some food in her body. She probably didn't eat anything."

She for sure didn't eat anything. Her anorexia is well-known gossip.

DeMarcus passes her over to me. I help sit her down, holding her by the waist. Her face scrunches together. "Hailey?"

"Yep."

She tries to sit upright, and I catch her before she tumbles over on her side. "You might want to let me help you."

I take out another tissue and wipe the remaining vomit off the ends of her tangled, sweaty hair. Removing the hair tie from my wrist, I quickly braid her long locks.

"Why are you being nice to me?" she slurs out.

Her dewy eyes are glazed over, and suddenly I feel sorry for her. "You don't know what you're saying."

She falls into me, her head hitting my shoulder. "What's going on? Are we still at the party? Where are my friends?"

All this time I've spent wondering what it would be like to peek behind the door, to live the popular "It" girl life, and now I feel like Dorothy when she meets the wizard. This is it? "DeMarcus and Blake are gonna find your friends, and they will help you."

She blinks, batting away the tears welling in her eyes. "No, they won't. They don't care about me. But I'm taking nasty shots to impress them."

Good to know hard booze isn't the way to go. I'm learning so much tonight.

"What's going on with you and Blake?" she asks, her words slurring again.

I almost choke on laughter. "Nothing. We're just friends."

She slaps her hand on my arm. "Leah saw you running with him and sent a pic around. Bree went *pyscho*. And now they're back together. She's telling everyone his mom told him to be nice to you."

This can't be true. They're back together? Why didn't he tell me? And he's hanging around me because his mom asked him? No, no, no. This sounds all wrong.

But it could be true; it probably is true.

I squint to hold the tears in and fight off the emotion ready to pour out of me. I get it now. God, I'm such a fool. "Thanks for the heads up on Bree, but Blake and I are just friends."

Her eyelids droop. "I think I'm gonna take a little nap."

I roll my eyes. I'm so over and done with my first high school party. I gently tap her cheeks. "Caroline, do not fall asleep. You need to stay awake until you get some food and water in your body."

"But I'm sooo sleepy."

As I fight to keep her awake, Blake and DeMarcus reappear. I stand and Caroline slumps over. I grab her arms and help her up, and then pass her over to Blake.

"Hey, what are you doing?" he asks.

"Can I have the car keys? I'm not feeling well, so I'm going to head home," I say in a flat voice.

Blake holds Caroline by the waist, but his eyes are on me. "You're going to leave? Now? Are you sure? We haven't even watched the fireworks."

I stare at my shoelaces. "Yep."

He hands me the keys, and I avoid eye contact. I leave him standing there with drunken Caroline.

I'm approaching Betty when a voice calls my name. "Hailey, wait."

I stop and stand in place before slowly turning around. DeMarcus.

"Did something happen?" he asks.

I fold my arms across my chest. "No, I'm just tired."

"You're a terrible liar."

I don't even know any of these people. Why did I ever think hanging out with them would be a good idea? He must already know the whole sad, unpopular Hailey thing, so why not just add to my humiliation, and ask him the question eating me up. "Did you know Blake is only hanging out with me as a favor to his mom? Like I'm some freaking charity case."

DeMarcus laughs, loud and bright. Let's just pile on the embarrassment. Tears build in my eyes, but I take deep breaths to make them disappear. I will not let DeMarcus see me cry.

"Who told you that?"

"Caroline. Bree told her."

"Girl, you have that all wrong. Bree is just salty because Blake is hanging out with you."

I smirk at him.

"I'm not lying."

"Why did Caroline tell me they're back together?"

DeMarcus shakes his head and rolls his eyes. "That's another Bree lie."

"What he said is true."

Blake.

He steps toward me. DeMarcus lightly squeezes my hand, then pats Blake on the back. "Y'all work this out. I'm going to go check on Caroline and make sure her friends are taking care of her like I told them to."

DeMarcus disappears into the night. It's just me and Blake.

Blake stands with his hands in his pockets and rocks on his heels, a half-smile showing a half-dimple. "I'm sorry if those girls were mean to you. It's my fault. It's not about you at all, it's Bree being Bree."

I climb into Betty's driver's seat.

"What are you doing?" he says. "You can't drive home. You don't have your license yet."

I keep my eyes forward. "It's five minutes to Gigi's house. I'll be fine."

He squats down, resting his elbows on the driver's side door. "I promised your grandmother I would take care of you and this car, so you have to let me drive you home. It's the right thing to do, so you need to let me make sure you and Betty arrive back to your grandmother safely."

"But you'll miss the fireworks."

"I think we've already had plenty of fireworks tonight."

He's right about Gigi. She would kill me if I drove the car home alone.

He touches my arm. "Please let me drive you home. I don't want the night to end like this."

I rub the heels of my palms over my eyes, gathering my thoughts and emotions. I can't break Gigi's trust.

"Fine." I swing my legs over to the middle of the seat, scooching my body over to the passenger side while Blake climbs into Betty.

"Let me text DeMarcus we're leaving and make sure he can catch a ride home," he says.

We sit silently for a few seconds and then his phone pings. "Okay, he's good."

He puts her in drive, and I turn the radio on.

"I thought it was required to listen to The Beatles while in Betty?"

"Only if Gigi is in the car with me."

"I like her rule. Will you put the *Help!* album on?"

The radio is all static, so I grant his request. He skips over to the song that I've been listening to on repeat lately, "You've Got to Hide Your Love Away." We listen to John Lennon's beautiful voice sing the first verse over a strumming guitar, the simplicity of the acoustic song making his poetic words more powerful. The evening air blows through my hair, and I feel the stress and anxiety of high school drama fade into the night's darkness.

"I love when the tambourine comes in," he says

I love the tambourine as well, but I don't tell him that. I turn the volume up and raise my eyes toward the stars, singing the chorus.

He stops in front of Gigi's house and cuts the engine off. "I'm sorry tonight was such a cluster."

I don't respond. My armor is up.

He pivots his shoulders toward me. "I'm glad we've gotten to know each other." He reaches over, his thumb runs over my palm. "I like hanging around you."

I'm not playing the fool any longer. I move my hands to my lap. "I'm glad I've been able to help your running."

He squints his eyes, a laugh falling out. "So, we're running buddies?"

"Yep."

Silence hangs between us. We're locked in a staring battle, but my nerves get the best of me. I blink first. "And you've been a nice friend, you know, helping me with the research."

"A nice friend? Who helps you with research?" he says, a smile creeping to his eyes.

He's way too close. But I don't move.

"So how can I upgrade my status with you?"

Is this another game? Or does he really want to spend time with me? "Well, we don't really know each other. Tell me something no one else knows."

He shakes his head, a playful smile on his lips. "Sorry, but nice friends don't get access to the vault."

"You're more than a nice friend to me."

His brows rise. I can tell he smells victory.

"You're my research assistant."

He jabs me in the ribs. "Ouch. But since you did share your family history with me, I guess it's my turn. But I'm trusting this secret stays between us."

My heart shifts into overdrive. "Of course."

His beautiful eyes pierce into me. "Ms. Hughes came on to me last year."

"*What?*"

Ms. Hughes is the young art teacher known for her style. She wears funky dresses and tortoise-rimmed glasses, her long black hair frequently streaked with bright colors. She's a favorite among students, allowing her classes to listen to music and use their phones.

He runs his hand through his hair. "Yeah. She asked me to stop by after school a few times and then the flirting intensified, and she started, um, sexting me."

My mouth hangs open. "Are you serious? She can get fired for that. I mean, she could go to jail if something happened between you two! Wait, *did something happen?*"

He takes his lower lip between his teeth. "It could have. It crossed my mind for like two seconds, but I was with Bree, and I'm not totally stupid. Teachers are off-limits. I just deleted the messages and ignored her."

"You never spoke to her about it?"

"Nope," he says. "But I'm not signed up for art this fall."

Good call on that one. "How did Bree react to this news?"

"I didn't tell her. D doesn't even know. It's too risky. It could ruin her career and ruin my reputation, even though nothing happened. Rumors like these never die once started."

He's so right. A story this juicy spreads like wildfire and lingers for years.

He then adds, "You're the first person I've told."

Electricity rockets through me. He trusts me as much as I've trusted him.

He cocks his head to the side. "What about you? What's something no one else knows?"

Do I share with him what's on my mind? I peer at Gigi's house and think of her encouragement. I decide possible humiliation is worth the risk. "We have opposite secrets. Mine is totally embarrassing, I . . ." Doubt creeps in, and heat flushes my face. *Step off the ledge.* "I've never had a real kiss. I mean, I've kissed a guy, but only did it to rid myself of virgin lips. Uninspiring kisses don't count."

He doesn't say anything. Does he think I'm a loser? He touches my hand, a lopsided grin appearing. "I can help you out with that, you know, if needed."

The amber of his brown eyes reflects off the streetlight's

dim light, his face inches from mine. We study each other like two people meeting for the first time.

"Yeah?"

He rubs my palm. "Yeah." He pulls back, removing his hand. "But, wait, I'm only a running buddy."

"Actually, it was nice friend." I raise my finger and tap my cheek. "Or was it research assistant?"

He places his hand behind my neck, softly pulling me closer, his fingers running through my hair. Our foreheads touch and I'm tingling *everywhere*.

"We need to find you a new title," I say.

His lips graze my cheek. "I'm open to suggestions," and then his lips are on mine. "This okay?"

I mumble out, "Mmmm."

Tongues are swirling and I'm not sure if I'm doing this right, but his mouth feels amazing. We share soft and slow kisses. I finally pull away, breathless, a minty Blake aftertaste lingering. I know I have a rosy tint and I don't care.

I wipe the corners of my mouth and run my finger over my lips. I smile sheepishly at him.

His eyes are bright, his dimple on full display.

"On that note, I think I should go now," I say.

"Then I should go as well because this isn't my car."

I laugh. "Right."

We both step out of Betty. "It's okay to leave her on the street?"

"Yes, Gigi said to make sure the top is up."

He cranks the convertible top, and we secure it, checking and rechecking the roof before locking the doors.

He outstretches his hand, giving me the keys. "Thanks for letting me drive your car."

"You mean Gigi's car."

"She's lucky to have you."

My cheeks sting from the ginormous smile I'm wearing. "I'm the lucky one."

We walk up the path to Gigi's house, his hand holding mine, and he kisses me one more time. "Happy Fourth of July."

"Happy Fourth of July."

I close the door and lean against it, my body exploding in its own fireworks show. I just had my first real kiss, in Betty, listening to The Beatles.

And it was perfect.

CHAPTER THIRTEEN

I'm still buzzing from last night when I get a text from Dad that he's on the way to pick me up at Gigi's house. Now that the Fourth is over, I need to get my act together and focus on discovering more about Jack and trying to locate his hideout.

We only know two facts about the hideout: a barn sits on the property, and it's located somewhere around Malone in Central Texas. We're basically talking about every piece of property over at least a hundred square miles. I've got to dig deeper and find a few more clues.

Dad is unusually quiet in the car. He doesn't ask about my night or the fireworks finale. A Fourth of July fireworks show is just the kind of topic that gets my dad excited. He loves to analyze the show's elements, giving an Olympic figure-skating judge critique on timing, colors, loudness, and height. But not today. We drive along silently listening to NPR. I'm starting to get an uneasy feeling.

We arrive home, and Mom is waiting in the doorway. "Dad and I need to speak with you."

I was right. Something is wrong and it must be about last night. Technically, I didn't do anything other than go to a high school gathering where alcohol was present. My mind races, trying to figure out what to say. I think I can spin last night into a Good Samaritan tale because I was helpful to Caroline.

The three of us retreat to the living room. I drop down onto the sofa, but they both remain standing. Mom crosses her arms in front of her chest, and she nibbles on her lower lip.

"We need you to tell us what's been going on," she says in a stern voice, her forehead covered in lines.

I look to Dad for help, but he wears the same troubled face as Mom. "I don't know what you mean."

Mom throws her hands up. "Hailey, enough. Just tell us the truth."

My stomach twists in knots. "Okay. I went to the golf course last night with Blake and DeMarcus. Some kids were drinking, but I was strictly tipping back Dr Pepper. Caroline Chase was there and super drunk, so I helped take care of her, and made sure she sobered up. But I didn't drink. I swear I'm telling the truth."

Mom's eyes widen. "That's not what I'm talking about. We will revisit last night *another time*. I'm talking about you driving Gigi's car on a road trip!"

Crap. I struggle to process what she just said. How did she find out? "May I ask who told you that?"

"No. What matters is that you lied to us, and you didn't have our permission to go. You don't even have your driver's license yet!"

"Did you talk to Gigi?"

I know that can't be it because she hasn't spoken to her in all the weeks I've been going to Gigi's house. And then it hits me. She's been checking my phone. Anger streaks through me. "Did you take my phone and read my Instagram messages? Did you really invade my privacy?"

Mom's face reddens, like steam is about to explode out of the top of her head. "Excuse me? That phone is our phone, not yours. We pay the bill, and we own the phone. Your father and I *allow* you to have Instagram and other social media but have always reserved the right to take it away if you abuse the privilege. Our job is to protect you, and I will read your messages anytime I'm concerned about your welfare.

"Gigi should not have let you drive that car on the interstate. Your father convinced me that since you never got to know his mother, you needed to get to know mine." She turns to Dad. "I knew this was a bad idea. My mother has no judgment."

Is Mom going to blame Gigi? "Whoa, this isn't Gigi's fault. I lied because I wanted to go with her to visit Malone. She's been researching some family history and needed my help. Gigi is amazing, and I've learned so much from her."

"Well, the history lessons are over. You're grounded for the next two weeks. No Gigi. No leaving this house."

This is total garbage. I stand and step toward her. "But nothing bad happened!" I shout. "Gigi was with me the entire time. I'm only spending time with her because you two asked me to help her!"

"It was a mistake. She's manipulating you like she does everyone in her life."

"She doesn't manipulate me."

"Really? Has she not made you fall in love with her, the car, and The Beatles? You aren't the first young girl to fall under her spell. But it's all fake."

Mom's words sting. "Stop saying such mean, horrible stuff. Why are you so jealous of her? Betty and The Beatles bring joy to the world. Gigi has brought so much happiness into my life. A lot more than you ever have!"

She whips her head back. I see the hurt in her eyes. "You know what I see when I look at that car? My five-year-old self chasing it down the street as she drove away in it. That car and Gigi broke my heart. She would load it up and leave me with Nana. Gigi coming and going in that damn car was my entire childhood."

Dad reaches for her, and Mom falls into his arms. She's sobbing, and my eyes flood with tears as well. I shake my head and flee the room.

I lie in bed and doodle in my journal, making notes of what Mom said about Gigi. I feel so confused because the person Mom was describing isn't the Gigi I know and love. I'm still not clear what Gigi did, but it hurt Mom very badly. And what does she mean when she said, "It's all fake"? Has everything between us been lies?

A light rapping at my door startles me from my thoughts. Dad walks in. "I wanted to check on you."

I sit up, and the tears fall from my eyes. "Is what Mom said about Gigi true?"

Dad sits down beside me, and I sink into his arms. He hugs me tightly. "Life is complicated, and we all have our flaws, even moms and dads and grandmothers. Gigi is a good person but made some bad mistakes and hurtful choices when Mom was young."

I pull back. "Like what kind of mistakes?"

His brows push together, and he massages his neck. Will he tell me the truth? "After your grandfather walked out on them, she left Mom with Nana and Papa. She would come back, but then leave again. Even though they were wonderful grandparents, it was incredibly hard on your mom to be abandoned by both her parents. She has a right to be angry and sad, but we never wanted you to be tainted by her experiences. That's not fair for us to pass her burden on to you."

He pats my back as I try to suck in my sobs, but they won't stop spilling out. "I love Gigi so much. She's fun and interesting and likes me the way I am. Mom's always trying to improve me, her disappointment in me is obvious."

He lifts my chin up. "You have that all wrong, Hales. Your mom is proud of you and loves you so much."

And then I ask the question I can no longer run from. "Does Mom not love Gigi?"

He lets out a sigh. "She loves her mom, but there are a lot of things for them to work through. Sometimes you can love a person but not like them. Look, this is adult stuff you shouldn't have to worry about. Being a teenager is tough enough. I've been trying to patch them up for years, but it's not my relationship. And maybe I shouldn't have pushed for you to spend time with Gigi, but I just . . ." His voice trails off.

"What is it?"

Tears fill his eyes. "I would give anything for one more day with my mom." He softly pats my cheek. "It kills me that she never got to meet you and Kyle."

I touch his hand. "I'm sorry about your mother. I wish I could have met her."

He nods, pulling me into another embrace.

Wiping my eyes, I suck in the snot building in my throat and nose. "One last question. I'm grounded for two weeks?"

"Yes."

"But can you drive me over to Gigi's so I can explain to her what's going on? I owe her an apology. I think I've made things worse between her and Mom."

"I'll need to ask your mom first." He squeezes my thigh before rising to leave.

He grabs the door handle and then turns back to me with sympathetic eyes. "Oh, and I need your phone. Mom said no phone for two weeks either."

So that's why he came. To ruin my life even more. I pitch the phone at him and bury my head in my pillow, the tears running over my cheeks like a waterfall.

Mom has agreed to let me see Gigi to apologize. I knock loudly, and then fidget with the hem of my shirt, my muscles twitching as my heart races.

The door swings open. "Hailey! Oh, my, why the long face? Come in, come in."

I step inside and she wraps her arms around me, but I don't hug her back, my arms glued to my sides. Gigi and I retreat to our living room spots, me in the wingback chair and Gigi across from me.

"What's going on? Why do you look so troubled?"

The tears are building again. "Mom read my DMs and . . ."

"Your what?"

"Direct messages. It's how most teenagers communicate on Instagram. She found out we took the road trip to Malone and is furious I lied to her."

Gigi appears unphased. "I see. It's not good to lie to your parents, but you know that. We had a wonderful time. That's what we'll both remember."

"She's grounded me for two weeks, and I can't come over to help you during that time."

Gigi's eyes darken and her lips turn down. "Your mother is punishing me, too."

"I'm sorry if I've made things worse between you and Mom. But I think I know why Mom doesn't know our family history."

I'm nervous, scared, angry, and sad all mashed into one confused state. I can't keep my feelings bottled up anymore. "It's because you left her just like Jack left you!" I lash out.

Gigi flinches, and her lips part slightly like she is going to say something, but nothing comes out.

I suck in my tears. "How could you abandon your daughter? Mom told me about you leaving in Betty. At least now I understand why Mom keeps her distance with you."

She is quiet, but her hands tightly grip the arms of her chair. "I made a lot of mistakes as a parent. I was a terrible mother. Nana was better for your mom, and I knew it."

Is that her answer? Just a cop-out response?

"But why did you leave?"

She fiddles with a loose string on her linen pants and yanks it out. She does not avoid my eyes but bores into them. "When your mother was four years old, your grandfather left me for another woman. He shattered my heart, and I fell apart. I had finally found someone who I loved deeply, who I adored and trusted, and he threw me away like yesterday's trash. We didn't have the Internet, or cable television, or Oprah talking to us about things like depression. I had fallen into a very dark place. Betty and The Beatles were my refuge from the hurt and anguish. I tried to drive away from my problems."

She takes a deep, heavy breath. "But the earth is round, and you always end up where you started. I did come back, but I would leave again, and your mother never forgave me. I don't blame her. It took years for me to get my head on straight, but too much damage was done to our relationship.

"Your mother is resilient and smart and brave. She created a beautiful life with your father. I always hoped that having the family she dreamed of would open the door for me to atone for my sins."

Her gaze moves past me, like she's staring into the past.

"I wanted to be in your life from the time you were born. I think she felt she was protecting you by keeping me at a safe distance. But I love you so much, Hailey. Spending time with you these last few weeks has been a highlight of my life."

It's been a highlight of my life as well, but now it feels like someone's taken a Sharpie and blackened it out. "Why doesn't Mom know about Jack and Ilse? You've evaded answering my questions, but I need to know."

She nods. "You're right. You deserve the truth. That begins with the decisions that were made to protect me."

Why do adults always think kids need protecting?

"When I arrived in Texas in the late 1940s, I was brought to a small town during a time when Jewish people were discriminated against in the South. This was before the Civil Rights Movement, and people who were seen as 'others' of any kind were treated differently. I wouldn't have been allowed to go to church with Nana, or invited to friends' houses, or be included in groups and organizations. Being Jewish in the Bible Belt of Texas in the 1950s was a black mark. I don't fault Nana and Papa for letting me believe I was theirs and raising me with their Christian beliefs.

"When my life fell apart, Nana and Papa came to Dallas and took care of your mother. I was in and out, but they stayed; they were her parents, and they loved raising her.

"I have made a lot of mistakes, but I wasn't going to strip away her identity as Nana and Papa's granddaughter and tell her she shares no bloodline with the man she considered her father. When Jack told me his story, it sliced me open. I knew it would do the same to your mother, and she had already been through too much. I haven't told her to protect her heart."

Her explanation makes sense. But that's the thing about Gigi. She knows how to weave a tale. After hearing the hurt in Mom's voice, I don't know what to believe. "I'm confused about a lot of things but thank you for the answers." I stand to leave. She rises as well, but I raise my hand to stop her. "I'll show myself out."

Her eyes have lost their luster. "I'm sorry if I've disappointed you or hurt you, Hailey."

The waterworks are back. I swipe a tear and close the
door behind me, the lyrics of a damn Beatles song repeating
in my head.

*I thought I knew you, but what did I know. You don't look
different, but you've changed. I'm looking through you,
and you're not the same.*

CHAPTER FOURTEEN

The days pass slowly. Mom and Dad banned me from all electronics, so I haven't been able to get on the Internet or watch TV.

I've been taking a lot of long, hot showers. The steaming water beats down my back and distracts me from the aching in my heart. I often slump to the shower floor and the water flows over me as the tears fall from my eyes. I'm so confused about Gigi. She's not who I thought she was. The person I know would never do something so hurtful to her own daughter.

Other questions slosh around in my mind. Why hasn't Mom forgiven her? It was years ago, and doesn't Mom always tell me people deserve grace? What happened to second chances? Does Gigi not get any?

And then there's Blake. We were just getting to know each other, and now I'm completely cut off from him. We kissed, and I've disappeared. What does he think of me now?

I put on real clothes for the first time in days. In my boredom, I play with my makeup and knot a waterfall side braid into my hair. I'm painting my nails for the second time this afternoon, when Mom pushes the door open and peeks her head in. She gives a hesitant smile. "You have a visitor at the front door. You're still grounded, so make it fast."

I sprint down the stairs, excited for some human interaction. I would happily take a conversation with the mailman at this point. I'm shocked by who stands on our front porch.

Blake.

"Hi," he says.

He's here. He came to see me.

"Hi."

I lean my shoulder on the doorframe, my hand gripping the handle. "I'd invite you in, but I'm grounded."

"I heard."

I step outside and close the door behind me. We sit down together on the front steps, leaving a sliver of space between us. He fidgets with his sports watch, adjusting the clasp. "I was so confused when you ghosted me."

Our eyes connect and my heart swells. I've been so anxious to speak to him. "I would never ghost you. Mom found out about my road trip with Gigi and grounded me for two weeks and took my phone and computer."

"Yeah, your grandmother told me."

"You saw Gigi?"

"I stopped by to check on you after a few days of not hearing back. I was worried I did something wrong on the Fourth." His knee touches mine.

I don't move my leg. It feels so good to have him close. "I'm so sorry, but I had no way to communicate with you."

"So, we're cool?"

All I can think is, *Hell yes, we're cool*, but then I wonder what does "we're cool" mean? Are we friends who shared a kiss or are we something more? "Yeah. I'm sorry if I seem out of it, but I've had a rough week. I've learned some stuff about Gigi that's upsetting."

"Like what?"

I stretch my legs out and cross my ankles. "That she was a horrible parent who abandoned my mom, driving away in Betty and leaving her with my nana."

His jaw falls open. "Wow. I didn't see that coming."

"I know. But it explains why Mom is always so icy toward her. I'm so confused because that's not the Gigi I know. This person that did all those bad things years ago doesn't seem real to me. She's been so wonderful and loving toward me."

And I'm crying.

He wraps his arm around me, and I press my cheek into his shoulder. When he drops a kiss in my hair, I tingle all over.

"I think you need to judge your grandmother based on your experiences with her. I feel sorry for her. She's been through a lot, and it seems like you two have a special bond. I wouldn't throw that away because of her past."

Blake is so calm and thoughtful; I wish I could rest on his shoulder forever. But I pull away from him and wipe my eyes. "It's complicated." I've used up my fifteen minutes and I need to get back inside before Mom barges out and embarrasses me. "Thank you for stopping by. It means a lot."

He leans in and kisses me softly. We part and I cover my mouth with my hand, trying to hide the grin escaping from my lips. I guess that's what "we're cool" means.

"I've got another week sentence here. The only time I'm allowed to leave the house is to train, so I'm doing long, hard runs twice a day." I nudge into him. "You better get ready for me to kick your butt when I'm free again."

He laughs and grabs my hand, taking it within his own. "I've missed you, and I've missed our runs. Do you think your mom would let me join you?"

"I doubt it. I'm in the doghouse with her, so I'm too scared to ask. I'll text you as soon as I get my phone and life back."

We both stand, his hand still holding mine. "I'll swing by and check on Gigi next week."

"Thank you. She'll love a visit."

But I'll love it more.

The longest two weeks of my life are over. What have I learned? I really like Blake Alexander and I really miss Gigi.

Dad has agreed to drop me off at her house this morning. I'm not sure how she'll react to my visit since we ended on bad terms. I hope she's happy to see me. As I approach her front door, nerves course through me. I tap the bronze knocker, and she opens the door. Her eyes twinkle and her smile is extra big. "Hailey."

She doesn't get another word out because I launch myself at her, wrapping my arms around her. She hugs me back tightly. "I missed you, Gigi," I say.

"I've missed you as well." Her voice catches in her throat, and she has a little wetness in her eyes. "You look as though you're dressed for a run."

I hold her hand in mine. "Yes, but I wanted to have a chat with you first."

"Are you running by yourself?" she asks.

"No, Blake is meeting me here in a few minutes." I bite my lip, trying to stop the grin forming on the edges of my mouth.

We move to our living room spots.

"He is such a polite young man. He came by last week to see if I needed help with anything. I realize I'm charming, but I suspect it had a lot more to do with his affection for you."

I'm unsure of what we are or how to address him. "He's very thoughtful and a nice friend," I say.

I redirect the conversation to the purpose of my visit. "I've had a lot of time to think these past two weeks. And although it pains me to hear about what happened with you and Mom, and I don't really understand it, what I do understand is that you are a wonderful grandmother and I want you in my life. You have brightened my world and taught me so much in our short time together. I want to help you find out more about Ilse and Jack and find the hideout."

And I mean every word of it.

Gigi wipes a tear away, her face wrapped in a grin.

The doorbell rings. "That's Blake." I try not to smile, but it spills out with his name.

We both rise. I can't help but hug her again, unspoken words passing between us.

We separate and I say, "I was hoping to come by tomorrow and have us pick back up on our weekly routine. There are only three weeks of summer left, and I want to spend them working on our family history."

Her wrinkles deepen as she bursts into a smile. "Sounds wonderful. We have so much to celebrate. Our favorite novels, the end of summer, and someone's extra-special sixteenth birthday."

"Yes, I will finally have my driver's license!"

The doorbell rings again and I race to the door, shouting over my shoulder, "See you tomorrow, Gigi!"

I'm so energized from my conversation with Gigi that I push us hard on the run, pacing us around six thirty. Blake grimaces but fights to keep up with me. I sprint off for the last hundred yards and beat him easily.

He catches me as I do my cool down walk. "What's gotten into you? You're Usain Bolt this morning."

I raise my hands above my head and exhale a deep breath. "I'm just happy to have my life back. But I have this weird thing that happens when my adrenaline kicks in. I drop into turbo speed and my mind shuts off from the pain.

I feel like I can push through a brick wall. It's the reason I win races. My legs could be on fire or completely cramped up, and I won't feel a thing until I cross the finish line. It just happened now."

I give a quick jab to his ribs. "Just so you know, a better analogy would be Mo Farah, Deena Kastor, Shalane Flanagan, or Galen Rupp. Sprinters and distance runners are completely different species. It's like comparing a wide receiver to an offensive lineman."

His dimple pops out. "Here I was thinking I would impress you by throwing Usain Bolt into the conversation."

We sit on the curb outside Gigi's house, our arms stretched behind our backs. "Are things better with you and your family?" he asks.

"Sort of. I eavesdropped on my parents arguing over me last night. Mom's not happy I still want to spend time with Gigi. Dad was trying to convince her to let me since school starts soon, and I'll be too busy to spend much time with her. He trusts me to make my own decisions, where Mom thinks she knows what's best for me." I smile at him. "I'm here, so Mom must have come around."

But I know my mother, and she'll be watching my every move.

I pop out of bed when my alarm sounds. I'm so excited to get back to our routine and leave behind the mess of the last two weeks. Back to Gigi's and back to finding out more about Jack and Ilse.

Dad drops me off a little before eight. I ring the doorbell but no answer. Walking down the porch, I peer in the windows but don't see Gigi. I loudly knock three times before I give up and grab her hidden key.

Pushing open the door, I call out Gigi's name, but no response. I walk into the kitchen and my heart drops.

"Gigi!"

She's on the floor, her arms splayed out. Blood drips down her forehead and out of her mouth. Her eyes are shut, and she's not moving. I pull my phone out of my bag, and my hands tremble as I dial 911. "Yes, I need an ambulance! My grandmother is unconscious, and I don't know what happened. Yes, 82 Oxford Street."

I hang up and call Dad. "Hey, Peanut."

I'm crying and screaming as I kneel beside her. "It's Gigi! Something terrible has happened! I've called an ambulance, but she's unconscious!"

"I'll be right there."

Bending down to her face, I cover her with kisses. "Please, Gigi, you gotta hold on. Help is on the way."

Her skin is cool to the touch. What is happening to Gigi? Is she dying? I need to do something. I jump up and grab a kitchen towel to wipe the blood from her face, but I'm shaking so badly I can hardly get my arms to move together.

I hear a siren and sprint to the door and then direct the EMTs to the kitchen.

They check her vitals; I hear them say she has a pulse, and they work diligently to secure her neck and place her on the gurney. An oxygen mask is placed over her mouth and an IV put in her arm. They ask me her age and name as they work. Raising the gurney up, they roll her outside, and I walk alongside them, holding Gigi's limp hand. "Can I ride with her?"

They open the back and lift her up into the ambulance. "Sorry, but only adults are allowed to ride with us," says the female EMT.

"But she can't go alone." I choke on my sobs.

The male EMT opens the driver's side door. "We're very sorry, but no kids allowed."

"Where are you taking her?"

"Presbyterian Hospital."

Standing alone on the sidewalk with tears streaming down my face, I watch the ambulance drive away. I'm violently shaking, my stomach turning over and over. Gigi is sick. Gigi is dying. I'll never see her again. They're taking her to Presbyterian Hospital. What if I never see her again?

Dad drives up and jumps out of his running car, and I collapse into his arms. "Presbyterian Hospital. We must go now."

He cups my cheeks. "Go grab her purse. We need her ID and health card information."

I'm in and out of her house in less than a minute. Dad quickly rolls through the neighborhood stop signs, and then guns it onto the freeway. I close my eyes, praying to God the entire way.

CHAPTER FIFTEEN

The next few hours are a blur. Mom shows up, her forehead covered in lines, her hands trembling. There are lots of doctors, and they do lots of tests. The head doctor comes out and speaks to us. His expression is serious, his body stiff. "Your mother had a massive stroke."

Mom's face drops at his words; sobs pour from her lips as she bends over at the waist. Her arms grip her stomach like she's been sucker-punched in the gut.

The doctor gives Mom a moment before continuing. "Her brain is extremely swollen, and the extent of damage is unknown. It's a waiting game, but she is sedated."

"What about her earlier TIAs?" Mom asks. "Was she on the wrong dosage? What happened?"

My body shakes and anger rips through me. *Something like this has happened before? Why hadn't they told me?*

The doctor taps his pencil on the clipboard. "Unfortunately, we don't know with strokes. When the swelling goes down, we can take her in for an MRI to see if the stroke affected the same side of the brain as the earlier TIAs. But this could be a separate event."

He walks away, and Mom's eyes drip tears. She turns to me and Dad. "I'm stepping outside to call her primary doctor. The cell reception is terrible in here."

Dad and I sit back down. "What's a TIA?" I ask.

His eyes are wet like mine. "It's like a ministroke. You temporarily go through a period of stroke-like symptoms. Gigi had suffered a few in recent months."

I'm shaking again. "Why didn't you tell me? How could you not let me know? Is that why you asked me to help her out?"

And then I remember her alarm and her medication. She said without her alarm, she forgets to take her meds. If I had known, I could have monitored her to make sure she didn't miss a dose. How could they not tell me?

"We were trying to protect you," Dad sighs.

I'm so tired of adults thinking they know what is best for me. What if I caused this? What if me upsetting her made things worse? What if this was all my fault?

The doctor comes out with an update, and we're told we have to wait a few more hours before we can see her. Mom passes through crying fits while Dad remains stoic. I'm there, but I'm not. I'm numb all over. I can't shake the image of Gigi on the kitchen floor, covered in blood, helpless and in pain. She must have been so scared when it happened.

She was alone, and it's my fault.

I can't just sit here any longer. I text Blake and ask him to pick me up. "I'm going to get some of Gigi's stuff," I tell Dad, gathering my bag. "Blake's coming to get me. I'll be back in an hour." He squeezes my hand, but I don't squeeze his back.

I step outside the hospital and finally catch my breath. The stale and sterile environment of the waiting room, with its blinking fluorescent lights, old magazines, and cold, metal chairs, left me feeling faint. I look up to the sky and the glaring sun beats down on my face. I feel uncomfortably hot, but it distracts me from the pit in the bottom of my stomach that Gigi might not be okay.

Blake's truck pulls up and I climb in. He leans over and kisses my cheek, and we drive in silence, only the low sound of the radio sits between us. With one hand on the wheel, he rests the other on my thigh, and I wrap my hands around his fingers, holding them tightly.

We walk into Gigi's house and it's eerily quiet. I avoid the kitchen, going straight to her bedroom. I grab a suitcase from the closet and fill it with some clothing, her slippers and robe, her fancy hairbrush, and every personal hygiene product I can find.

Blake stands in the living room, twirling his car keys on his finger. "All set?"

I nod and we exit her house, locking it up with the hidden key still in my pocket.

The days have started to run together. Gigi's been at the hospital six long days with little change. I'm there every day from sunup to sundown. We have a routine. On my portable speaker, I play The Beatles for a stretch every morning and every afternoon. I sing and talk about what the songs mean to me. I brush her hair with the silver antique brush and braid her hair.

I read to her from *The Great Gatsby* and *Twilight*, but mostly I talk to her. I tell her about Blake and what's going on at the dinner table and about how much I miss her. I tell her I need her to get better because we have to find Jack's hideout and find Ilse and her family. Holding her hand, I stroke my fingers over her palm and make promises to paint her nails once she's back home. The mean nurse says nail polish isn't allowed on patients, but I secretly paint one toe because I know Gigi would appreciate it.

The nurses tell me they think my energy is lifting her spirits, but all my efforts start to feel futile. Even though Mom steps into the hallway to speak with the doctors, the loud male voices carry through the thin walls. They say her brain is showing significant damage. But they also talk about a strong heart and good lungs and miracles.

We're on day seven when my prayers are answered. Gigi's eyes begin to flutter. I yell to the nurses, and they rush in. They speak to her in soft voices, telling her where she is and what happened. They take her vitals, shine a light in her eyes, and listen to her heart. They nod and smile and call for the doctor.

I sit down beside her, gently taking her hand within mine. Gigi looks so much older since arriving here. A week without food has taken a toll on her petite frame; she is withering before my eyes. Her voice croaks out when she asks for a sip of water. But she is speaking! And her eyes are open! And I'm smothering her in kisses as tears fall down my face.

Gigi has been in and out of consciousness for two days, but there have been no real conversations yet. She mostly wakes up, sips water, and falls back to sleep. I'm playing her favorite Beatles album, *Abbey Road*, when her eyes blink open, and her hand moves in mine.

"Gigi, I'm so happy to see you."

She tries to raise her head and I quickly move to adjust her neck and prop an extra pillow behind her. I return to sitting beside her, her hands inside mine.

"Hailey?"

"Yes?"

"All you need is love," she says, her breathing labored with each word.

I cough out a loud laugh. Her eyes twinkle. "All you need is love," she repeats.

I kiss her hand. "All you need is love and love is all you need."

A tear trickles down her cheek. "It's time."

My breath catches in my throat. She can't mean it. This isn't happening. "You mean it's time for you to get better, right? I need you here."

Gigi takes a gasp of air. "Hailey, you have made this old woman so happy. You brought love back into my life. I want to thank you for loving me."

Her eyes are heavy, struggling to stay open. Panic overtakes me. "Gigi, you *must* stop talking like this right now. You have so many years left, and we still have to celebrate our favorite books, the end of summer, and you must be here for my sixteenth birthday. Oh, and you're going to watch me run cross-country this fall, and you promised to show me the bluebonnets in springtime. And you have to help me get ready for prom. Who else would match my lipstick perfectly to my dress?"

"I'll be watching," she says. "I'll be with you always. This body is ready to release my soul."

I struggle to breathe. "You can't leave me. I need you, Gigi. You're the only one who gets me. You've given meaning to my life." I gently move my hand across her face, kissing her cheek as I say softly, "You're my best friend."

Her eyes blink open and shut. "All you need is love," she says in a gravelly voice.

I shake my head, my sobs blocking my voice.

She's panting and her eyes water. "Always remember to fill your life with love. All you need is love. Say it with me."

"All you need is love," we say together, her voice shallow and weak.

The machines beep loudly, drowning out my weeping. My face is next to hers, my lips on her cheek. "I'm hearing the trumpets. Never forget how much I love you."

Her hand stills. The twinkle is gone. My world goes black.

CHAPTER SIXTEEN

I'm in a daze, floating outside my body, unaware of time or space. I know I've been in bed for days, unable to eat, tears flowing from me like a fast-moving river.

There's a knock at my bedroom door and then Dad walks in. He gently touches my face and picks up the glass of water on my bedside table. "You need to drink something, and you need to get out of bed. Gigi wouldn't want you to waste away like this."

I don't move.

He sits down beside me and pushes my messy hair from my eyes. "The funeral is tomorrow. Mom wants to make sure you have something black to wear. So come on, let's get up. We need to do this for Gigi."

I think there were a lot of things we needed to do for Gigi, and now it's too late. Something else I know is that my colorful grandmother wouldn't want us wearing black at her funeral, but I remain silent. Sitting up, I wince in pain. My legs, back, and neck ache down to my bones. "Everything hurts."

He stands and takes my hand to help me out of bed. "You have a broken heart. The pain is the grief of losing someone you love."

We walk over to my closet, and I search for black. I haphazardly select a black top, a black skirt, and rummage through my shoes for black flats. "Can you get approval for this outfit, please?"

"How about you ask Mom?"

I roll my eyes. "No, thanks."

"Your mother is hurting as well. You can't ignore her forever."

I move to my bed, climbing back under the covers. "Are we finished?"

"Mom wants you to practice the Scripture from Corinthians II you're to read at the service."

"Has she reconsidered playing The Beatles at the funeral?"

Dad's forehead creases. "Mom doesn't think that's the right tone for the service."

"I told her I'm not reading some Bible verse if she won't play The Beatles."

"Not even for Gigi?" he says softly.

I want to scream at him that none of this is for Gigi! This is for Mom and tomorrow will be a big joke and no one will talk about the wonder and magic of Gigi, but they will jabber on about how she's in a better place and all that other crap that gets said when a loved one dies.

"No." I turn my head toward the wall and close my eyes.

As expected, the church service was somber and sad, a gathering of slumped shoulders and red eyes. The only part that came remotely near capturing Gigi was when a few of her favorite hymns were played, "Joyful, Joyful We Adore Thee" and "Lift High the Cross," but even the singer's voice failed to match the beauty of Gigi's perfect pitch.

My family of four shares a limousine ride to the grave-
side. Gigi only has three family members left in the entire
world. Ilse was one of five siblings, but she was the only survivor. Jack was one of three, but Billy didn't have kids and
neither did Nana. Jack only had Gigi and then Gigi only had
Mom. We're all that's left of her, all that's left of Jack, and
all that's left of Ilse's entire family. Two huge family trees
reduced to Mom, Kyle, and me.

It's a steamy morning and everyone is sweating as we
stand around waiting for the minister to arrive at the cemetery.
The funeral home has pitched tents around the gravesite, but
a crowd has formed, and several guests are left to melt in the
sun. I recognize a few neighbor faces and spot lots of old ladies.
They must be friends from her Sunday school class, bridge
group, or book club. Gigi had lots of acquaintances, but I don't
know if any of them were close friends. Gigi wasn't one to let
too many people in; she liked to be alone. But maybe it was
because a solitary life was all she knew?

Our family is seated in a row of chairs in front of her
casket, and strangers bend over and kiss me to offer their
heartfelt condolences. I hide my eyes and tears behind my
sunglasses, curiously scanning the crowd, guests oblivious to
my stares. And then I spot them.

Blake and DeMarcus.

They stand toward the back of the crowd, beside Blake's
mom. I bite down hard to fight my quivering lip. They're
dressed in suits, eyes covered by sunglasses with sweat
dripping down their faces. DeMarcus takes off his shades
and wipes his eyes.

The minister draws the crowd to attention, a few more
Bible verses shared. We say the Lord's Prayer, a soloist sings,
"Amazing Grace," and then it's over. No mention of The
Beatles or her ability to play music by ear or her gorgeous
singing voice or her love of books. No one spoke of Betty or

Gigi's exquisite taste in clothes and interior design or her love of caramel coffee ice cream or baseball or her beloved rose bushes or her beautiful, twinkling eyes. The stories of her amazing life were not shared and will soon be forgotten.

But not by me. I will always remember.

They tell us they will lower her into the ground after we leave. She will be going six feet under alone, and the idea of this shatters my heart.

Mom is hosting the reception at our house, and I'm required to attend. I ask to retire to my room, but I'm told that would be disrespectful to Gigi. I wander around our house, trying to avoid conversation with strangers. How many times can I answer what grade I'm in and where I go to school? I circle around the buffet spread—most of the requisite funeral food is disgusting. When are deviled eggs sitting out for hours ever a good idea?

My gaze travels across the room, curious how the rest of the family is faring. Mom and Dad are occupied by a barrage of well-wishers, and Kyle is stuffing his face from the dessert table.

When will the torture end?

I pass through the living room to the kitchen searching for the only thing that remotely appeals to me: a cold Dr Pepper.

Pulling the tab back, the can pops and the drink fizzes. I take a sip, but even Dr Pepper can't lift my spirits today.

Then I see them walking toward me.

DeMarcus smiles widely, but Blake is more cautious. DeMarcus grabs my hand and wraps his arms around me, my face crashing into his chiseled chest. He strokes my hair, and his heart beats loudly. He's a mumbling, incoherent mess. "Hailey, I am so sorry. Man, I just can't believe it. It's awful, so terrible, but remember God has a plan. He always does."

DeMarcus and his raw emotions are the first reactions that have felt pure to me. He understands how much I miss her.

He flicks away a tear, shaking his head with laughter. "Don't be telling anyone you saw me cry. But, man, that burial took me out! When the lady started in on 'Amazing Grace'? I was bawling like a baby!"

I laugh and he laughs, and, for a moment, I feel like myself again.

Blake leans in and takes me in his arms, and I squeeze him tightly. I've been terrible to him. He's texted me multiple times and I've given one-word responses. We separate and he drops his hands to his pockets. "The church service was nice."

"What did you think of the service?" I ask DeMarcus.

He bounces on the balls of his feet. "Um, well, ugh, it was good."

"You are both terrible liars," I say, with a half-grin. "It was horrible."

"It wasn't horrible, it was just very *traditional*," replies DeMarcus.

"It definitely didn't capture the essence of your grandmother," adds Blake.

I nibble on my lower lip as a tear slides down my cheek. DeMarcus wraps his arms around me again.

"Thank you both so much for coming today. Gigi would be thrilled, and it means a lot to me. But I insist that you leave now. This entire day has been excruciating, so please go since I'm forced to stay."

"You know where I'm going tonight?" says DeMarcus. "To have dinner with my grandmama. I was out there today thinking about her and feeling lucky to have her."

A soft cry falls out of me. "You are lucky."

Blake leans in and kisses me on the cheek. "I'm here if you need me," he whispers in my ear.

A few more painful hours pass before all the friends and neighbors leave. Mom is cleaning the kitchen, while Dad and Kyle watch a Texas Rangers baseball game. I sit by myself in the living room, staring into oblivion, feeling sick that Gigi is alone in the hard ground.

The doorbell rings, and both Mom and Dad yell for me to get it. It's probably the next round of kind neighbors dropping food off. For the last few days, a nonstop procession of casseroles and crockpots have quietly arrived at our doorstep.

I pull the door open, and Blake Alexander stands in front of me.

He's no longer dressed in his fancy suit but still looks nice in a polo and shorts. He gives a hesitant smile. "Hey, I know this might be a bad time, but can I steal you away for a few minutes?"

I suddenly realize how desperately I need to get away from this house. "I would actually love to get out of here. Let me go tell my parents."

I'm still only communicating with Mom on an as-needed basis, so I stick my head in the TV room. "I'm going out for a bit with Blake. Is that okay?"

Dad smiles warmly at me. "Yes, of course. Don't stay out too late."

Exiting the house with Blake by my side, I'm shocked to see the car sitting out front.

Betty.

I squint to make sure I'm not seeing things. I haven't eaten or slept in days and visions of Betty might be an illusion brought on by delirium. I walk over to the curb and run my hand over the side door. There is no doubt that this car is really here.

"How did you get Betty?"

"I asked your dad earlier today at the reception. He gave me the keys, and I drove her here."

"Why?"

He opens the door for me, and I slide in. He circles the car and drops into the driver's seat. He turns toward me and drapes his right arm over the back of the seat. "Because today was kind of crappy, and that shouldn't be your final goodbye to Gigi. I figured Betty needed to say goodbye as well."

My heart splits in two from his kindness. I thought the well was all dried up, but the tears return, dripping down my cheeks. He places the key in the ignition. "Which Beatles album for the drive over?"

This is the first time I've felt good about any decision in days. "Definitely *Abbey Road*."

The air is hot, but the breeze from the convertible flows through my hair, cooling my body and calming my soul. We drive in silence, listening to the music, and I'm flooded with memories of Gigi, singing and smiling as she played her favorite songs on our first trip in Betty.

We pull into the cemetery and stop on the curb next to Gigi's plot. The tents are still up, but the casket has been lowered into the ground, a large pile of dirt covering it. Fresh sod will be laid in the coming days.

Stepping out of Betty, I slowly close the car door and then walk over to the grave. My legs give, and I fall to my knees. "Gigi, I'm so sorry that I didn't keep my promise and play your song today."

"The day's not over. You're keeping that promise."

Blake stands behind me, his guitar slung over his shoulder. He sits down beside me in the grass, and I struggle to find my voice. "What are you doing?"

"You mean, what are we doing? I'm going to play this guitar and you're going to sing, 'In My Life.'"

I lunge at him, throwing my arms around his neck so forcefully we fall to the ground. He lets out a laugh. "Easy, now. You might bust the guitar and singing this song acapella is tough."

I pull back, a smile hanging on my lips, as tears stream from my eyes. "Do you really know how to play 'In My Life'?"

"When your grandmother passed, I taught myself." He pauses. "I wanted to do something special for you and for her."

His words break me wide open. I'm weeping again.

He swings the guitar from around his back, sliding the pick out from between the strings. "Ready?"

I nod and take a deep breath to gather my composure. I clear my throat and roll my shoulders out; I'm ready for my solo. He strums the first few chords and I close my eyes, images of Gigi filling my mind as the words pour out of me. As I sing the verses, I think of all the places that have their moments, with lovers and friends, some that are dead and some that are living, and how I've loved them all. And no one does compare to Gigi.

He's playing the bridge, and I raise my eyes toward the sky. I sing the chorus again and sing to Gigi. That in my life, I loved her more. I feel love for her in the deepest part of my soul, in the string of DNA that connects her to me. As he strums the last note, a wave of peacefulness passes through me. I touch his hand. "Thank you. That was everything."

He removes the guitar from his shoulder, his hand not releasing mine. "Oh, we're not finished."

"We're not? What's left to do?"

He reaches in his pocket and pulls out two rocks. "I'm being a little presumptuous here, but considering you and your grandmother are technically Jewish, I thought we should make sure and bless her soul with a Jewish custom."

I choke on a sob.

He reaches over and wipes my tears. "Am I good to continue?"

I squeeze his arm, unable to find my voice. It's been swallowed by my heart.

"In Judaism, we leave a small stone at the grave of a loved one as an act of remembrance and respect." He hands me a stone. "We place it on or around her headstone with our left hand."

"Why the left hand?"

"I actually don't know," he says. "I'll say a Jewish prayer and then we place the stone and say, 'I remember you.'"

He speaks in Hebrew and then he places the stone on the marker. "I remember you."

I recite the only prayer I know, the Lord's Prayer, and set the stone next to Blake's. "I remember you."

I step back and we stand in silence together.

"I'm going to give you a moment."

I squat down, and my hands run over the dirt, the soil covering my fingers. The dirt feels cool, even though the air is hot and heavy. Brown specks stick to my nails. "I painted them red for you. I tried to match my lipstick, but of course not as well as you would do."

I release a heavy sigh, the aching in my chest making it hard to breathe. "I'll never forget you, Gigi. I'll never forget our summer together and all the fun we shared. You opened my eyes to the world and to love and to the trinity of a perfect day: read a good book, listen to a great song, drive around in a cool car."

The tears spill from my eyes. "We had just said hello and now we're saying goodbye. We didn't get enough time together; I didn't learn all your stories. I know you taught me to let it be, but I can't on this one, Gigi. I promise you that I won't stop looking for Ilse and our family. I won't stop searching for answers."

I look up to the sky, and a bird soars by. Maybe that's Gigi?

CHAPTER SEVENTEEN

Another week has passed, though time has no meaning for me. Minutes fall into hours, which bleed into days, and I fail to snap out of it. I'm back to watching hours of TV and staring at my phone. Mom and Dad lifted my electronic time limit restrictions since they'd rather I troll the Internet than cry in bed.

The only comfort I've found from my grief is going for long, hard runs. I run until I puke, trying to get the pain out of my body, to stop my heart from hurting. But the pain is always there, like it's planted roots, weaving deep inside my bones.

School begins next week, and I'm hoping a fresh start will help me shake off the sadness. I'm trying to refocus my attention on Ilse and Jack, but every time I open my laptop and see their names, I think of Gigi, and it hurts too much. I think I just need more time.

A few taps on my door and it pushes open. Mom stands in the doorway, leaning on the frame. "Can we talk?"

I don't feel like talking, but what choice do I have?

I shrug and pause the show on my phone, the most hospitable I've been to her since Gigi passed.

She sits down at the footboard while I'm upright on my pillows.

"Are you going to give me the silent treatment forever?" she asks, raking her hand through her long blond hair.

I don't respond.

"I'm hurting, too. She was my mother."

I can't even buy this trash. "You weren't even nice to her. You would text me to come to the car. You couldn't be bothered to spend five minutes with her."

A tear drops down her cheek. "Gigi and I had a complicated relationship."

I won't let her off that easily. "You're an adult, and you didn't act like one. You treated her terribly, and she wanted to be back in our lives. You wouldn't let her."

Mom's body crumples like a wounded animal. "You have no idea what you're talking about." Her voice is small, and her eyelashes bubble with tears.

"Gigi was pure and good, and I know you didn't trust her, but I did. I know she made mistakes when you were young, but we have a great life, and you should have forgiven her. You kept her from me to hurt her. I missed out on having this amazing person in my life because you were petty and mean."

Mom stands, her body trembling. "You have it all wrong. I kept her from you to protect our family. She's not who you think she is; she's a liar and everything is a façade. You scratch the surface with Gigi and it's fool's gold."

I don't even understand what she's talking about, but I'm tired of her making decisions for me, and I'm going to hurt her like she hurt Gigi.

"You're the one that has it all wrong. She kept things from you to protect your heart. Did you even know that Nana isn't her real mother? Uncle Jack is her father and her mother died in Paris after the war."

"Oh, Hailey, this is what I'm talking about. This is textbook

Celeste. She makes up fantasies and then pretends they're real. Uncle Jack never married, and he wasn't her father."

"Yes, he did!" I say, my voice exploding out of me. "I have a book with an inscription to his wife, Ilse. They met after the war, and she was Jewish and we're Jewish and I was trying to help Gigi find her. When Jack was arrested, he was trying to get back stuff from Nazis in South America."

Mom raises her eyes to the ceiling and shakes her head. "Do you hear how ridiculous it all sounds? What proof did Gigi have for this story? There's none. This is a figment of her imagination. Gigi always wanted a glamourous, adventurous life and could never accept that she was the daughter of a schoolteacher and a mechanic, a working-class, ordinary girl. She exaggerated her life and told wild stories, but nothing is ever true with her. Jack was a petty thief who went to jail for fencing stolen goods."

Her words blindside me.

"I'm so sorry, sweetie," she adds softly. "I know you loved her, but everything she told you is a lie."

Mom's words rip through me. A sledgehammer straight to my battered heart. I'm trying to grieve, and she's destroying everything I'm grieving for.

"Did she tell you about going to India and riding elephants and meeting George Harrison? Because she came home after one stretch and told that tall tale. Did she tell you about all the men she dated with the private jets and chalets in Switzerland?"

She never told me those things. "But Jack served in the war. I have a picture of him in his uniform."

"He did, but she stretches and bends the truth. You only knew her a few weeks, and she showed you the side of her she wanted you to see."

Mom walks over to me. Leaning down, she kisses the top of my head. "I'm sorry, sweetie. For your sake, I wish it were all true."

She turns and leaves, and I'm left more confused than ever. Who was Gigi? The adoring, amazing grandmother I knew, or this stranger Mom described?

I bury myself in reruns and running. I no longer listen to The Beatles and have stuffed my research in the bottom of a drawer. I've tucked *The Great Gatsby* away in my closet, shutting the door on the past. I try to think about school and resuming my former life.

My phone buzzes.

Here.

I fly down the stairs and throw the front door open.

Livi is back from exile.

I jump into her arms, hugging her like a soldier returning from war. I'm crying and she starts crying. "Why are we crying?" she asks.

"I just missed you so much."

"I missed you, too." She squeezes me extra tight. "I'm so sorry about your grandmother. Mom told me when I got home."

A sob falls out of me. "It's been really hard."

I pull back, taking her all in. Her shiny black hair has dulled, and her olive skin has darkened from the sun. Cuts of muscle definition curve into her arms, and her posture is more upright. Is she taller? My gaze travels to her hands, and I gasp. Colorless, jagged nails bedded in puffy cuticles blind my eyes. I point at her fingers. "Um, we have an emergency situation going on right there."

Livi flashes her hands at my face. "Ugh! It was barbaric how I was forced to live, like total medieval! They wouldn't let me have a nail file! And look at my hair. Six weeks without a hair dryer, flat iron, or a deep conditioner. I had to use a two-in-one shampoo!"

I grab her arm and lead her inside. "We can work damage control on your fingers and then move to your toes. But I'm a little scared to see them."

"I'm not gonna lie, it ain't pretty."

Taking the stairs, side by side, I ask, "But was it okay?"

She halts on the steps, her hazel eyes bulging. "It was horrible. I was outside *all day*. You know I'm not outdoorsy. I was sweating all the time and I had to wear dirty clothes and sleep on the ground. But there were some cool parts. It was good to step away from my life and try to figure out what matters."

This is intriguing. Did Livi really see through the trees and find her inner peace? We continue up the stairs. "Like what did you figure out?"

"*Like I love having good hair.*"

We break into giggles. Same old Livi. "Having good hair is important."

"*Essential.*"

We enter my room, and I lock the door behind us. I pull out the box of nail colors from beneath my bed, and we plop down on the floor. "So what else did you figure out?"

Livi rifles through the colors. "I definitely was forced to reflect on my life and bad choices I've made. I own them; they're mine and I can't go blaming my parents or some jackass boy. I realized I give way too much credit to what others think of me. What matters is what I think of myself. I control the narrative of my life. But . . ." her voice trails off.

"But what?"

Her brows lift. I know that glint in her eye. "There were some super-hot counselors that made reflecting a lot easier. I totally hooked up. *Like a lot.*"

We both giggle uncontrollably.

Returning to the box, she selects a shade, handing me a bottle of OPI's Teal the Cows Come Home. "I have so much to tell you. Like *teal the cows come home.*"

I smile at her. Same, girl. Same.

Today is my sixteenth birthday and the last official day of summer. School begins tomorrow, so it's back to the grind of high school and junior year: race season, SATs, ACTs, and thinking about college. I'm trying to pretend this summer never happened, but the grief hangs over me like a black cloud. No sunlight is allowed in my life.

Mom and Dad said they have a surprise for me. I'm not expecting a sweet-sixteen party but have no clue what they could be planning. Dad told me I wouldn't be getting a car today but possibly for Christmas if I keep my grades up.

I walk downstairs. The living room is covered in balloons. I peek out the window and Mom has rented one of those god-awful yard signs that reads, "Happy Sweet Sixteen Hailey!" paired with a balloon arch with the number sixteen. Although I want to give it a big eyeroll, and I find it totally embarrassing, I say, "Wow. Thanks so much. I love it."

Dad sits down with me on the sofa. "What's the plan for today? Don't forget our dinner reservation is at six."

"I won't forget. Livi is coming over, and we're going to shop and get coffee."

Mom smiles at me. Neither one of us has breathed a word about Gigi since our big blowup. I did overhear her and Dad discussing Gigi's house. They plan to pack it up soon and put it on the market.

The doorbell rings. Livi is right on time, which is a miracle because the girl runs at least twenty minutes late to everything.

"Have fun, girls," Mom says. I wave and we leave.

We shop for a couple of hours, each picking up a few new things for school. I buy a pair of Vans and some nail polish, and she finds a cute skirt and top for the first day. We then head over to our favorite coffee shop and curl up in our regular booth.

I blow on my decaf caramel latte, and she sips her espresso. Livi loves the hard stuff; she'll soon be bouncing off the walls.

"You seem better today," she says. "I mean, it is your birthday, but you don't seem as sad."

I swirl my drink, licking a dollop of foam milk from the top. "I'm feeling a little better. Going back to school and getting back in a routine will hopefully help take my mind off the summer."

She leans in. "Have you heard from Blake today?"

My stomach drops, and I fiddle with my coffee cup. "No. It's just been weird between us since my grandmother died, and he's so busy with football."

I'm lying to Livi. I let her think he's the one ditching me, but the truth is that I haven't responded to his messages in a week. I can't go back to flirting with Blake like nothing happened. Gigi *died*. We can't be the way it was before. Everything feels different now.

She grabs my hand. "Well, his loss. We're going to have the best junior year! I still can't believe you had a little summer thing with Blake Alexander. Do you think he's back with Bree?"

I gulp down my coffee. "I have no idea what's going on with them, but it wouldn't surprise me if they're back together."

If Blake's back with Bree, it wouldn't surprise me, it would stun me. But if that happens, it's all my fault.

Returning to the house, I change into a simple black dress and my favorite Converse high-tops. Mom and Dad then take me to a fancy steakhouse for my sixteenth birth-day. We have a nice time, and Kyle manages to not be a total embarrassment at the table. When we're back home, Mom asks for a picture in front of the birthday sign. Taking a photo with Kyle and Dad is the last thing I want to do, but I humor her, and we end up making silly faces and laughing. For a moment, it almost feels as if things are back to normal.

We approach the door, and I abruptly stop. My heart jolts. "Look at the beautiful flowers," says Mom, her voice rising an octave.

She picks up a vase off the front porch and hands it to me. "I assume these are for you."

I don't say a word, heading up the stairs to my room with the gift in my arms. Setting the vase on my desk, I gawk at the flowers and think of Gigi. She would know every variety in this wild bunch. She would be able to tell me where each flower grows and whether they like sun or shade. And she would think me receiving flowers was the most marvelous thing to ever happen.

I open the card and read, "*Happy 16th birthday, Hailey. I hope you had a special day. I miss you. From, Blake.*" A tear slides down my cheek. I miss him, too. But everything is so jumbled together these last few weeks. I can't make up from down or left from right. Some days I don't even know how my heart keeps beating it hurts so much.

I should reach out to Blake and thank him for the flowers, but every time I think of him, I see Gigi. We're forever connected to her, and it's too painful to try to pick up from where it ended, no matter how kind and wonderful he is. I can't shake the memories of that horrible day when I found her lying in the kitchen, and I feel responsible. My flirting with Blake caused the fight with my mom, which led to my harsh words to Gigi. I know I hurt her; I know I caused her stress and then she had a stroke.

A knock on my door startles me, and I quickly wipe my eyes and suck in the tears. Dad peeks his head around the door. "Can I come in?"

"Sure."

"Beautiful flowers. Who are they from?"

"A friend."

"A friend on the football team?"

I say nothing. He knows a response isn't necessary.

I sit at my desk and take off my shoes. He relaxes on my bed across from me. "I have something for you."

He hands me an envelope, and my body freezes.

Hailey

It's her handwriting.

Dad reaches over and pats my leg. "I found it when I was over at her house yesterday. It was in a bathroom drawer with her nail polish, which seems like an odd place to keep a letter."

Not strange at all if you know me and Gigi. She knew I would go looking for nail polish and find the card. I bet she had a plan to surprise me.

Dad stands and kisses me on the cheek. "Happy birthday, Peanut. I'm so proud of you. I'm going to give you some privacy now."

He leaves and my hands tremble; I'm mesmerized by Gigi's penmanship. She suddenly feels alive again. I remember what she told me, how a person's handwriting is unique like their DNA. Seeing her penmanship, her mark on the world, is a reminder that she was here and was real.

I run my finger under the envelope flap and gently pull out the folded-over sheets.

My Dearest Hailey,

Happy Sweet Sixteen, my dear angel. I wanted to write you a letter and express to you all the joy and love I have for my beloved granddaughter. You are a light, a force for good in this crazy world, and a beauty to behold. You have warmed my old soul and brought a skip to my step. You are a talented and thoughtful young woman who I pray will have a happy and fulfilling life.

Our time together this summer has been one of the true blessings of my life. I feel we know each other, that we are connected by that invisible string that runs between us, that runs in our blood. Thank you for listening to my story and wanting to help me find my parents and my peace.

Now the reasons and purpose for this letter are threefold:

First, I wanted to make sure and wish you a Happy Birthday. I hope this rotation around the sun is your best year yet!

Second, I wanted to set forth my birthday gift to you. I want you to have Betty. She's a lot to handle, but I have complete faith in you. Take good care of her and always remember that driving around with the top down while listening to The Beatles can solve most of life's problems!

Third, and most importantly, I wrote you this letter to ensure you have the experience of receiving a love letter once in your life. I know I'm not your sweetheart, but you are one of the great loves of my life. I love you with all my heart. Endlessly. I hope you can feel my heart and soul in this letter and in my words to you.

Always and forever,
Gigi

* * I've sprayed a little Chanel No.5 on here for you!
* * * A drawing for you as well!

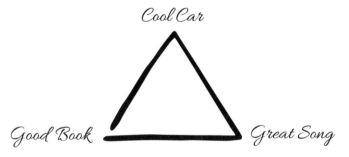

Cool Car

Good Book   Great Song

The Trinity of a Perfect Day!

I raise the letter to my nose and take in a whiff. It's as if Gigi is standing beside me. I hold the letter to my chest, hugging it tightly as my grief crashes over me like a hundred-foot wave, barreling me to the bottom of the sea.

CHAPTER EIGHTEEN

Today's the first day of junior year, and Livi is picking me up. Livi's always excited for the first day of school while I'm more reserved, but I'm ready for a change this year.

I'm still waiting for a verdict from Mom and Dad on whether I get Betty. Mom claims she's hesitant because of her size and the maintenance involved with a classic car, but I think she doesn't want me to have a connection to Gigi.

Standing on my front porch, I glance at my watch. Of course, Livi is late because Livi always runs late. She pulls up, and I jump into her car. I give her a quick hug and say, "Let's go. We're cutting it close."

She squints one eye shut. "Don't kill me, but I still have to make a Starbucks run. But I placed the order on my app, so you just have to dash in and grab it."

"Livi! We're gonna be late, and it's the first day!"

"Being fashionably late is totally acceptable."

"At social events, not for school where they take attendance, and you get in trouble for missing class!"

"It'll be fine. Hales, you worry too much. Sometimes you gotta just let it ride."

She gave me the same speech before sending Caleb those photos.

I race to AP English but still don't beat the tardy bell. The teacher, Ms. Mason, gives me a disapproving look, and I slide into the only open seat left on the front row. I scan the classroom, searching for familiar faces and spot the usual AP class crew: a few band kids, the artsy/Goth crowd, the orchestra nerds, some dance team girls, and the token jock, Blake Alexander.

He's sitting right behind me.

He smiles and I smile, and I quickly turn back around.

"Welcome to junior year AP English," announces Ms. Mason. "We have a lot to accomplish this year, but my number one priority is getting your writing in shape so every single student in this classroom can rock their college essays next year. I want us to start this first day with a writing exercise to get a sense of each student's skills.

"Take out your spiral notebook. This will be your writing prompt journal for the year. I'm going to go light on you since it's the first day. Today's topic is simple: my summer. I'm giving you twenty minutes to write whatever pops into your head."

I pull out my journal and tap my pen on my desk. Oh, the irony. Having to write about my summer with Blake Alexander sitting behind me. I should write about Gigi, but I can't. I can't write down that my grandmother died. Writing my feelings would probably be helpful, but it's too personal and too raw. Instead, I dance around Gigi; I draft broad strokes about The Beatles and a car and meeting a hot guy.

Ms. Mason bangs a ruler on her desk. "Everyone, pens down, please."

She points her ruler at students, pairing them up. Irony strikes again. I get partnered with Blake.

"Now read over your classmate's work and edit and correct any errors you see."

Blake and I exchange notebooks.

With red pen in hand, I carefully review his paragraphs for mistakes. His first page is entirely dedicated to football and their summer training schedule. His grammar is strong; I find only a few errors. Who knew that someone could write so much about protein shakes and dead lifts?

The topic changes slightly, and the next few sentences throw me. "I kicked up my training by running with a girl who is an incredible athlete. She pushed me hard, and we became good friends, and I thought maybe there was something more between us. But then her grandmother died, and she shut down and shut me out. But I don't blame her; I just miss her."

I make a few notes about run-on sentences and commas versus semicolons, but what I want to write is, "She misses you, too."

He passes my journal to me. "Who's the hot guy with the guitar?"

I feel my cheeks flush. "Who's the incredible athlete?"

He sighs. "Just someone I used to know."

His words send a shooting stab to my heart, and I quickly turn back around.

Another week of school has gone by and still no decision on Betty. However, I did pass my driver's test. I'm a fully licensed driver with a cool car and an overprotective mother who won't let me drive it. The best argument I have going for me to get Betty is that Livi is perpetually late, and I haven't made it on time to school yet, but Mom doesn't appear concerned with Livi's tardiness.

The good news about being late is I miss awkward small talk with Blake, since I roll in after the bell most days and bolt out the door at dismissal. English is the only class we have together this year. Although I see him a few times throughout the day in the hallway and exchange smiles, we haven't had any conversations.

I'm standing at my locker before lunch when I hear his voice. "Hey."

I turn my head to his beautiful smile. "Hi."

His backpack is casually slung over his right shoulder, his hair flopping down over his forehead. He lifts his hand and swipes it from his eyes. "I wanted to tell you congrats. I saw your time for the first race. You were on fire."

His words warm my entire body. Why does he have to be so great? Why does he take the time to tell me he's paying attention? Can't he see I'm trying to avoid him? "Yeah, well, remember how I told you I can't feel pain when racing? I'm so numb these days that I'm not feeling *anything*, so I'm Superman out there, faster than a speeding bullet." I give a fake laugh at my weak joke.

But he's not laughing. His smile drops. "So that explains it."

"What do you mean?"

"The not feeling anything. That's the reason you've been ignoring me."

His words knock me off guard. I wish it were that simple.

With students whizzing by us and lockers slamming loudly, this isn't the time for a confessional, so I quickly change the subject. "Congrats on the two touchdowns Friday night. That was a great win for the team."

"You were there?"

"Of course, it's Friday night lights, baby. *Texas forever.*"

"Clear eyes, full hearts, can't lose," he says.

We share a smile.

"You ran a lot of good routes during the game. Cody missed you a few times when you were wide open, but you looked fast out there."

"I had a good training partner."

Bree walks up, and the queen bee is buzzing. "Hey, Blake, you're needed for this pep rally thing with the football captains. *Like now.*"

She casts her gaze my way. "Hi, Hailey." Her friendly tone doesn't match her eyes.

"Hi, Bree."

"Sorry, but we've got to go." She drags him by the arm, leading him away.

I watch them leave, hoping he might look back, but he doesn't.

DeMarcus walks up and gives me a hug. "Hey, girl. What's up?"

"The sky?"

"You know that's not what I meant. What's up with you and my boy?"

"Nothing."

"*Exactly.* He brought you flowers for your birthday and no response? That's stone cold."

I do feel like a jerk. My thank-you text was pathetic.

He wraps his arm around my shoulder. "Don't let her win. He likes you, not her. But he won't wait around forever, and Bree wants him back." He winks, giving me his million-dollar smile.

"Thanks for looking out for me," I say.

"I told your grandmother I got your back."

His words tug at my chest. I think how Gigi is still sort of with me.

It's Saturday night, and I ran another great race that morning. I finished first in the girls' division. Dad is over the moon. The problem is now all he wants to talk about is running. From my diet to my sleep schedule to my mental fortitude, the man thinks he's building an Olympian when the truth is I'm just a girl running away from her problems.

Livi has convinced me to go to a party tonight. It's a field party about an hour away at a guy's hunting lease. I don't even know if it's safe, but Livi says it's fine and we'll be cleared out of there before the guys with guns show up.

We have the GPS going. Hearing the British lady's voice makes me think of Betty, Gigi, and the roadmap. But I tell myself to stop going there, stop wading into troubled waters. I try my hardest to push Gigi and the summer from my thoughts.

The car bumps up and down a dirt road. As the darkness deepens, I tap my feet on the floorboard and chew on my lower lip. This was really a bad idea. What if we get lost? This desolate road is exactly the type of place a serial killer would live. But then the Brit tells us we've arrived, and we spot two trucks blocking the gate.

Livi is on the list, so we pay our entry fee and park with the hundred other cars in the open field.

Kids are drinking from kegs and bottles and Solo cups, drinking anything they can get their hands on. We roam around, and I listen to conversations more than I participate. I look across the fields, searching for familiar faces, which is nearly impossible in the darkness. As we inch toward the bonfire, the large flames light the night.

I then see them and my heart drops. Bree is hanging on Blake, and he's smiling and laughing. They're definitely back together.

I look away, too embarrassed I'll get caught staring at them. DeMarcus sees me. "Hales! What's up, girl?" He jogs over and hugs me. I still can't believe I'm buddies with DeMarcus Thomas.

"Another great game. Two hundred yards rushing and three TDs! You might break a couple school records this year."

His brown eyes dance from the compliments. "Thanks, but my priority is winning a state championship and signing with a D1 school. You know I plan to take over the world."

I laugh and have no doubt DeMarcus will rule the universe.

His face changes, his eyes and nose pinching together. "But did you see what's happening over there? She has her claws in him. I told you to get on it!"

I saw and I know, but I don't have any fight in me. I'm gutted by it, and I like Blake a lot, but he raced back to her fast. But we couldn't work, anyway. It's all tied to Gigi and our connection is mired in lies and sadness. "Yeah. It must be what he wants."

His eyes turn to slits. I know he doesn't buy it. Before he can argue with me, he's dragged away by a group of superfans.

I join Livi at the bonfire. She tilts her head in Blake's direction. "Did you see that? So typical that he goes back to her. You're so much better than Bree, other than chest size. But the rest of her? Bleached hair, spray tan, lash extensions, and acrylic nails? She's plastic. Everything is real with you."

The girl does go through a lot of work to look good.

Livi leans into my ear. "Do you want me to go pretend to accidentally bump into her and spill my drink down her dress? Because I would totally risk the wrath of Bree for you."

I wrap my arm around her. Livi's a true friend. "Thanks, but no need to make a scene. Let's talk about you and Ethan."

Livi's face lights up as we chat about the guy she likes. I'm playing lookout as he flirts with another girl. But then he walks our way and sits down next to Livi. They're lost in conversation while I'm the odd man out. I tap her arm. "I'm gonna grab a drink."

Roaming the open field, I search for a bottled water but discover it's the only beverage not at this party. Eventually, I stumble over a cooler of sodas and energy drinks. I'm guessing it's the mixer's station and I happily grab a Dr Pepper. I pull my phone out of my pocket and scroll Instagram while sipping my soda.

"You made it to another party. I thought after the Fourth, you'd never come back."

I look up and Blake's amber eyes are still visible in the dark, the gold around the rims shining at me. "Yeah, well, a new year, a new me."

I feel like he's studying me. It's unnerving. I clear my throat. "You had another great game last night. Congrats."

He smiles. "Thanks."

As I gaze at him, unsure what to say, Bree walks up and slides her hand over his shoulder. "Hi, Hailey. Oh my God, is this, like, your first party?"

I give a closed-mouth grin, a smirk on the edges.

"What are y'all talking about?" she asks.

"We were just discussing the game. What do you think was Blake's best play?"

Her hand massages his neck, her body rubbing against him. She's a dog marking her territory. I guess that's one tactic to hold his interest. "Oh, the touchdown, *of course.*"

I slowly sip my Dr Pepper. "I thought it was when he did the cutback and got loose from the cornerback that was completely holding his jersey the *entire game.* Those refs were terrible! That he could make that incredible reverse route and gain the much-needed first down on third and fifteen and get us in the red zone while having someone hold him was unreal. That might have been the play of the night."

Blake looks away, and I know he's trying not to smile.

"Yeah, that was great," replies Bree. "It's hard for me to see all the plays because when you're cheering on the sideline, you have to keep the fans engaged."

Oh, the trials and tribulations of a cheerleader. "Really? I thought you watch the game and then rally the crowd at key moments?"

"It's a delicate balance."

I take a swig of my Dr Pepper. "Yeah, cheering requires skill and grace. I mean, not just anyone can yell, 'Go, Team, Go' at the right moment."

She's so dense that she can't tell if I'm teasing or being serious. But then Blake lets a laugh slip, and she catches on. I now have daggers shooting at me with such intensity I think I'm watching my own murder.

"Great to see you both," I say. "I need to check on Livi."

Throwing my shoulders back, I walk away with a little swagger. A girl like her used to intimidate me, but this whole "not feeling anything" is empowering. I couldn't care less about Bree Billings.

CHAPTER NINETEEN

Fall Sundays are lazy around our house. Dad watches football all day and Mom works on home projects. I have a ton of homework but I'm in heavy procrastination mode, pushing my work off because I have a few hours to burn before it's crunch time.

Sitting on my bed, I open my side table drawer and pick up my journal. Tucked in the back cover is my birthday letter from Gigi and the Polaroid photo of her from our trip to Malone. Raising the letter to my nose, faint traces of her perfume linger. I study the photo, my fingers running over the edges as her beautiful green eyes draw me in. What was behind those eyes?

I reread her letter to me, tears bubbling on my lashes. The words she wrote about finding her parents and searching for peace tug at my heart, a sliver of hope resurfaces that maybe part of her story is true. Maybe she did lie about a lot of stuff, but not Jack and Ilse?

I power up my laptop and click on my family tree. Flashbacks of our trip to Malone and details of Gigi's stories flood my mind. Grabbing the stacks of ancestry.com research out of my desk drawer, I then flip through the pages and hope for some nugget I overlooked to jump out at me. I review all the papers but it's another dead end.

I next search the Holocaust Survivors and Victims database. There are hundreds of Ilses listed, but I don't know any details other than her name and the camp. What am I missing? What can I do to find them?

I pack up my papers and stuff them in my bag. I can't just try to forget Gigi or our family history. I need answers, which means I must return to the one place I've resisted visiting these last few weeks.

Gigi's house.

I'll go back to dig into Gigi's past and search for clues. I hope Mom and Dad haven't packed everything up. I hope I'm not too late.

I still have her house key. I lie to Mom and Dad and tell them I'm hanging at Livi's house, but instead I drive the Volvo over to Oxford Street.

Only a few weeks have passed but stepping inside her home makes it feel like yesterday, like nothing has changed, even though my entire world is different. I walk into her living room and lower my body into my spot, across from Gigi's club chair. My heart pounds so loudly in my chest I can feel it in my brain. Faint traces of her hairspray, her Chanel No. 5, and her favorite coffee hang in the air. I shut my eyes and picture her sitting across from me as she reads a book, plays the piano, types in her office. But I open my eyes and I'm all alone.

I rise, pushing off the pain, and focus on the purpose of my visit. Starting in her office, I pull open desk drawers and dig through her file cabinet. Sifting through old bills, receipts, and medical records, I search for clues but find nothing useful.

In her bedroom, I find the first evidence that Gigi no longer lives here. Mom has stripped the sheets from the four-poster bed. I choke up when I catch a glimpse of her silver hand mirror, bottle of Chanel No. 5, and clanging bangles still laid out on the vanity. But I can't waste time wallowing; I have work to do.

I pull out books from her bedside table drawers and uncover old letters in boxes on a closet shelf. A few letters are from someone named Tom, mostly dated in the 1960s. Could this be my grandfather? The man writes about her eyes and how much he loves her. But none of the letters mention Jack or Ilse.

I pilfer through her bathroom cabinets but come up empty-handed again. My frustration builds. I close my eyes, searching my memories for tidbits of information she shared with me, a detail I might have overlooked, something said in passing that might unlock these unsolved mysteries.

Nothing comes to me.

I step outside and check on Betty in the one-car garage. Her top is down, and she's gathering dust, so I crank the top up and place the tarp over her. It feels like I'm burying her, but I tap her side and say, "I'll be back for you."

I pack up a few things I will be the best caretaker of— sentimental items like her bangles, her antique hand mirror, and her Jackie O sunglasses. I also make sure and take the two mementos of Jack: the framed photo and his Medal of Honor.

I make one more loop through the house before locking it up in defeat. Reality sets in that I might not ever find answers. I might not ever know whether Gigi was telling the truth about our family.

As I load the small bag of keepsakes in my car, a pickup truck passes by.

Blake.

I wave and he waves back.

Blake reverses his truck and pulls in front of the Volvo. He steps out and walks toward me. With his baseball cap pulled down low, his eyes are barely visible.

"Hey."

I lean against Dad's car. "Hi."

"What's going on?"

I shrug. "Just tying up some loose ends."

He leans next to me. "I could use that as well."

"I'm sorry?"

He crosses his arms, causing his biceps to bulge out. "Some loose ends tied up. You've dodged me for weeks. Can you tell me why? Because I've been trying to understand why you shut me out, yet you come to my games and give a better play-by-play analysis than even Joe Buck could."

"I prefer to be Erin Andrews. She's way hotter."

He smiles, nudging my shoulder. "I miss you. I miss us hanging out." He takes his hat off and runs his hand through his thick locks. He throws a gorgeous, cocky grin at me. "How do you not miss me?"

I miss him so much that every cell in my body hurts. Just like it hurts from losing Gigi. I lost two loves at once, and one hurt bleeds into another hurt. It's like my heart is split open and gushing blood and I can't stop the hemorrhaging.

But why is he saying this to me? He has a girlfriend. "I heard you and Bree are back together."

"You heard wrong."

What does that mean? "You two looked awfully cozy at the party."

"We have history; and she's a big flirt." He adds, "You never answered my question."

My stomach twists. I have to come clean and tell him the horrible truth, so he'll understand why I avoid him. I haven't been ready for him to see the real me and to reject me.

"You're right. You deserve an explanation."

I stare at his beautiful eyes and his full lips, memorizing every detail of his face since it will be our last conversation. I take a deep breath, bracing for the official end of whatever was between us. "I'm a fake and a phony. Gigi made up all the stuff I shared with you. I told you I was Jewish, and my family was in the Holocaust and Nazi hunters and with Bonnie and Clyde and it was all a big lie. Gigi played me for a fool, and I sucked you in and everything we shared was based on untruths and an old lady's need to feel special."

His body shifts, his eyes studying me. I continue, "It's horrible and awful because there are real people who suffered unthinkable tragedies and their lives matter, and she belittled them with her tales and with her lies. And I was complicit in spreading the lies. I wanted so badly to be a part of a big adventure, an epic story, and played right into it. I'm humiliated and embarrassed about what you must think of Gigi and of me."

I fiddle with my shirt. "There's another reason I've avoided you. The one that slices me open. Even if you felt like you could get past the lies, the fact is that every time I look at you, I see her. And it hurts too much. You and I are forever linked to Gigi. Every memory I made with you is also a memory of Gigi."

The tears build, but I fight to keep them in. "Mom read our messages and then told me things about Gigi I didn't know. I yelled at Gigi and didn't see her for two weeks, causing her pain and stress. And then she had a stroke. It's my fault, and it's because I was messaging and flirting with you."

And then I tell him what's deep in my soul. "I'm sad every day. I'm no good to be around. I'm not the same person I was before Gigi died and what if you don't like the new me? I can't have my heart broken again. It's already in pieces from losing Gigi."

A tear falls down my face. I brush it away, sucking in my breath and my heart.

He doesn't say a word, but the way his eyes narrow tell me everything I need to know.

I climb in my car, and he walks toward his truck.

Arriving home, I creep up the stairs, hoping to avoid my family. I'm emotionally exhausted and want to crawl into bed, into a cocoon and hideaway until I metamorphose into an adult like a caterpillar turns into a butterfly. Yeah, right. Nothing beautiful is coming out of me.

I change into pajamas and climb into bed with my homework. I try to focus on my pre-calc assignment, but the numbers jumble together in the mush that is my brain. I can't shake the image of Blake's amber eyes and how they stared at me, the disappointment and disgust visible on his face.

A few knocks at my door and Mom and Dad walk in together. This is not a good sign, but typical of the day I'm having. They stand a few feet away from me, a united front.

"We need to talk to you," Mom says.

I look to Dad and his face is a blank slate. He's on her side on this one. I'm on my own.

"Your father and I have made a decision that we feel is in your best interest and wanted to tell you together. We're selling Gigi's convertible and will use the money to buy you a safer car."

I want to scream at her, *The car is named Betty!* Mom and her callous tone. I try to process another loss in my life. "But she left the car to me."

Mom rubs her hands together. "No, her will left all her assets to me."

Mom is such a jerk. I'm enraged but try to remain calm. "Dad, you saw my birthday letter. She wrote that right before she passed, and she wanted me to have Betty. She was supposed to be alive when I turned sixteen, and she was going to surprise me."

Dad, the attorney, should be on my side on this one. I know I'm right legally. "Hales, let's not fight about this."

I push myself out of bed and stand in front of them. "Okay, tell me why I can't have her? What's the problem with Betty?"

"The car is old and not safe for a teenager, *a new driver*, to have on the road," Mom says, her voice amplifying with each word. "And the car attracts trouble. Dad told me about the donuts and then the road trip. I'm sorry, but we all need to move on from that car. It's for the best."

My hands tighten into fists, and I dig my nails into my palms. Adults and their belief that they know what's best for me. This decision about Betty is bull, but I simply climb back into my bed and pick up my math book. "Fine."

Dad walks over and kisses the top of my head, but Mom knows to keep her distance. They leave my room and I try to focus on my homework, tears dripping onto my paper.

A few hours have passed and I'm still on the same math page. Screw school and screw my mom. She cares about my grades more than I do, so let's see what happens if I start failing all my classes.

The problem is I don't want to fail my classes. I like school and want to go to a good college and get out of this town. I want to move far, far away and start a new life, a great life, and not have to think about Mom, Betty, or Gigi again.

I squint, trying to focus so I can finish my homework, but images of Betty run on a loop in my head. She'll be gone soon. My link to Gigi and our summer together erased. All that will remain of our time together is the copy of *The Great Gatsby* she gave me.

A panic overtakes me. Where did I leave the book? I hop out of bed and dash over to my closet. Reaching to the top shelf, I frantically search the sweaters and winter clothes until I feel the binding beneath my fingers.

I return to my bed and sit with the novel in my lap. I think about Jay Gatsby and am struck by the similarities to Gigi. Mysterious and charming, a person who desired more out of life than given to her, yet she blurs the truth, her past unclear. My finger traces the inscription Jack wrote to Ilse. Did Gigi really make up such an elaborate story and go to such lengths to carry out a lie? She would have to purchase a first edition copy of the book and write a fake inscription. Was Gigi that much of a con artist?

My phone flashes. I have a message from Livi.

I'm so sorry! His loss.

I click on the link she sent me, and my heart drops. It's Bree's Instagram post with a picture of Blake kissing her.

Can't wait to dance with him again this year! #pvhshomecoming #gomustangs

Can life get any worse?

I throw my phone hard onto my bed. Then I do the unthinkable: I chuck Gigi's book across my room, and it slams into the wall. The binding pops, and the pages pull apart.

Betty is gone, Blake is back with Bree, and the book is in pieces. It's like last summer never happened. I guess I got my closure.

CHAPTER TWENTY

As I take a few deep breaths, I taste the salt of my tears. I pick up my phone and text Livi back.

Not surprised.

I shouldn't be surprised after our exchange this morning. He moved on fast, but I'm learning life can change quickly. One minute, life is great, and the next the world is a minefield, bombs exploding all around you.

I stare at the collapsed book on the floor and pangs of guilt course through me. Ruining a first edition book is just wrong, even if I have a good reason. The busted binding has pulled the cover away from the pages, but they hang on by a few threads on each end.

As I bend down to inspect the damage, a speck of white catches my eye. It's inside the binding where the glue was holding the pages in place. My hands shake as I pick up the book. I raise the spine to eye level, and I see it. There's a note hidden inside!

I try to gingerly pull on the paper, but I can't get it loose without tearing it. *Think, Hailey, think!* I race to my bathroom and grab my eyebrow tweezers. Sliding them into the binding, I pinch at the note. After solidifying my grasp, I slowly inch the paper out with each gentle tug. Success! I scurry to my desk and flip on my table lamp.

I unfold the edges and flatten the note. The paper is pristine, the ink smudged only slightly. Oh, sweet Jesus! It's a map!

My heart gallops in my chest, a Kentucky Derby race underway as I study the details. Written in cursive penmanship, I read:

Celeste,

I hope it is you that finds this note. You are to be the caretaker of my efforts to help your mother and the others. I'm sorry I wasn't a better father. I'm sorry you never knew your mother. Make things right for both of us.

—Jack

The map sets out a few roads, with markers for Malone and Irene and Hubbard, places I've visited with Gigi and a town called Penelope. At the bottom of the page sits a large tree with a thick trunk and spiraling limbs. It's not hand-drawn, it looks more like a stamp or watermark. Written across the top of the tree reads, "Tree of Life."

Celeste,
I hope it is you that finds this note. You are to be the caretaker of my efforts to help your mother and the others. I'm sorry I wasn't a better father. I'm sorry you never knew your mother. Make things right for both of us.
– Jack

Irene ⊙

Malone ⊙

X- - - - -

Penelope ⊙

Hubbard ⊙

TREE OF LIFE

Robert Storey
RA 2-6844

In the right bottom corner is a name and series of letters and numbers. Robert Storey RI 2-6844. What does it mean? I turn on my laptop and Google his name.

Multiple pages of hits come up. I click the first link.

Robert Storey served as Dean and Professor of Law at Southern Methodist University in Dallas, Texas, from 1947 to 1959. His work as executive trial counsel at Nuremberg focused on crimes committed by the Nazi secret police (the Gestapo) and the Third Reich's looting of priceless European art. He was awarded the US Medal of Freedom and the French Legion of Honor for his work.

My head swirls and my legs shake.

Jack was telling Gigi to ask this man for help. He worked on the Nuremberg Trials and lived in Dallas.

My mind fires through all the players and moving pieces, but it all finally makes sense. Jack was insistent Nana give the book to Gigi, but we never understood its importance. He told Gigi the book binds their family together. Jack hid the map inside the book's binding that told Ilse's story. The book was the link to the treasure. Gigi was telling me the truth. I knew it! I knew it in my heart.

A million things run through my head, but only one thing truly matters to me: finding Jack's hideout.

My hands tremble as I type on my computer. I pull up Malone on Google maps and study the surrounding area.

I pound my desk and let out a silent scream. The maps line up!

I think I've found the land that holds Jack's hideout.

CHAPTER TWENTY-ONE

I t's Friday afternoon, and I've spent the week formulating my plan. I'll take Betty on one final trip to uncover the past.

All week, I worked out logistics in my head during class and then raced home to scribble notes on my laptop. I've packed my supplies and printed out every map of Malone I could find on the Internet.

I've filled a bag with snacks, a twelve-pack of Dr Pepper, a sleeping bag and pillow, and put every cent to my name in my wallet, which is exactly $585.25. I'm regretting all those years of blowing birthday and Christmas cash on clothes. Although I have a debit card from Mom for emergencies, I'm not bringing it, because one thing I've learned from countless episodes of *CSI* is never leave a paper trail.

I've put a lot of thought into how to dodge Mom, since she tracks my every move. Livi is on board to help me, but I haven't told her specifics. My plan is to leave tomorrow morning, but I have to keep some normalcy to my schedule. I'll do my Saturday run with Dad and then shower and "head over to Livi's."

Sitting in my living room, I use the Find My Friend app on my phone and track Livi's car. She's en route to pick me up for the homecoming football game. I really don't want to go because I'm so wound up about heading to Malone tomorrow, but I can't raise any suspicions.

Mom walks in. "Are you excited for this weekend?" she asks.

If she only knew how excited I am, but I play it cool. "I guess. Homecoming is kind of awful with all the silly traditions, but whatever."

I might have added that comment to dig at her. Mom probably lived for homecoming. She was the queen.

"Well, it should be a fun football game with a packed crowd."

I give no response and return to staring at my phone.

She clears her throat. "Can we talk for a minute?"

I raise my eyes, my fingers still typing a message to Livi. "Sure."

She sits down next to me on the sofa. "I wanted you to know we have a buyer for Gigi's convertible. He's stopping by Sunday afternoon to check the car out in person."

Shoot. Sunday afternoon. That really shortens my weekend deadline.

"I was hoping you might reconsider selling Betty," I say, in a semi-friendly tone.

Her mouth remains tight. "I think it's for the best."

"Well, I don't, and I think this decision makes things worse between us."

"Sweetie, don't you see Gigi and this car are coming between us?"

"Then don't let them. You're the one choosing sides. You need to understand that Gigi was important to me, and I love Betty. Gigi died, and I lost someone I loved very much, and now you're taking Betty from me. Don't make me lose both."

Mom is quiet. Maybe she will reconsider? "Oh, Hailey. You have that all wrong. I'm not trying to hurt you."

"Have you considered what the car means to me rather than what it means to you? Maybe if you let me keep Betty and see how happy it makes me, it will turn a bad memory into a good one."

"Maybe," she says, her voice laced with doubt.

My phone buzzes. "Livi's here."

Mom touches my arm. "I don't want tension between us. I love you."

I say nothing and walk out the door.

Dad and I head out for our morning run at eight. I hope my desire for an early start doesn't raise any suspicions. We start jogging and Dad asks, "How far today?"

"I didn't sleep well last night, so can we make it a shorter run? Maybe just three or four?"

I, in fact, did not sleep well, but I've run many times on bad sleep. I just need to get out of town.

"That's fine," he says. "Was the game fun last night?"

He's digging for Mom. I used to find it slightly endearing, but now I find it annoying. Dad showed his true colors with the Betty blowup. "Yeah, it was a good game."

"Are you excited for the dance?"

Play it cool, Hales. "I guess. Livi loves this stuff and always makes dances fun, even if they're kind of cheesy."

He lifts his chin like he gets it.

"I wanted to tell you something," Dad says. "I'm working on Mom about Betty. This is a tough thing for her, but I'm trying to persuade her to reconsider. The car is special, and Gigi wanted you to have it."

I glance over at him. "Seriously?"

He smiles at me. I throw my arms around him, halting our running as we hug in the middle of the street.

He's my person. How could I have ever doubted him?

I shower quickly and text Livi to come pick me up. Waiting downstairs, I have my homecoming dress slung over my arm and pretend my overnight bag is for Livi's house.

My phone buzzes. It's a DM. I swipe over to my Insta app.

Hey. Can we talk? I need to tell you something.

Blake.

What could he need to tell me? He's back with Bree, they're going to the homecoming dance together, and I've got too much to worry about to add him to the mix.

So I ghost him.

I yell to my parents that I'm leaving. Mom rushes into the hallway from the kitchen. "Please send me photos. Are you sure I can't come by for a few snaps?"

I've got to shut this down and fast. "Livi's older sister is home from college for fall break and she's taking our photos. No offense, but old people aren't so great with filters, angles, and light."

Mom seems to buy it, and I scoot out the door and into Livi's car.

As we cruise over to Gigi's, I run over the plan with her one more time. "You must remember to keep my phone on you. Mom tracks me all day, so your house, the coffee shop, the dance, wherever you go, my phone goes!"

Livi releases a hand from the steering wheel, elbowing me in the ribs. "I love this wild and naughty side of you."

"Make sure and send her a photo of us in our dresses right before the dance starts."

She squeals. "That fake photo shoot was brilliant, by the way. You're way sneakier than I would've ever guessed."

I smile and raise my eyebrows. You have no idea, Livi. "I'll take that as a compliment since it's coming from you.

Remember to send the photo to Mom from my phone, not yours. Don't be mushy or too friendly because we aren't on great terms at the moment. And make sure to check in with her the next morning, but not before ten or eleven. She won't expect to hear from me until then."

"Got it. Anything else?"

I tap my index finger to my lips. "Check my phone throughout the night for any messages from her. You don't have to respond to each one, but definitely give one response by the end of the night."

"Got it. What if I need to reach you? And where are you exactly?"

I should leave her with a few details, in case of an emergency. "I'm going to a place called Malone, Texas, to track down something for my grandmother. I'm taking her phone and I'll text you later, so you have my contact number. But it's an old flip phone so don't respond with a picture message or meme or send me a link because it won't go through. It's best if you call me."

"Call you?" she scoffs. "Who in the world calls anymore?"

We stop in front of Gigi's house. I lean over and give her a hug. "I owe you big time. Thank you for helping me. I'll be home tomorrow."

She squeezes me back. "Good luck. I promise I won't blow your cover!"

I step out of the car and wave goodbye as she drives off.

Betty is sitting out in front of Gigi's house with a "for sale" sign in the window. Mom really has a stone heart.

I enter Gigi's house and pull out my checklist: Betty's keys, a cooler filled with ice, flashlights, batteries, bath towels, paper towels, toilet paper, and Gigi's flip phone.

I open the car's trunk and load my supplies. My next round includes tools from Gigi's backyard shed: gardening gloves, shears, a shovel, outdoor trash bags, and a machete she used to trim her thick bamboo trees. I'm not sure what I might need to break into or tear apart.

I'm leaning into Betty's trunk, wrapping the tools in beach towels, when I hear a voice.

"Hailey?"

I pop up and Blake stands in front of me. His hair sticks out the sides of a backward baseball cap; a Mustangs football logo is plastered across his chest.

"What are you doing?" he asks.

I need to throw him off my tracks. "What? I could ask you the same thing."

"We just finished Saturday practice to review last night's film when I drove by." He smiles at me. "You and Betty are hard to miss."

Don't fall for his charm. I need to stick to the plan.

He points at Betty. "What's all that?"

I move, trying to block his view of the trunk. "Oh, I'm just running some errands."

"With a machete?"

"It's a long story."

He cocks his head to the side. "I DM'd you after I saw the 'For sale' sign on Betty. What's going on?"

I lean against the trunk and throw my arms up. "Mom is selling her, which is a bunch of bull because Gigi left her to me."

"For real?"

"Yep. The car is technically mine but would require a fight in court and we both know that's not happening, even though my father, the attorney, has pretty much admitted I have legal rights to her."

"I'm sorry."

"Yeah, it sucks."

"That's not the only reason I messaged you. I was hoping we could talk." He takes a step toward me.

I bite down hard on my lip. Although a part of me would love to talk to him, I don't have the time or the emotional wattage for a heartbreaking conversation. "I'm kind of on a time crunch today. Can we talk later?"

"Yeah, cool. Text me when you get a chance."

I finish packing the trunk and slam it shut. I spin around and then stumble back. Blake is standing in front of me. "You scared me."

"You know what? I can't leave yet. I need to clear the air, so please hear me out. I only need five minutes."

Leaning against Betty, I raise my hand to shield the sun and take a deep breath. "Okay."

"I was pretty stunned by what you told me the other day, but you bolted before I had a chance to respond. I've thought a lot about it, and I think you have it all wrong.

"You said you were a phony and a fake because you're not Jewish and feel embarrassed by your grandmother's lies. But you were duped as much as me. And I couldn't care less whether you're Jewish. I admit it seemed like an amazing win-win when you told me, but other than making my mother extremely happy, it doesn't matter to me."

The amber of his eyes and the depth of his words hypnotize me. "And then what you said about not spending time with me because I remind you of your grandmother, well . . ."

He shakes his beautiful head, his thick locks flopping up and down. "That's just not right. It's the exact opposite. Our relationship is special *because* of our connection to her. I'm someone in your life who actually got to know her. I understand how important she was to you. And her stroke wasn't your fault. She was so happy when you saw her the day before. I was there with you right after you two made up. I remember."

Blake's words surprise me. Does he still care for me? But then I think of the picture of him and Bree kissing just a few days ago, and I'm back to a state of confusion. "Thank you for the kind words. But can I ask what's the point of you telling me this?"

"So you don't have any more excuses to avoid me."

"What about Bree?"

"What about her?"

"I saw her post earlier this week. Aren't you going to the dance together tonight?"

"No."

My heart races. "I don't understand."

"She posted that so I would feel guilted into asking her to the dance. She's used to controlling our relationship, but I'm over it."

I'm floored. "She made that up? Man, she's straight up diabolical."

"Yeah, that pissed me off. But she's a mess right now. Her parents are getting a divorce, and it's really hard at home."

Now I kind of feel bad for Bree. Her life isn't as perfect as it seems. "That's terrible."

"I'm trying to still be her friend, but she knows my feelings have changed." He eyes lock on mine. "And that I like someone else."

Why does he do this to me every time? Pulling me back toward him when I try to run away. "I'm not involved in that equation."

"Yes, you are. Ever since I met you, I can't get you out of my head. We connected this summer, and I know you felt it, too."

Of course I felt it. He stole my heart this summer and then playing "In My Life" for Gigi and blessing her soul, and now declaring he has feelings and fighting for me? I'm gone for this guy, like homerun-out-of-the-ballpark gone for this guy, and I hate baseball.

Our eyes meet, and he closes the gap between us. His arms wrap around me, and it feels as if I belong there. Our faces are inches apart; my stomach somersaults.

But then I remember Jack and Ilse. I break our embrace. "Can we pick this up when I get back? Because I need to get going. I'm running out of time."

"Where are you going?"

"Well, um, yeah . . ." I stammer, trying to figure out a good lie, "it's better if you don't get involved."

He grabs my hand. "I'm involved."

Do I tell him everything? I look over my shoulder, and then whisper, "I found it."

"Found what?"

I peek over my shoulder again. "Jack's hideout."

He draws back, his amber eyes flare. "*What?*"

"Mom had said everything Gigi told me was a lie. I was so angry that I threw Gigi's copy of *The Great Gatsby* into a wall. The binding broke, spilling out a hidden note from Jack. The note was for Gigi and contains a map. He wanted her to find it."

His smile is so wide it steals his face. He repeatedly pounds his fist on Betty. "Yes! Well, I'm coming with you. You can't do this alone. It could be dangerous, or you might need help."

"No, you can't come. If we get caught and end up in trouble, it could ruin your football season. It's not worth the risk."

"I'm not taking 'no' for an answer. This is bigger than you. This is part of my history, too."

It does seem fated that he would take this adventure with me. What did Gigi say about the earth is round and you always end up where you started? "Okay, but we've got to get going. Grab a change of clothes in case we stay the night and anything else that comes to mind. I have money for food and gas, and you saw my supplies in the trunk."

He gives a wicked grin. "Now the machete makes sense."

"Make sure and leave your cell phone. Livi has mine. I don't want parents tracking us."

His amber eyes glow. "You've thought of everything."

I really hope so.

CHAPTER TWENTY-TWO

I slide into the front seat of Betty and bring her to life. I haven't driven her since the evening Blake and I said goodbye to Gigi at the cemetery. This will be my last ride with her.

Blake waits for me on the front porch. He pitches a bag into the backseat, but doesn't get in. "Can you give me a minute?"

"What are we waiting for?"

"You'll see."

An SUV rolls up behind me.

DeMarcus.

The guys fist pump and hug. "Hey, hey, hey. Glad to see you two listened to me and worked it out," DeMarcus says.

"You're always right," I tease.

He points his finger at me. "Exactly. Hailey, guess why I'm here?"

"No clue."

"Because we all get by with a little help from our friends," he sings in his deep baritone voice.

I choke on laughter. "You're a Beatles fan?"

"Girl, ever since Blake met you, he's been playing them in the locker room nonstop. I gotta admit, I'm hooked on a few of their songs." He punches Blake's arm. "Pass it over."

Blake tosses his phone to DeMarcus. "I'll take good care of it. But how are y'all going to survive without phones?"

I reach into my backpack and pull out Gigi's flip phone. "We have this old thing for emergencies."

His eyes pinch together. "Y'all are crazy. Driving around with no GPS and no smartphone. Blake knows my number if you need me to come save you."

DeMarcus hops in his car and waves through his rolled-down window as he drives away. Blake climbs into Betty's passenger seat. "So where are we going?"

"Back to Malone. On the map, Jack marked the hideout along the road between Malone and Penelope, another small town a few miles away. I found the spot using Google Maps, but there aren't any old barns in the area. Even more confusing is a tree that Jack labeled 'The Tree of Life.'"

Blake stiffens. "Like the Hebrew Tree of Life?"

There's a Tree of Life in Hebrew? "I don't know. I Googled it and the definition said that it's a connection between heaven and earth. And then I read that there was a Tree of Life in the Garden of Eden, and it was the source of eternal life. I couldn't make heads or tails of it. What do you know about it?"

"In Judaism, it can symbolize the Torah itself, or it can be used as a term for wisdom."

I'm not sure how that relates to the map. "Well, that just adds to the puzzle."

I decide to share the big news. "There's a name and some numbers written on the map. I looked the guy up, and he's the former Dean of SMU Law School." The excitement is too much for me. I grab his arm, squeezing it tightly. "He worked on the Nuremberg Trials, prosecuting Nazi war criminals!"

Blake stares at me like I have three heads. "Seriously?"

"Yep. And guess what one of his main areas of focus was?"

Before he can answer, I blurt, "*The Third Reich's looting of priceless European art!*"

His beautiful eyes bulge. "Wow."

"I know. All the dots are connecting."

I rifle through my bag and hand him the map. Blake studies the details. "What do you think the numbers and letters mean by the name?" I ask.

"I don't know. Maybe the code to a lock? Or maybe a phone number? It's two letters and five digits, which could be a seven-digit number, but there's no way it's still a working number."

He taps his finger on the map. "This tree is drawn in a distinct manner. Did you do a search to find this exact tree?"

"Yes. I tried to look for unique trees on Google maps in Malone and Penelope but didn't find anything."

He hops out of the car, map in hand. "We aren't leaving just yet."

I open the car door and chase him. "Wait, why?"

A huge grin spreads across his face. "Because I know how to find the exact location of the hideout."

I'm so confused. What does he see on the map that I don't? "How?"

"Follow me. It shouldn't take long."

He takes the stairs two at a time, and I try to match his pace. We enter his room, and he powers on the computer at his desk. I've never been in a teenage boy's bedroom before. I gaze at Blake's private world.

His room is surprisingly tidy. No dirty socks on the floor or empty potato chip bags or soda cans lying around. His queen-sized bed is made and covered in a navy comforter. His dresser has a few trophies and medals, a guitar sits in the corner, and framed football jerseys hang on the wall. My eyebrows arch up at the familiar names: Irvin, Sanders, Pearson, Bryant, Owens, and Cooper. Basically, the Dallas

Cowboys all-star wide receiving team. I point at the hall of honor. "That's an impressive collection."

He stops typing on his laptop. "My grandfather gives me a jersey every year on my birthday. Okay, this is it."

What does he think he knows?

I peer over his shoulder. "How is Google Earth going to help? I already printed all the maps."

He spins his chair toward me. "My family's Sunday afternoon ritual is to watch an NFL or NBA game together, followed by *60 Minutes*, and then we debate the show's stories at dinner. We tune in every week. When you told me about the hideout, I remembered an episode from a few years ago about the new way archeologists are discovering ancient artifacts."

I'm still not following.

"Satellite imagery. It's a new field they call space archaeology. The archaeologists study satellite images, looking for changes in topography on the pictures that aren't visible from the ground's surface. Subtle variations of the soil could mean something underneath.

"I'm betting if there are no structures on the property, the hideout is in the ground, hidden from view. If Jack was the last one to visit the hideout, it's been over sixty years since anyone was there. If you factor in the tornadoes that rip through this part of Texas, and the gentle change of topography over time, the hideout could be obscured from the ground's surface; it might have always been obscured. A cave. A bunker. A storm shelter. So, let's zoom in on the property using Google Earth and see if we notice anything."

Blake searches the area of land I pinpointed as the likely location of the hideout. He slowly plods through, and I lean over his shoulder to help, but my adrenaline is in overdrive. We're wasting valuable minutes that should be spent getting our butts down to Malone.

He magnifies a picture on the laptop's screen. "See this? It could be nothing, but the land changes color in this one rectangular area. Why would the land be less healthy than the surrounding area?"

He's so smart. I finally catch on. "Because there's a physical structure underneath it. Not just miles of soil."

"Exactly." He pounds his fist on his desk. "Look! There's a tree a hundred or so feet away."

I wrap my arms around his neck. "Yes!"

"Let me print these photos and let's get out of here and go find that hideout."

I'm confident I can get us back to Malone on my own, but we have Gigi's roadmap with us. We cruise on Interstate 35 with the top down. The wind blows fierce, making it impossible to talk.

I peer over at Blake and can tell he is deep in thought, trying to help me unravel my family's mysteries. I pray we can piece it all together.

We stop for gas, and I fill the tank while Blake loads up on drinks and snacks for us. He returns to the car and passes me a Dr Pepper. "I took a wild stab on this one. How did I do?"

"You catch on fast," I tease.

I toggle out the last few bits of gas. Blake relaxes in the passenger seat, chewing on Twizzlers. "Want me to drive the rest of the way?"

We don't have far to go, but my stomach cramps from anxiety. I'm terrified my parents are going to have the police looking for me soon. But I'm more scared this is a wild goose chase and I'll look like a fool, sucked in by fantastical Gigi stories.

"Yeah, that would be great. And let's crank the top up. We don't need Betty calling even more attention to herself."

We drive through Malone and turn on the Farm-to-Market Road toward Penelope. I study the map and am thankful the roads seem consistent. We drive a few miles and then the road curves left, and a gravel farm road appears, matching Jack's map. We take the country road and make it about a hundred feet down when we're greeted by a barbed-wire fence that blocks the road completely.

Blake stops Betty just shy of the fence. We both step out and walk over to examine the four-foot-high blockade. Blake studies the perimeter, walking a few hundred feet in each direction. "The fence runs along the entire property line. Should we leave the car and hop the fence? Or is it better to cut through it? If we cut the fence, I can pull the one wood post out, move it, and move it back. Someone would have to be paying close attention to notice the damage."

I stare at the barbed wire, eyeballing the height. "I don't think I can hop this fence without getting cut up. And there's so much rust on the metal. One prick and we could be gushing blood and get tetanus."

His eyes narrow. "I can help lift you over, but our bigger issue is we can't just leave Betty out here with all our stuff. It could be a long walk. That map isn't an accurate scale. It could be fifty yards or two miles to the area we're looking for. And we need food, water, and supplies."

He's right; we need Betty with us. "Decision made. Let's take the fence down."

Blake pops the trunk, and I unwrap the beach blanket filled with Gigi's garden tools. I have a couple pairs of sharp shears, wire cutters, and the machete.

"Hand me those wire cutters," says Blake.

"Do you think they'll work on metal?"

"Let's hope so."

After working for a solid thirty minutes, Blake finally rips through the metal. He then lifts the wood posts out and over. He cautiously drives Betty through, and then we work together to put the posts back.

He expertly navigates the potholes, weaving the car back and forth like a slinking snake. The gravel crackles under the tires as we bump up and down. We slowly travel another half mile, then the road ends, and we hit open land, but it's protected by an iron gate. The gate extends into another barbed wire fence that ropes off another swath of land. We hop out of Betty and walk over to examine our latest obstacle.

"Am I seeing this correctly?" I ask.

"Yep," says Blake. "It's not locked, which is basically the same thing as an invitation."

He pushes the gate open, and we drive Betty inside. I hop out to close the gate behind us. We drive another few hundred yards, and open grassland spreads to the horizon. We park Betty and climb out, each stopping to scan the flat prairie. I examine Jack's map with the satellite printouts, searching for common markers. "The topography of this entire area looks the same. I don't see any big trees here, do you?"

"No. But let's fan out. We need to explore by foot and look for traces of torn down trees, chopped down trees, or remnants of the barn."

We spread apart about thirty yards and then crisscross the land of wildflowers and weeds with our attention laser-focused at our feet.

"Do you think someone owns this land?" I shout at him.

He stops. "I thought your family owned it?"

"If this is where the hideout sits, they did at one point. They might still own it, but I couldn't find the property records."

We continue another thirty minutes with no discoveries. My frustration grows. "Do you think we're in the wrong place?"

He drops to his knees and runs his fingers through the dead grass. "The maps line up. We just need to go over every inch of this property. And remember how much time has passed. A lot can change in sixty years."

"But the map is clear about a Tree of Life."

Blake stands and rotates his head over his shoulder. "I don't know. There aren't any trees out here."

"Wait, look to the right, beyond that pond. There's a tree."

Touching the horizon sits a single tree. It's small, without a thick trunk, and only a few branches. We both run toward it, and I sprint ahead.

"Beat you again," I tease.

He bends over, breathing heavy. "Barely. And, just so you know, I let you win."

"Sure. And I believe you."

He reaches his hands to touch the tree's trunk. "This is a baby tree. There's no way this has been here sixty years. We could still dig it up and check what's in the surrounding ground?"

"He wouldn't build an underground hideout next to a pond."

Blake nods and we keep searching the property.

Late afternoon arrives and still no luck. A chill whips through the air as the sun begins to fade. A shiver rings through me, and I raise my eyes to the sky. "We only have a few hours of sunlight left."

We continue to comb over the land but find no clues to a Tree of Life or underground hideout. My disappointment boils over. "I don't understand because the satellite images showed a difference in the land's topography, but everything looks the same out here."

"It could have been those satellite images were from spring or early summer," he says. "We're coming off August and September when everything is burnt up, especially out here with no fertilization or water system."

My hope sinks.

We march on, looking for the Tree of Life. Another hour passes, and we've circled back to where we began. I climb into Betty, fighting to hold in my tears.

"Hey, don't give up. We need to regroup and rethink the map. There must be something we're missing."

"Like what? The map is clear on where the land sits. We have the road markers; we're in the correct spot. But there is a huge tree on the map, and we don't have any trees, or downed trees, or tree stumps."

Blake pops the trunk and lifts out the cooler. He pitches me a Dr Pepper and opens himself a bottled water. We sit together in Betty, the afternoon sun fading behind us.

"We must have the Tree of Life wrong," he says. "It's the only piece of the puzzle that could be off. It's not a marker on the map, it's just stamped at the bottom. Maybe it doesn't mean what we think."

I pull out the map and place it on my lap. I sip my Dr Pepper and stare at the Tree of Life. What was Jack trying to tell Gigi? His handwriting is controlled, and his words carefully chosen, mentioning her mother twice. I think about Gigi, about Ilse and Jack, and then it hits me. "You're right; we have it all wrong. It's not an actual tree marking the spot, it's just a symbol for what's here. My roots. Our ancestry. Their story. All the Jewish families whose possessions and family histories are here. That's what the Tree of Life means."

I read Jack's words aloud to Blake. "'I hope it is you that finds this note. You are to be the caretaker of my efforts to help your mother and the others. I'm sorry I wasn't a better father. I'm sorry you never knew your mother. Make things right for both of us.' See, it's about family. It's about *our* tree of life."

Blake jumps out of the car. "I like it. But we still didn't see anything."

I join him. "Yeah, but we were so focused on finding a

tree that we might have overlooked the topography changes, especially like you said, with the land burnt up from summer."

We spread out and start a new search. We switch sides to get a new set of eyes on the property. I'm staring so hard at the ground, trying to will the hideout into being, my head throbs from the intensity of my focus.

Another hour passes.

We loop back to each other, and both shake our heads in silent frustration.

No dice.

I take the last sip of my Dr Pepper and throw the can to the ground.

"Did you just hear that?" asks Blake.

He's right. I did hear something. "Throw that can again," he says.

I pick it up and pitch the Dr Pepper can as hard as I can into the ground. A loud smacking sound follows.

We look down. We're standing in dirt, the grass all dead, just like it is all over this field. He squats to the ground and frantically pushes the dirt away. I join him and do the same.

We stop and lock eyes.

Solid concrete.

"Blake, is this it?"

He jumps up and runs toward Betty. "What are you doing?"

"Getting the shovel and the rest of the tools!"

We work for the next thirty minutes in silent solidarity. Blake grunts as he shovels the dead grass and ground beneath. Wearing Gigi's gardening gloves, I work with my hands, pushing away dirt. And then we see it. I stagger back, shocked.

The concrete slopes down. The beginning of a staircase.

We stare in wonder. What in the world is down there?

"This could be it!" I shout.

Blake brushes his arm across his forehead, swiping away the sweat. "Let's hope so. We only have about an hour of daylight left. Do you want to pack up before it's pitch black out here and return at dawn?"

Pack up? There is no chance I'm leaving this place. "We can't leave. I can't go home without answers."

"How do you plan to work in the dark? There's absolutely no light pollution out here to help us."

"I brought flashlights. Or we can turn Betty's lights on."

He looks over his shoulder, scanning the property. "Let's do it. But, at some point, we'll need to call it a night and sleep for a few hours. I'm a little concerned about wild animals coming out when the sun goes down."

My stomach tightens. I'm terrified of most dogs, so the thought of wild animals makes me jumpy. "What kind of wildlife are we talking about?"

He scratches his head. "Coyotes. Foxes and skunks. Wild hogs."

Did he just say coyotes? And *wild hogs*? "Let's work until we get spooked."

I dig out dirt with my hands, and Blake scoops out large chunks with the shovel. As Blake scrapes out the stairs, a structure appears. We dig and dig, and now at least six stairs are visible. A loud wind howls over the open land.

I scream and my body tremors, terror overtaking me. Was it the wind or something else? Blake stops working. "You okay?" he asks.

"That noise freaked me out."

We walk back to Betty, and Blake shines his flashlight around us. "I don't see anything. What time is it anyway?"

I check my watch. "A little before nine. We were working so hard we lost track of time."

Betty's lights have been on us the entire time, guiding and protecting us.

"I'm starving. Let's take a break and eat," says Blake.

I step into the back seat and sit on the trunk of the car,

stretching my legs out. Blake joins me, hoisting the cooler into the space between us. He reaches down and pulls out a few items. "I worked incredibly hard preparing this meal for us."

He hands me a bag of Munchos potato chips and a container of beef jerky.

"Solid choices," I say. "If only we had a bag of Combos, it would be a five-star meal."

He holds a finger up. "I'm saving the best for last."

Flipping his hands from behind his back, he holds two packages of Grandma's Double Chocolate Chip Cookies. "In honor of Gigi."

Warm fuzzies cover my body. He smacks it out of the ballpark again. Gigi's here with us. And Blake remembers her.

"Do you mind if I put some music on?"

His amber eyes give their approval, and I reach over into the glove box. I know exactly what song to play. I pop the *Let It Be* album in the eight-track, clicking over to my choice. "Gigi was a big believer in finding the perfect song to set the mood or to memorialize an occasion."

"Across the Universe" plays and we both smile. What's more perfect than John Lennon's voice, a strumming guitar, and a sky full of stars? We both lift our gaze toward the full moon, an astronomy lesson on display. I point and say, "There's the Big Dipper."

Blake takes my hand, moving my finger to the left. "There's the Little Dipper, and that bright star is Mars."

Listening to John sing that nothing will change my world matches my mood, that regardless of whether we've found the hideout, things will be okay. The note proves Gigi's story is real. I know these people existed and their story is a part of me.

Blake yawns. "I think we should get a few hours of sleep."

He's right. A few hours of rest are needed to power through tomorrow. "Dawn will be at five or so, and we should get back to work as soon as we have a sliver of daylight."

We raise Betty's top, leaving the windows cracked for air. I prop my pillow behind my head and lay across the back seat, a beach towel pulled up to my chin. Blake rests his arms behind his head, his body opposite mine. Our legs intertwine, and I give him a playful tap with my foot. "Hey, Blake."

"Yeah."

"Thank you for coming. I couldn't have done any of this without you."

He rubs my foot with his. "Hey, Hailey."

"Yeah."

"There's no place I'd rather be."

A giant smile crosses my lips. I close my eyes as I lie in Betty, with Blake, closing in on Jack.

I jerk awake, momentarily forgetting where I am. Peeking out the car window, the sun is inching up over the sky. I disentangle my legs from Blake, gingerly climbing into the front seat, and out of the car. I shake my arms and legs out, roll my shoulders, and crack my neck. Every part of me is stiff from a night of cramped sleep. My mouth is dry, a rancid taste lingers from last night's dinner of Dr Pepper and beef jerky.

The morning is perfectly still, the sun piercing through the clouds. The air is crisp and cool, a dew covering the grass. I walk to the front of Betty, and my jaw dangles down at last night's progress. The staircase is clearly visible in daylight. We've dug out eight steps. How many more can there be?

I grab the shovel and start digging.

"I thought that was my job."

I look up to see Blake's smile. His hair is a disheveled mess, his clothes rumpled from sleeping. He takes the shovel from my hands, and I move over to scrape more dirt from the stairs. We work diligently, the sun rising behind us.

"Hailey, look!"

He's reached the last step. Twelve steps down and then the stairs stop at a metal door.

"What is it?"

Blake taps the door with the shovel and a loud clanking sound echoes through us. "An underground shelter."

"You think this was from Bonnie and Clyde?"

He bangs on the door again with the shovel. "No, I think their hideout was a barn on this land that no longer exists. My guess is this is a bomb shelter, built in the 1950s by Jack."

I remember we learned in US History that during the Cold War paranoia of nuclear war had people on high alert, and underground shelters were common. Towns would sound alarms, and people ran for cover. "He could have built this bomb shelter, and no one would have thought anything of it," I say.

"Exactly."

"What are we going to do about that lock?"

He pitches the shovel onto the stairs and grips the door handle. He wiggles and shakes it, but the door doesn't budge.

"It's jammed. The door handle rotates, but I can't get it open."

I push him to the side. "Let me try." Lifting the handle, I ram my shoulder into the door, trying to open it with force. I then kick the door, but that just hurts my foot. Hopping around on one leg, a few curse words slip out.

"Did you really just try to kick in the door?"

"Hey, it always works in the movies!"

"Let me try."

He leans his shoulder in and I cry out, "Wait, don't! You could hurt your arm. I won't be responsible for our school losing their star wide receiver."

He steps toward me and kisses me on the cheek. "Cute, but I'm not afraid of this door."

He pushes his body into the door and twists the handle with force. It creaks open.

"You did it!"

"Almost there," he says. He continues to thrust himself into the door until it's completely ajar.

He turns to me, his smile bright. "Admit it. You need me."

"What I need is your big shoulders," I say, and I wrap myself around him.

"Okay, let's do this. Pitch me that shovel and grab the flashlights."

I quickly do as he instructs. He places the shovel in the doorway, creating a door jamb. "We don't need this closing on us." He touches my hand. "Ready to go in?"

I nod, a mixture of fear and excitement choking my voice.

I'm shaking as I step in front of him. My heart beats so fast, I think it might explode. I'm slightly terrified of what might lay inside. Please no dead bodies, snake pits, wild racoons, or an infestation of giant rats. I shine my flashlight into the pitch-black bunker.

The light illuminates an empty room, a cot in the corner. The room is unusually cold, and a musty odor hangs in the air, but no dead bodies so far. I whip around to make sure Blake is behind me and am relieved to see his face. I beam my flashlight straight in front of me, exposing a corridor.

"The door is secure, right? Like we can't get trapped in here?"

"We're good. I have it blocked, but I don't think it locks anyway."

I take a deep breath. "Well, I have the flip phone in my pocket to be safe."

"Yeah, I don't think you're going to get reception down here."

My nerves and adrenaline are making thinking difficult.

"Keep going," he says.

We walk down the dark corridor, bending our heads to avoid knocking into the ceiling. My light flashes on the end of the tunnel.

"Another door."

"Yep."

I push it open, and my flashlight slips from my hands. Shaking, I bend down, my fingers fumbling for the light. Blake beams his light down and I pick it up. I shine my flashlight into the room.

Standing behind me, Blake touches my shoulder. "Is this for real?" he whispers.

I gasp, trying to find my voice, but it's left my body.

Paintings are rolled and stacked against the walls, leather-bound books lie in boxes, gold candlesticks and silver serving pieces line the ground, and even a few fur coats lay in a pile. This room is a window to the past; things thought lost are suddenly found.

I stop my light and hold it still. Three old machine guns are propped against a table. Could those have belonged to Bonnie and Clyde?

My flashlight travels along the four walls of the rectangle space, and two massive steamer trunks sit in a corner. "Blake, over there. Look."

We walk toward the trunks. Blake bends down, examining the wood slats and metal hardware. "They're unlocked."

He lifts the brass latches and opens the first trunk. I shine my light down.

"Whoa." I stumble back, my legs giving, and I fall to the floor.

"This can't be real! Is this real?" Blake asks.

Jewelry made of rubies, sapphires, and diamonds sparkle and shimmer under the light. A single large antique key hangs off a black ribbon. "It must be the key to the trunks."

I run my hands through the necklaces, earrings, bracelets, and watches. I then push aside a layer of jewelry, exposing stacks of currency.

Blake hands a wad of bills to me. Examining the money under my light, I'm thunderstruck. I think I've forgotten how to breathe. "This is German currency. It says Deutsche Mark, Berlin, and is dated 1955."

Blake moves over to the next steamer trunk. "What do you think is in this one?"

I shake my head and my throat constricts, strangling my voice. He pops it open, and inside lay piles of books.

He picks one up and flashes his light on the cover. "What language is that written in?" I ask.

"Some are in Hebrew and others in Yiddish. These are really old."

"From the war."

"No, much older than that."

As he studies the writings, I move my light around the room. A single framed painting leans against the wall. Blinking my eyes, the image comes into focus. I flinch, the flashlight shaking in my wobbly hands. It can't possibly be true.

The painting is a young woman in a white fitted gown set against a hazy background, her dark hair pulled back with ribbon, cheeks dotted with freckles, haunting eyes gazing directly at me. She's light as air, like a ghost. Could it really be the painting Ilse said hung over their mantle?

I walk toward it, running the tips of my fingers over the frame. Tears fall down my face.

Blake wraps his arm around my waist and pulls me toward him. "I think this was Ilse's."

He thumbs my tears away, his face is next to mine. We kiss in the dark, so much spoken without words.

Our mouths part, and I hug him tightly. "Thank you for being my friend."

"Does that mean you'll stop avoiding me now?"

I laugh. "Yes. I promise."

Flashing my light around the room again, I make sure this isn't a dream, that the treasures are real.

"What now?" he asks.

I think of Jack's note to Gigi. "I need to find Dr. Storey."

"Hailey, he must be dead. He worked on the Nuremberg Trials in the 1940s."

He's right. There's no way he's alive. "Well, someone knew him and must know what to do."

"I know who can help us," says Blake.

"Who?"

"My grandfather."

CHAPTER TWENTY-THREE

Exiting the bomb shelter, I blink my eyes, the sun's rays blinding after the darkness underground. Blake and I make multiple trips to Betty, carrying out handfuls of treasure in our arms. We arrange the rolled-up paintings in the trunk, buffered by the towels we brought with us. We fill the rest of Betty with as much silver serving ware, crystal glasses, and gold platters as we can fit. We then stuff jewelry and stacks of German bills into our overnight bags.

Blake carries out the framed painting of the woman in a white dress and places it in the backseat. We also line the car's floors with the ancient texts and books, and more rolled up artwork. Blake then covers the loot with a fur coat.

I grab my Polaroid from Betty and snap a few pictures of the outside of the bomb shelter. With Blake shining two flashlights, I take a few snaps inside the shelter of the remaining treasures.

"Do you think we cover the entrance back up with dirt?" Blake asks.

I shrug. "We don't have time for that. We just have to pray we can get back here before anyone else finds this place."

We both take a moment to study the bunker one final time, and then Blake slams the metal door shut.

As we walk toward Betty, a loud sound crashes over us. Was that a gunshot? I frantically scan the open land and catch sight of a figure approaching. A horse gallops toward us, the rider raises a rifle in the air. I yell at Blake. "Run!"

Another shot fires and we both freeze. I'm fast, but not quick enough to beat a bullet.

"Don't move! I'll shoot!" shouts a deep voice.

The horse has slowed its gallop to a trot. Blake moves toward me, placing his body in front of mine.

"Whoa, whoa, there, boy." The horse abruptly stops, its front legs kicking up dirt.

An old man sits on the horse; his face covered in folds and creases. His skin matches the rawhide of his saddle, and his eyes are black as night. Removing his cowboy hat, he wipes his brow and spits a wad of tobacco on the ground.

"This is private property. Y'all are trespassing."

I step out from behind Blake. "No, sir. We're allowed to be here. My family owns this land."

His eyes narrow. "Who's your family?"

My legs shake, but I try to hold my voice steady. "The Webers."

The horse snorts, pitching a few steps to the right. "Now, young lady, it's not good to lie, especially to your elders. I have lived in this town since I was a boy, and I can tell you no Webers have been here in Malone for over fifty years."

Crap. He's on to us. Maybe I can trick him. "Sir, you're wrong. My grandmother told me this land is ours. You need to let us pass and we'll be on our way. I'll have my grandmother sort this out with the county."

"Not so fast." He cocks his rifle toward us. "What have you been digging up?" He points his finger behind us at the pile of dirt visible by the steps.

Poker face, Hailey. "Sir, we didn't dig anything up. We found it like this."

He spits another nasty wad of tobacco to the ground. "What did I say about lying? You aren't the first person I've caught sneaking onto this property. Everyone in Malone knows the rumors about Bonnie and Clyde and Otto Weber. My granddaddy said Otto was up to his ears in corruption. A German traitor and a criminal. Where do those stairs lead?"

My head spins at the mention of Otto, but I don't flinch. "It's just an empty bomb shelter from the 1950s. Bonnie and Clyde died in the 1930s. Sorry to disappoint you, but there's no connection."

He squints his beady black eyes. I swear they have icicles hanging on them. "So if I go down those stairs, it's nothing but an abandoned bomb shelter? Be careful, young lady. I think it would be wise for you to come clean."

Blake steps forward. "Like she said, it's empty. Now, if you'll excuse us, we were just leaving."

He points the rifle at us. "Don't be rude, son. We were just getting to know each other."

He shifts the reins to the left and trots over to Betty. "This is a mighty nice car. Where'd you get a classic beauty like this?" I grab Blake's hand, squeezing it tight. The old man hops down from his horse and peeks in Betty's window. "Well, what do we have here? Looks like y'all have some explaining to do."

With his gun pointed at us, he swings back onto his horse. He's awfully spry for someone so ancient. He reaches into his pocket and pulls out a cell phone. "I'm going to need some help unloading this car."

I lean in toward Blake, lowering my voice. "We can't lose Jack's work. We need a distraction so we can make a run for it."

"I know. We've got to act fast," he whispers.

The man chatters on his phone. "Get your butt out of bed and over here. You're not gonna believe what these kids found."

"I have an idea," I say.

Blake lifts his chin. "I'll follow your lead."

Go time.

I take off in a mad dash at the horse, waving my arms wildly, my voice screaming every expletive I know in the highest pitch I can reach. I'm yelling in dolphin. The horse stomps its feet and pitches its neck back, then violently throws its front legs up, causing the cell phone to slip from the old man's hands.

"Whoa, whoa!" yells the old man. He's still got the rifle, but he's barely holding on. I run in circles and pump my arms, screaming curse words. The horse reacts, bucking up and down.

"Blake, get to Betty!" I yell out.

"Almost there!" he shouts.

Sticking my fingers in my ears, I let out the shrillest scream I can muster. I'm pretty sure I just broke glass. The horse bucks hard and the old man flies off. He's flat on the ground, moaning in pain. The horse flees out of the pasture, and I run over to the rifle and grab it with both hands. I aim it at the old man.

His cold eyes meet mine. With the rifle pointed at him, I kick his cell phone out of reach. I then slam the butt of the gun into the phone, smashing it to pieces. He won't be calling his friends now.

But I'm not done defending my family. "What you heard about the Webers is wrong. Otto was a good man, and he loved this country!"

Betty roars to life, and Blake pulls her up next to me. "Let's get out of here! Now!"

I jump in the car, and he peels Betty out of the open field, kicking up dust in our wake.

Blake's wild eyes meet mine. "We almost just died," I say. I try to catch my breath, but I'm panting loudly, my adrenaline pumping in light speed.

"Yeah, that was a close call." He weaves Betty down the gravel road, dodging potholes right and left. "You were amazing. Are you okay?"

I pat myself down. Face is fine and my arms and legs are still intact. "I think so. We gotta get the hell out of Malone. His friends are headed this way."

"I'm working on it," Blake says, revving Betty's engine, as he swerves the car onto the Farm-to-Market Road. We speed down the road, winding our way back to the interstate. A pickup truck blazes by us, two men in cowboy hats in the front seat. One of the men had the same black eyes as the old man. "Blake, I'm betting that was his goons. Drive faster!"

He slams his foot on the pedal, and Betty flies down the road. I rip open my backpack and dig out Gigi's flip phone.

"Should we call the cops?" I ask.

"And tell them what? That we were attacked by an old guy with a rifle, but we happen to have thousands of dollars of missing art and other loot in our car that we found while trespassing? Oh, and the map we used to find the loot is from a guy who went to prison for selling fenced goods?"

He makes a good point. "What about the rest of the stuff in the bunker? They're going to get it."

"You destroyed his cell phone. Hopefully it will take them awhile to find him. But we can't worry about that now. We just have to get ourselves safely out of here. Whoever that old man was, he wasn't smart enough to get a tag number. Yeah, he knows the car make and model and that you're a Weber, but you're not. You're a Rogers. We're fine. He can't find us."

I hope he's right. Checking over my shoulder, we seem to be in the clear.

Blake turns Betty onto Interstate 35, but he's going the wrong direction. "Blake, hello, Dallas is I-35 North, not South."

His eyes don't veer from the road. "I know."

"I thought we were going to your grandfather's house."

"We are. He doesn't live in Dallas."

What? I wasn't expecting a detour. Between the old man with the rifle and this, my simple plan has gone up in flames. "Where does he live?"

"Llano."

"Where the heck is that?"

He glances at me, a smile crinkling his eyes. "Take out your grandmother's roadmap. It's about eighty miles northwest of Austin."

I grab the map off the floorboard and flip it open. "How long will it take us to get there?"

"I'm not sure. It's about four hours from Dallas to Llano, so I'm guessing about two-and-a-half from here."

"But I have to get back to Dallas with Betty. Mom is meeting that buyer later this afternoon."

"I think what we discovered today trumps returning Betty to your mom. Betty's not leaving us."

Us. Not leaving *us* is what he just said. Are we a couple now?

But he's right about Betty. I won't let Mom sell her, especially after everything that's happened. I push Mom from my thoughts. I'll worry about that problem later.

"Tell me about your grandfather. Why do you think he can help us?"

"He's brilliant. He knows about everything: from sports to literature to philosophy . . . he's a bit of a legend."

Now I'm super intrigued. "You've just set the bar awfully high. I hope I'm not disappointed."

He smiles. "Grandpop was a big-time surgeon in Dallas and on charity boards and in other community organizations. I'm not entirely clear about what happened, but when my grandmother got sick and died, he just gave it all up. He moved out to his ranch in Llano to fish, hunt, and paint. And, well, he never came back."

"How long has he been out there?"

"Awhile. Maybe seven or eight years? He lives off the grid on a lot of land and has become somewhat of a recluse."

"When was the last time you saw him?"

He taps the steering wheel. "About five years ago."

"*Five years?* That's a long time."

"Yeah, he doesn't really like people."

"But you're his grandson." I remember the hall of honor in his room. "Wait, what about all those jerseys you have from him?"

"They arrive every year on my birthday."

All I can think is why are we going to see someone he hardly knows? "What makes you think he'll be there?"

"He's there. He never leaves. He doesn't have a phone, but he sends Dad letters every few months."

This man is starting to sound mentally unstable. "But why do you think he can help us?"

"Because he's the smartest person I know. He loves art and history, and he'll guide us in the right direction." He touches my hand. "And we're Jews from Poland. This is our history, too."

It's late afternoon when we arrive at our destination: the Triple A Ranch. Blake steps out of Betty and pushes on the iron gates. Locked. Moving over to the security gate keypad, he presses a few numbers, and the gate swings open.

"How did you know the code?"

"I tried a few family birthdays and then realized my grandfather wouldn't take the time to personalize from the factory setting. He hates technology. I entered the magical combination of 1-2-3-4 and *ta-da*."

Blake drives Betty down the long single lane dirt road. We pass shallow, rocky soil and dirty creeks, and then the land morphs into green-and-brown hills, the ground covered in wildflowers and fallen leaves. We bump up and down the hilly road for at least another fifteen minutes before winding our way back to the homestead, a limestone ranch house with a wraparound porch dotted with rocking chairs.

Blake parks Betty in the circle drive. We both step out of the car and slowly walk to the front door.

As we stand on the porch, I tug on Blake's arm. "Are you sure this is a good idea? He's not expecting us, and you haven't seen him in years."

He takes my hand in his, gripping it tightly. "Trust me."

With his free hand, he bangs on the door. A few moments pass, but there's no response. Blake knocks again several times.

"He may be painting in his studio." He jerks his head to the side. "This way."

We circle to the back of the house, and an old barn sits in a pasture. Blake peers in a window. "We have a winner," he says.

He pushes the barn doors open and we walk in. A man with his back to us sits on a stool, his body hunched over a canvas, a paintbrush in motion. His white hair hangs shaggy around his shoulders. He wears overalls, and his cowboy boots are propped on the stool's legs.

"Grandpop, it's me, Blake," he says in a loud voice.

The man's hand stills, and the brush drops to the ground. He turns around, his face covered in wrinkles and a white scruffy beard and Blake's amber eyes.

"What in the hell, son? Are you trying to give me a heart attack?"

Blake smiles and walks toward him. The old man steps off his stool, sticking his hand out. His fingers are covered in color—shades of blue, green, and white. They shake hands, and Blake's grandfather grabs his arm, and then touches his face. "You're a man now. The last time we were together, you were a boy." His gaze travels past Blake and settles on me. "Hello."

"Hello," I croak out, my voice scratchy.

"This is my friend, Hailey," interjects Blake.

"I'm Alan," his grandfather replies gruffly. He crinkles his nose, and his eyes narrow. "I have to say y'all gave me quite the surprise. Let's not beat around the bush. Why are you here?"

Well, that was blunt. He hasn't seen his grandson in five years and doesn't even offer to have a chat or give us a meal?

Blake grabs my hand, and his grandfather spies our connection. "We need your help."

The old man rubs his neck. "Have you two run away together? Because I can't get involved in domestic disputes with your parents."

Blake laughs loudly. "God, no. Grandpop, we have so much to tell you. We wouldn't be here if it weren't important."

He points his finger over his shoulder at the easel behind him. "Well, I was also in the middle of something important. I've been waiting weeks for inspiration, and it arrived this morning."

"Please," Blake pleads.

His grandfather stands stoically and stares at us. Is he going to send us away and not help us? "Well, come on, then," he says. He waves his hand, motioning us to follow him. "Let's go to the house, have a drink, and you can tell me everything."

Blake's grandfather walks slowly, his cowboy boots kicking up dirt with each step. We enter the ranch's back door and stop in a galley kitchen. Dirty dishes line the farmhouse sink, open shelves hold a few plates, and a kettle sits on the gas stove.

"Would you like some coffee or water? That's all I have."

"Water would be great," Blake says.

His grandfather reaches up to a shelf for two glasses, rinsing them out before filling them from the tap. He hands them to us without a word and moves into his living room.

He lowers himself into a recliner while Blake and I choose the brown leather sofa across from him. The room has a rustic charm with wood beams that cut across the ceiling and large bay windows with views of the prairie. A buck's head with eight-point antlers is mounted above the stone fireplace; a brown bear rug lies on the floor. Books are piled in stacks around the edges of the sparse room. He could really benefit from a few bookshelves, end tables, and window treatments. Mom would have a field day with this place.

He holds a glass of brown liquid in his hand that I'm pretty sure is whiskey. "Well, lay it on me."

I raise my eyebrows, letting Blake know to go ahead. "What we have to tell you is going to sound absolutely insane."

"Son, I've lived a long life and seen it all. Nothing you can say will shock me."

Buckle up, big guy. This one is going to blow you over.

"Hailey became close with her grandmother this summer, and she shared an old family secret. Her grandmother's parents met during World War II when her great-grandfather helped to liberate the Dachau concentration camp as an American G.I. Her great-grandmother was a German Jew at the camp."

Alan's body stiffens; his drink slightly shakes in his hand.

Blake continues. "He nursed her back to health, they fell in love, moved to Paris, and had Hailey's grandmother, but then her mother died. Her father brought Hailey's grandmother to Texas to be raised by his sister."

Alan takes a sip of his whiskey, his eyes locked on me and Blake.

"Her father then went to get vengeance and hopped a boat from Galveston to South America to hunt Nazis."

Alan's face is frozen, but he's so old and wrinkly, it's hard to see a change in expression. I'm still pretty sure Blake just shocked him.

"Hailey's great-grandfather recovered items stolen from Jews and brought them back to Texas to a hideout, but then went to prison and died shortly after that."

Blake takes in an enormous breath, and I'm mesmerized how he remembered every detail of Gigi's story. "Hailey found a map hidden in a book her great-grandfather left for Hailey's grandmother. We used Google maps and found the hideout. He made a bomb shelter on some land about two hours from here. We broke into the shelter and found the recovered Jewish property."

I gaze over at his grandfather and his jaw hangs open. We definitely shocked him. He places his drink down. "Son, this can't be possible."

Blake stands and I join him. "We have about half of the items from the hideout in our car, but we couldn't fit everything. There are more paintings, books, and other recovered possessions still in the bunker."

I speak for the first time. "The map had a name and phone number on it that we believe my great-grandfather left to my grandmother as a contact to help her. Robert Storey. I looked him up and he was—"

"I knew R.G.," says Blake's grandfather, cutting me off.

We both wait for more, but Dr. Alexander stares out the window.

"You really knew him?" Blake asks.

He directs his attention back to us. "He worked on the Nuremberg Trials. Every Jew in Dallas was aware of his work. Our synagogue helped fund various efforts to search for art looted from Jewish families by the Nazis. He and I had many conversations about his work in Nuremberg. He was a friend. But he died at least thirty years ago."

My body twitches, and my foot wildly taps the floor. How is it that my world keeps colliding with Blake's? Even our pasts seem connected. His grandfather knew the man that Jack had told Gigi to reach out to for help.

"Well, follow us," Blake says. "We have a few things to show you."

We walk outside and over to Betty. Blake opens the trunk, removing a fur coat to reveal gold plates and candle-sticks, silver serving pieces, and rolled art.

Blake's grandfather reaches in, slowly moving his hands over the items. He rubs his beard repeatedly. "Impossible."

"There's more in the back seat," Blake adds.

"Bring it all inside," he says.

The three of us work silently, carrying the recovered items into the living room.

His grandfather unrolls the paintings, but the edges curl after sixty years rolled up. He dashes to the kitchen, returning with plates and glasses to hold the four corners of each canvas flat.

We empty the last treasures from Betty, and then Blake and I dump our overnight bags of jewelry, gold and silver coins, and German currency onto the floor. I survey the room and my eyes glisten. To see all the recovered possessions set out together, in daylight, is mind-bending.

His grandfather wears his reading glasses and studies each piece of art. He intently focuses on a painting of a young man in a beret, wearing a blouse of some sort. Blake's grandfather drops to his knees. He bends over the painting, his eyes tracking every detail. I'm not sure why this painting catches his attention more than the others. I prefer the painting of the ballerina and the colorful impressionist painting of a street scene.

He turns to us with wide eyes. "Do you know what you've found?"

Blake and I shake our heads.

"This is Raphael's 'Portrait of a Young Man.' It went missing from a Polish Museum during the war. Most art historians consider it the most significant missing art piece from World War II. This was painted during the Renaissance, around the early 1500s, and is estimated to be worth over a hundred million dollars."

I think I might pass out. How did Jack find it?

His grandfather takes his time, moving from painting to painting. He calls for Blake to bring him a pen and paper from the kitchen, and he meticulously writes notes about each work.

Blake taps his shoulder and hands him a stack of texts. "Grandpop, these are in Hebrew. I think they're incredibly old."

His grandfather studies the books, and then opens one.

"Why is he reading it backward?" I whisper to Blake.

"Hebrew is written right to left." He grins at me. "You have so much to learn."

His grandfather raises his moist eyes to us. "These are religious texts, most likely taken from a library or synagogue. Some are written in Hebrew, others in Yiddish."

He stands and clasps the book to his chest. "I thought I was done living, but you two are pulling me back into the world."

He reminds me of Gigi. He's full of mystery and deep thoughts.

"So does that mean you'll help us?" Blake asks.

He flashes a giant smile, his amber eyes glowing. "Yes. We need to catalog everything you brought."

I yank on Blake's sleeve and lean into his ear. "But I need to keep Ilse's painting."

"Of course."

Blake touches his grandfather's arm. "Grandpop, the painting in the frame belonged to Hailey's great-grandmother's family."

He moves his gaze to me. "Her name was Ilse," I say. "She told Jack about this painting. He must have searched until he found it. I'm hoping it can lead me to her and the rest of my family."

"I know someone that can help you," he replies.

"Like Dr. Storey?"

"Yes."

A few hours have passed. I worry about the time. We need to figure out a plan and fast. We have school tomorrow, and we need to get back to Dallas. I push Blake into the galley kitchen. "Should we leave everything here with your grandfather and head to Dallas? Except for the painting. I must take it with me."

Blake checks his watch. "I don't think we should leave. Do you?"

Blake's grandfather walks in. "It's getting late. You two shouldn't drive to Dallas in the dark, and we have some phone calls to make. I would like you both here to answer questions. Could y'all stay the night and head out in the morning?"

My parents are going to kill me. But I do want to know what steps are next because I'm uncomfortable leaving Jack's work so soon after finding it. I need to follow through and make it right, like he asked Gigi to do. And we still need to get the rest of the stuff we left behind. "I guess that makes sense."

"I agree," replies Blake.

"We need to tell him about the shootout," I whisper to Blake.

He nods. "Grandpop, one more thing."

"Yes?"

"We ran into a little trouble in Malone. As we were leaving, an old man on a horse showed up. He had a rifle. He threatened us, but Hailey was able to spook his horse, and we escaped. But I'm sure he's going to try and take everything we left in the shelter."

"You two had quite an adventure."

"That's the understatement of the year," I deadpan.

"Rest assured, I already called my old friend, Senator Stevens, and he alerted the FBI. A team from Houston was dispatched immediately to secure the bunker. Those guys won't get far."

"You have a phone?" Blake asks.

"Your father bought me one for emergencies."

His grandfather points his finger at us. "Now you both need to call your parents. Blake, I can speak with your father if necessary."

I know he's right. I need to call Mom and Dad.

I step outside, wanting privacy for what I know will not go well. The sun is setting here in Llano, which means Mom and Dad must have guessed I'm on the run by now and that I'm in Betty.

I realize Dad is the best path to peace with Mom. Taking out Gigi's flip phone from my bag, I dial Dad's number. "Hailey?"

He's smarter than I give him credit for. "Hi, Dad."

"Hailey, what in God's name is going on? Where are you?"

I can hear Mom's voice in the background, but he hasn't given her the phone yet. "I'm fine. I'm safe. I had to do this for Gigi."

"Do what? Where are you?" he yells, his voice tight.

I pace around Betty. "I'm in Llano."

"Llano, Texas?" he says, through exasperated breaths.

"Yes."

He repeats to Mom what I said.

"We're coming to get you."

"Dad, it's late and I'll be home tomorrow. You don't need to worry. I'm at Blake's grandfather's ranch."

"Why are you at his grandfather's ranch?" He's yelling again.

I have no idea what he must be thinking, but I'm sure it's not good when your teenage daughter leaves town with a guy she likes. "I found a note from Jack in the book Gigi gave me. It had a bunch of clues to our family history. Blake came to help me figure stuff out, and we ended up here in Llano."

A long silence follows.

"Your mom and I will be there tomorrow morning. Don't go anywhere. You promise, Hailey."

I sigh. "I won't."

"Give me the address."

I tell him the ranch's address and am thankful Mom hasn't gotten on the phone.

"You have a lot of explaining to do," he says, the anger in his voice palpable.

I know I do.

We stay up most of the night, helping Dr. Alexander to catalog the art, jewelry, and other treasures. Blake and I both fall asleep on the leather sofas, still wearing the same clothes of the last forty-eight hours.

I awake, unaware of the time, but the sun is peeking through the windows.

Blake's grandfather walks in, a cup of coffee in hand. "Good morning. Time to rise and shine. Your parents will be here soon. Anyone need coffee or breakfast?"

Blake yawns, stretching his arms over his head. "Coffee would be great."

I pop upright, but I'm not hungry. My parents' impending arrival has my stomach doing flip-flops.

I join Blake in the kitchen. I sip on coffee, trying to clear the fog off my brain, but the caffeine just elevates the anxiety coursing through my body. I decide fresh air would do me some good and excuse myself.

Leaning on Betty, I take in the beauty and stillness of daybreak on a ranch. Nature's dewy morning scent fills my nostrils, and the cool fall air chills my lungs. As I gaze upon the rolling grass and granite hills, my life of the last two days seems like a dream.

The house screen door creaks and then slams. Blake walks toward me.

"It's going to be fine. They're going to be angry, but once they see everything, all will be forgiven," he says.

I don't think Blake understands the depth of distrust Mom has for Gigi. Our discovery proves that Gigi wasn't a fraud, but I'm not sure Mom will believe it. Mom's reactions to everything the last few months have surprised me. But maybe now she will see Gigi the way I see her? Maybe she will finally forgive Gigi?

"How do you think your parents will react?" I ask.

"Utter shock and disbelief. But Dad will still want to make sure I get back to school in time for football practice."

"Yes, Texas football takes precedence over recovering millions of dollars of stolen art."

He smiles. "Always."

He touches my arm and slides his fingers to weave through mine. "I was thinking since I helped you uncover one of the greatest treasure troves of lost art of the last fifty years, we've crossed over into new relationship territory."

I fight off a smile. "True, but I have a feeling my status at school is about to rocket launch past every other girl. I think I need to wait and weigh my options." I playfully lift my shoulders.

"Okay, I'll get in line then."

He takes my hand, pulling me into him. Our eyes meet and I know he's the only one for me. "But the more I think about it, those other guys will just be after me for my fame, so I'd be a fool to even consider it."

He leans down and kisses me.

"Y'all better cut that out before your parents get here."

I might die from embarrassment.

We separate, and each quickly wipe our lips. "Grandpop, thanks for the heads up," chimes in Blake.

The three of us stand beside Betty, gazing down the long gravel road. Blake's grandfather sips his coffee, long and slow. "You two are something special. Y'all are going to change the world for so many families. Good is triumphing evil. Hailey, your great-grandfather is a hero."

His words hit me in the gut. Anyone who knew Jack thought he was a criminal who died a disgraceful death. But the truth will now be broadcast to the world. Jack was a hero.

He's my hero.

My parents' Volvo stops in the circle drive, right on Betty's bumper. Mom and Dad both step out, and I give a weak smile.

They stand in front of me as I shift from left to right, bouncing on my toes. I'm steadying for the verbal assault when Mom launches her arms around me. Dad's arms envelop hers, adding another layer around us both.

Mom pats my hair. "I love you, Hailey Jane," she says, her voice gentler than I expected. "I'm angry with you, but I was also terrified yesterday. Don't you ever put your father and me through such hell again." And she smothers me with more kisses, squeezing me tighter. "You're not off the hook, though. We'll discuss punishment when we get home, but I'm just so relieved you're okay."

I had a feeling this wouldn't end well for me.

Dad has tears in his eyes. "Yes, never again."

We separate and Mom chews on her lip. "Why did you take off? This is all because of Gigi and her ridiculous stories? I thought she had finally stopped spinning lies."

"They weren't lies."

Dr. Alexander steps forward. "I'm Blake's grandfather, Alan. I know these are unusual circumstances but it's nice to meet you both." He extends his hand to my mother and then my father. "Your daughter is a hero and about to be famous."

My parents exchange quizzical looks and then direct their gaze at me. Mom touches my arm. "Hailey, what is he talking about?"

An approaching car crunches up the driveway. Blake's parents are here. Dr. Alexander and Blake greet them, while we stand a few feet behind.

I take Mom's hand in mine. "Come on. We have a few things to show you."

We walk inside, the loot spread out before them. Blake's parents burst into tears. Mine haven't spoken for several minutes; their faces frozen in shock.

Mom and Dad circle the room, surveying the art and I trail behind them. "Do you know these artists? Degas, Pissarro, Van Gogh, and Reubens? Are these real?" Mom asks.

"We will have to get expert verification, but I believe so," says Dr. Alexander. "All these works have been missing since the war. When combined with the other items found in the hideout, it all makes sense, as inconceivable as Jack's story is."

His eyes are wet again. He removes his glasses, swiping at each. "Can you imagine that hidden in the ground in central Texas are treasures the world has been searching for the last eighty years?"

"What now? How do we get these items returned to their lawful owners and heirs?" Dad asks, falling into attorney mode.

Dr. Alexander returns his glasses to his face. "I took the liberty of making some phone calls last night. A team is arriving in a few hours to take everything to Washington. If that is permissible to your family?"

Mom and Dad are bug-eyed, so I answer for us. "Yes.

Jack's message was clear: Gigi was to make things right. Can I request we keep the painting that belonged to my great-grandmother's family? The one my grandmother told me about?"

"Yes. We will take photos and confirm its provenance for you," says Dr. Alexander.

"What painting?" Mom asks.

I take her hand and lead her to the framed portrait of the young woman in the white dress. "According to Gigi, Jack said that Ilse spoke of a portrait of a woman in white that hung over the mantle in their home."

Mom touches the frame. Her finger lightly traces over the girl's lace dress.

"Does that say Gustav Klimt?" she asks, her voice cracking.

I hadn't been able to decipher the scribble in the corner. But I've never heard that name before.

"Yes. I believe it's authentic," answers Dr. Alexander. "He painted several Jewish women during this time period."

Mom stumbles back, her hand covering her mouth. "My word."

"Remember the Bloch painting—"

"At the Neue Galerie in New York," interrupts Mom.

"Exactly," replies Dr. Alexander.

Dad wears the same confused look as me. I'm glad I'm not the only one uneducated and in the dark on this one. "What are y'all talking about?" I ask.

"A Klimt painting of a wealthy Jewish woman was taken by the Nazis during World War II as payment for alleged 'tax evasion' and given to the Belvedere Museum in Vienna," says Dr. Alexander. "The Nazis would make false allegations against Jewish families to justify their theft. The painting wasn't returned to her heirs until 2005 and only forcibly by the decision of a court.

"Jewish families have fought for decades to reclaim their art and other possessions stolen during the war. There are so many players in the game: the Nazis who originally stole the art, and then the unscrupulous art dealers and museum directors who purchased and sold the stolen art, the postwar governments that made recovery difficult for Jewish survivors, and let us not forget, the wealthy collectors who looked in the other direction. Thousands of pieces of art owned by Jewish families remain missing to this day."

How can people keep things that don't belong to them?

Dad has his arms around me. "We need a play-by-play of how this all happened."

Mom has joined the group embrace. A tear trickles down her cheek. "I have a lot to learn about my mother and her family, don't I?"

Mom's words shock me. I thought I had made things worse between them. I thought my mother would never see Gigi's beauty. Maybe what I found can mend old wounds. Maybe the past can heal the present.

Mom, Dad, and I walk out of the house, and I guide them around to the iron bench under the big oak tree. I have my bag with me and pull out the book and the map. Mom sets both in her lap, neither of us speaking as she reads Jack's note. She runs her fingers over Jack's handwriting and a tear drops down her cheek.

"I'm sorry if you were worried," I say. "I apologize for sneaking away like that and purposefully misleading you, but I had to do this. Do you understand now?"

Mom kisses my hand, nodding.

But they need to understand this isn't over yet. "I have two requests to make of you both. First, I'd like to keep Betty.

I have a boatload of currency we found that I can use to buy her from you. Now, given, I'll be paying in German marks, which I don't think exist anymore, so I'm not sure if they have value or what the conversion would be—"

"Hailey, you can keep her," Mom says, the ends of her lips curving up. "With some rules in place, of course."

That was too easy. This new heroism gig is paying off big time.

I nod, not showing the inner happy dance going on inside me. Poker face intact. "Cool. My second request is that I must keep going. I have to find her, and I don't want you to stop me."

Mom and Dad don't seem to be following.

"Ilse. We have to learn about her life. We have to do it for Jack and Gigi."

Mom inches toward me and touches my cheek. "I was hoping we could work on that together."

CHAPTER TWENTY-FOUR

I'm in Betty, driving over to Blake's house. I've relaxed Gigi's rules on music in Betty, stretching my repertoire to include John, Paul, George, and Ringo's post-Beatles music. I'm blaring Lennon's "Happy Xmas," as I'm full of Christmas spirit this year. But I'm about to switch holiday modes: I've been invited to the first night of Hanukkah with Blake's family.

Before ringing the doorbell, I run my hands down the front of my skirt, flattening the edges, although with my black tights nothing troubling is on display. I wet my fingers and slick down a few wild hairs. I've spent time with Blake's family for a few dinners, but this feels different. It feels meaningful.

Blake greets me with a smile and pecks my lips, before whisking me inside. His family is warm and inviting, and I receive a loving embrace from both his mom and dad. These past few weeks Blake and I have solidified our relationship status. He's officially my boyfriend.

We're in the living room where the family is about to light the menorah for the first night. A few blessings are said and then Blake and his sister each open a present. I enjoy watching Blake and his sister tear into their gifts, just like Kyle and I do on Christmas.

Blake then hands me a box. "You get a gift, as well," he says.

"Is it from you?"

"It's from our entire family," his mom says.

The present is small. I unwrap the gift carefully, salvaging the ribbon and square of paper for future use. Inside the box is a necklace. A tree hangs on the end of the silver link chain.

The Tree of Life.

This might be the most thoughtful gift anyone has ever given me. Blake helps me put the necklace on, clasping it around my neck. I rub my fingers over the tree charm, feeling once again connected to Gigi, like a part of her is always with me.

His mother announces dinner is ready, and we sit down to a feast of latkes and several other traditional Hanukkah dishes. The doorbell rings, interrupting the holiday meal.

Blake excuses himself to get the door. He pops back, his dimple on display. "We have a special visitor."

In walks his grandfather, Dr. Alexander.

Blake's father jumps to his feet. "Dad! What in the world? You never leave the ranch. Did you really come to celebrate Hanukkah with us?"

Blake's grandfather removes his coat, his cowboy boots rumbling on the wood floor. "It's serendipity that Hailey is here because she's the person I really came to see."

Although he's spoken to my parents a few times on the phone, I haven't seen him since we met the FBI in Malone to walk them through how we discovered the bunker.

Blake's father pulls a chair out, and Dr. Alexander joins us at the dining room table. He leans over his elbows, his wrinkles somewhat obscured by the dim dinner light.

"I have some exciting news to share. Hailey and Blake, you, and your families," he stops, pointing to Blake's parents, "that means you two and me as well—we've been invited to

Israel for a lecture series. The Prime Minister wants to hear Jack and Ilse's story firsthand from our two detectives."

The room breaks into cheers. I'm speechless. I've never left the country before. I don't even have a passport.

"That's not all." His eyes lock on mine. "We found her."

My fork clatters on my plate.

"I reached out to the Holocaust Memorial Museum in DC, and as soon as I told them Jack and Ilse's story, they put to work some of the best researchers on the cold case. I got word a few days ago and had a lengthy conversation with the director."

I'm overwhelmed he would do this for me, and that other people cared to help.

"Your great-grandmother's name was Ilse Klein," he says. "Her father, Jacob, was a professor of physics. Her mother, Hannah, was originally from Vienna and a music teacher. Ilse had three sisters and a brother."

My entire body shakes and my eyes fill with water. Gigi had told me Ilse had three sisters and a brother and that her father was a professor. All I can think is, *Gigi! We found her!*

Dr. Alexander wipes his eyes, and I'm touched by how deeply he clearly feels for my family.

"Hailey, I have a few more stunning developments to tell you. First, the painting has been verified. It is a Gustav Klimt."

I shake my head. My voice has left the room.

"Second . . ." His voice trails off as he chokes on his words. "Ilse's younger brother, Samuel, survived the war. He's alive."

My heart is in my throat. The room spins, and I grab the table to steady myself. I must not have heard him correctly. "*What?*" I mumble out, my voice pitching up and down.

"He was ten years old when their family was taken in 1942. The parents and girls were separated from him immediately. I don't have all the details, but he was hidden by a German family who then raised him. He immigrated to America as a young man and has lived here ever since."

I'm trying to do the math in my head, but my brain won't work. "How old is he?"

"Eighty-eight."

"Where does he live?"

"South Florida."

Dr. Alexander reaches his hand over and touches mine. "He's been notified about you and would like to meet but is unable to travel because of his declining health. If you would like, a friend has arranged for his plane to fly you and your family to Florida."

Gigi's uncle is alive. Ilse's brother.

The tears drip down my face. "Yes, I would like that very much."

I look around the table, and there isn't a dry eye in the room. Blake's mom claps her hands together. "Well, this is officially the best Hanukkah ever in the history of Hanukkahs! Hailey, you have to promise to come back every year!"

Mom and I are in the private car headed to meet my great-great uncle. Dr. Alexander had us do a DNA test before flying out to Florida. I gave him a hair strand from Gigi's antique hairbrush and the results were conclusive: Gigi and Uncle Sam are a match.

Mom and I had decided to make this journey together, just the two of us. We are both unusually quiet. The anticipation of this trip has been building for the past week, but Dr. Alexander made this happen fast. How ironic that we're meeting my Jewish uncle on the eighth night of Hanukkah?

We step out of the car and make our way up the short walkway. Mom and I hold hands as I ring the bell. A petite woman around Mom's age answers. Her eyes glisten with tears. "You must be Hailey and Stacey. I'm Sam's grand-daughter, Jessica."

We instinctively fall into her arms, familial lines pulling us like magnets toward one another.

She leads us into the living room where a crowd is gathered. We are slowly introduced to each person—lots of cousins and more cousins. We learn that Sam had five children of his own, and they each had two or three children who then had two or three more. Sam has fourteen grandchildren and twenty-two great-grandchildren. I'm surrounded by a massive group of people who all share my blood. My tribe. The glowing faces overwhelm me. And to think less than a week ago, I thought Mom, Kyle, and I were all that was left of Ilse's family.

A wheelchair is then rolled into the room. It's my great-great uncle, wearing a suit and tie. Thick bifocal glasses cover his eyes, and hearing aids stick out of each ear. He commands a young man for his walker, and he stands to meet us. He's barely my height. He grabs Mom's wrist with one hand and my wrist with the other, his body shaking so badly that ours join in the tremors. He chokes on sobs.

Mom and I both hug him, holding him tightly. He touches my dark curls. "You have her hair." His hand moves to my cheek. "And her fair skin."

He still has a German accent, his pronunciation of certain words difficult to follow. He points at Mom. "And you have her eyes. Ilse had my father's eyes. Twinkling, sparkling green eyes."

We sit down and Uncle Sam tells us about his life. Hours pass, and Mom and I sit transfixed by Uncle Sam's stories, sponges taking in every detail of our family's history. We learn about Ilse, my great-great-grandparents, and their life in Germany when the Nazis took power. And then we learn of the last day he saw his family and how he survived the war.

"I never stopped hoping, and praying, that I would see my family again," he says, his voice straining to get words out. He holds the back of his hand to his nose, sucking in a deep breath. "And my prayers were finally answered. My sister is here, in each of you." He reaches for us, squeezing our hands. Mom is covered in tears and I swipe my eyes.

I stand and say, "I have a surprise for you."

"I don't know how many surprises this old man can handle today," Uncle Sam says with a chuckle.

I hold my finger up. "Give me one second. Can someone please help me?"

A guy about my age joins me in the hallway. We lift the large frame and return to the room with the painting of the young woman in white. Uncle Sam pushes himself out of the chair, but then his legs give; a young man beside him catches his fall.

We set the painting down in front of him. Tears fall uncontrollably from his eyes. His chest heaves for a few minutes and then he reaches his hand over and delicately touches the frame. "Mother," he whispers.

The young woman in the painting is his mother. How did that part of the story get lost through the years? No wonder it meant so much to Ilse.

He smiles and cries at the same time. The young man holds his hand, and two others prop up his body. He removes his glasses and dabs his eyes with a handkerchief from his suit pocket. He then blows his nose loudly like a bull horn. "Although she still visits me in my dreams, I haven't seen my mother's face in almost seventy-eight years. This painting hung over our mantle above the fireplace. My grandparents had it painted before her wedding."

A shiver runs through me. The woman in white is my great-great grandmother in her wedding dress.

"How is this possible?" he asks.

"My great-grandfather Jack was determined to get this painting back for Ilse. We'll never know where he found it, but I hope returning this to you can heal a small part of your heart."

The corners of his eyes crinkle. "What do you mean?"

"Jack said to make things right. Those were his instructions to my grandmother. This painting belongs with you."

He touches my arm, and then my face. "I can feel her here in both of you. The knowledge I'm not the only one who survived and that my sister was loved and had a child is the greatest gift you could ever have given me. I will never forget what your great-grandfather Jack did for Ilse and for all of us in this room. But I want you to keep this painting. Jack's love for my sister is what saved it. Let their love live on in your family. As I reach the sunset of my life, I can tell you, love is all that matters in the end."

All you need is love. Love is all you need.

Just like Gigi said.

CHAPTER TWENTY-FIVE

I t's Christmas Eve, and I have somewhere important to be.
I step out of Betty and make my way to the big event.

I sit down beside her, with my party hat, a few balloons,
a bouquet of fresh flowers, my portable speaker blaring The
Beatles, and a slice of cake topped with coffee caramel crunch
ice cream.

Today is Gigi's seventy-fifth birthday.

I show her my necklace and tell her about my first
Hanukkah. Then I drop the big bombshell. I tell her about
her uncle and our reunion. "Every single fact Jack told you
was true. Ilse had three sisters and a brother, just like you
said, and her father was a professor.

"Gigi, guess what? Uncle Sam recognized the painting.
He cried and said it was his mother, Hannah. Her name was
Hannah, Gigi! The reason that painting was so important to
Ilse was because it's her mother.

"Uncle Sam shared with me all sorts of fun facts about
your mother. Ilse had perfect pitch and played the violin
masterfully. She loved books and had an infectious laugh. He
said her laugh was her trademark. Does that sound familiar?

"And you know what made me almost pass out? Uncle Sam said she was the fastest girl in their school. Now, they didn't have races back then because, you know, the world was sexist, but she loved to run and would race all the boys and beat them every time. Oh, and this was a big one as well: she wore her hair in braids all the time and was, like, a pro at it."

I smile through tears. "Oh, how I wish you were here, Gigi. You should have been here for it all."

I draw in a deep breath while I swipe the corners of my eyes. "Although I recovered a part of my heart when I found the hideout and found Ilse, nothing can truly fill the void that losing you has left in my life. I miss you so much every day, and I'm scared that my memories will fade, that our time together will diminish in my mind.

"But then I realize some people make such a mark on your heart and soul, that they will live on in you forever. Gigi, you are forever a part of me."

I kiss my hand and rub it over her name etched on the headstone. "Celeste Hannah Turner."

I light a candle and sing her Happy Birthday. I make a wish and blow it out on three. My wish for Gigi is simple: that in heaven, she's found the peace she was searching for on earth.

Let it be, Gigi.

Let it be.

ACKNOWLEDGMENTS

Writing this novel was an escape from the stresses of a chaotic and uncertain COVID world. I wrote fast and furiously in the fall of 2020. The entire plot came to me during a long beach walk while listening to a Beatles playlist on Spotify. So, thank you, John, Paul, George, and Ringo for the creative inspiration and for gifting the world so much beauty and heart.

Thank you to Brooke Warner, Samantha Strom, and the entire team at SparkPress for their encouragement and support on my publishing journey. I'm especially grateful to my publicity team at BookSparks: Crystal Patriarche, Grace Fell, and Hanna Lindsley. Thank you to the incredible She Writes Press community of writers, and most especially Emily Wolf. Your friendship and advice these past few years have been such a gift.

I'm greatly indebted to my talented editor, Jodi Fodor, for her detailed notes, pushing me to dig deeper, and making this story so much stronger in the process. I'm so grateful for my friends who read early drafts and provided feedback so essential to the fine-tuning of this story. Thank you, Halina

Zarczynski, Eileen Serxner, Alante Falkner, Molly Shah, Caty Winslow, Susan Kelly, Carrie Paul, Laura Robbins, Faith Martin, Debbie Cheatham, and my GoodReads friends. A big thank you to Susan Woeppel who cared so deeply for this story. A special thanks to Daisy Ross, Audrey Geric, Savannah Farr, and Penny Zarczynski who made sure I got my "teen speak" right!

To my grandmothers—the grand ladies of my life who inspired Gigi. They lived with grace, humility, and God's love as their guidepost. They were elegant, intelligent, funny, and tough. They were—and are—perfect in my eyes.

To my parents, Natalie and Tom, for the unwavering support and love. They are amazing role models and the best Stolly and Nama any grandkid could hope for. Their love has sustained me through so many ups and downs in my life. My mother was the first reader of the first draft and her encouragement and enthusiasm convinced me to charge forward. Thank you, Dad, for being my person. I can always count on you to tell me what you think and guide me in the right direction (literally and figuratively). No one knows Texas geography like you!

This novel wouldn't be what it is without the love and support of my best friend, my amazing sister, Jaxie. She has been my sage advisor my entire life and was an integral part of my creative journey with this story. My love and gratitude to my sister-in-law, Allyson, for her enthusiasm, keen observations, and astute feedback to make this story the best novel it could be. To my brother, Jeff, you are the smartest person I've ever met, and I value your opinion more than anyone on this planet.

To Janina Zarczynska, a brave, strong, loving, and kind woman, who shared with me her story of being taken by the Nazis and her time in a concentration camp. That day, and her words, had such a profound impact on my life.

A heartfelt thank you to the community of my childhood, Richardson, Texas. I grew up with an incredible group of teachers, coaches, and parents who had such a deep impact on my life. To all my childhood friends, you inspired many of the people in this story and each of you mean so much to me. A special thanks to Geri Farr for her love and confidence that I got this story right.

My deepest gratitude to my dear friend, Susan Kelly. Our weekly walks/counseling sessions through the rollercoaster ups and downs of my publishing journey were a saving grace. You were my sounding board and biggest cheerleader, and your friendship is such a blessing in my life. To Mel Intemann, my girl, for helping me get this book ready and for always lifting me up with love and encouragement. It means more than you know. To Betsy Wells, for pushing me to find my voice and for all the love and laughs over twenty-five years of friendship. To Cristi Navarro, for her incredible insight into the publishing world. Your support of this story meant everything.

To my Creative Club gang—Marcy Stoudt, Melissa Papock, Serena Schupler, Kirsten Martino, Susan Kelly, Lori Shapiro, and Christina Cush. Y'all have been so instrumental in helping me bring this novel to the world and I'm so grateful for your friendship and business savvy! A giant thank you to all of my wonderful PVB friends who checked in on me and supported my writing adventure. And to my original squad: Kim Weatherby, Erin Higman, Emily Cannon, and Geri Farr—we met when we were twelve and y'all still give me the loudest and deepest belly laughs of anyone in my life. I cherish our friendships and I'm so thankful for your love and support.

Finally, to my favorite people in the entire world, Kris, Penny, Luka, and Jaxie. I wrote this novel to share with the world the kind of love I feel for each of you. You four are my reason for everything.

ABOUT THE AUTHOR

Kate Stollenwerck is an attorney turned author. Kate graduated from Northwestern University and the University of Texas at Austin School of Law. A fifth-generation Texan, she now lives in Florida with her husband, three children, and a crazy cat. This is her first novel.

Author photo © Agnes Lopez

SELECTED TITLES FROM SPARKPRESS

SparkPress is an independent boutique publisher delivering high-quality, entertaining, and engaging content that enhances readers' lives, with a special focus on female-driven work. www.go sparkpress.com

A Song for the Road: A Novel, Rayne Lacko. $16.95, 978-1-684630-02-8. When his house is destroyed by a tornado, fifteen-year-old Carter Danforth steals his mom's secret cash stash, buys his father's guitar back from a pawnshop, and hitchhikes old Route 66 in search of the man who left him as a child.

The House Children: A Novel, Heidi Daniele. $16.95, 978-1-943006-94-6. A young girl raised in an Irish industrial school accidentally learns that the woman she spends an annual summer holiday with is her birth mother.

The Leaving Year: A Novel, Pam McGaffin. $16.95, 978-1-943006-81-6. As the Summer of Love comes to an end, 15-year-old Ida Petrovich waits for a father who never comes home. While commercial fishing in Alaska, he is lost at sea, but with no body and no wreckage, Ida and her mother are forced to accept a "presumed" death that tests their already strained relationship. While still in shock over the loss of her father, Ida overhears an adult conversation that shatters everything she thought she knew about him. This prompts her to set out on a search for the truth that takes her from her Washington State hometown to Southeast Alaska.

But Not Forever: A Novel, Jan Von Schleh. $16.95, 978-1-943006-58-8.When identical fifteen-year-old girls are mysteriously switched in time, they discover the love that's been missing in their lives. Torn, both want to go home, but neither wants to give up what they now have.

Beautiful Girl:A Novel, Fleur Philips. $15, 978-1-94071-647-3. When a freak car accident leaves the 17-year-old model, Melanie, with facial lacerations, her mother whisks her away to live in Montana for the summer until she makes a full recovery.